A CONFLICTED BETROTHAL

SCOUTS OF THE GEORGIA FRONTIER
BOOK FOUR

DENISE WEIMER

Copyright © 2024 by Denise Weimer

All rights reserved. No portion of this book may be reproduced or transmitted in any form or by any means - photocopied, shared electronically, scanned, stored in a retrieval system, or other - without the express permission of the publisher. Exceptions will be made for brief quotations used in critical reviews or articles promoting this work.

The characters and events in this fictional work are the product of the author's imagination. Any resemblance to actual people, living or dead, is coincidental.

Unless otherwise indicated, all Scripture quotations are taken from the Holy Bible, Kings James Version.

Cover design by Evelyne Labelle at Carpe Librum Book Design. www.carpelibrumbookdesign.com

ISBN-13: 978-1-942265-95-5

CHAPTER 1

Savannah, Georgia
September 2, 1765

"How are ye feelin' this evening, sir?"

The question, posed by the owner of the popular Savannah tavern, spiraled panic through Ansel Anderson. The man leaning on the bottom half of the Dutch door wasn't even speaking to him. But his manner, his tone, and the way the patron in front of Ansel eased forward to answer told him he should have been more prepared.

Clearly, a password was required for entry tonight.

Ansel had been right. The seedling Sons of Liberty group sprouting up in Savannah—calling themselves the Liberty Boys—were congregating here. Most likely, access to the ordinary had been restricted this evening because they would discuss what had happened today in Georgia's Commons House of Assembly. And he'd miss hearing it firsthand unless God granted him a small miracle right now.

What had the patron muttered? A single word, but one with several syllables. Whatever it had been, the owner, James

Machenry, backed up with an indulging smile, swinging the bottom half of his tavern's door wide.

Ansel wreathed his countenance with an answering smile—hopefully, one that conveyed ease as well as warmth—and started up the steps to trail the man into the dark interior. But the door swung shut.

The big Scot's benevolence had disappeared. He eyed Ansel's dusty light-wool suit and riding boots. "Traveled far today, have ye, me friend?"

"A piece. My family has a farm in St. George's Parish."

A true statement. Ansel held the man's gaze. If he told the shrewd tavern keeper where he'd actually ridden in from—Fort Argyle, nineteen miles west of the city on the Great Ogeechee River—he could save himself the trouble of wracking his brain for a password. Instead, he'd get a boot in the backside. And squander any chance of returning.

Maybe it hadn't been such a brilliant idea to get right to work sniffing out the revolutionaries before checking in with the man who had secured his promotion...and his secret assignment. But he could hardly bow out now.

Machenry raised a bushy brow. "What brings ye to Savannah?"

"A visit to a friend of my father's." He twisted his mouth to one side, leaning forward as if rendering a confidence. "In truth, my father hopes I might find a bride. His friend's daughter." Again, all facts.

A bark of a laugh answered his confession. "Then ye're in need of some spirituous courage, son. How are ye feeling about yer new bride, if I may ask? Is she bonnie?"

Ansel's throat worked. That was the entry question, though couched a bit differently. His mind darted here and there. He bought himself a moment. "I'm told both of the man's daughters are fetching, though I've seen neither in twenty years. I was too young to remember them and therefore find myself unable to judge if my father is attempting to pull the wool over my eyes."

"But if he speaks the truth, ye must surely be..." The tavern keeper widened his eyes.

A flash of a memory had him fighting to keep his own eyes from going wide—a snippet from Judge Scott's letter, which Father had read to him. *They call themselves the Amicable Society.* Could it be?

"Ye can give it to me in confidence, son." Machenry beckoned him closer.

Ansel obliged. "Amicable." He spoke the word with confidence and stepped back, holding his breath and searching his potential host's face for thunderclouds.

Instead, the man nodded. "I wish ye the best of luck. Come in and fortify yerself before ye go a'courtin'."

"Thank you." *And thank You, God.*

A few steps through the foyer, past the stairs that likely led to the family's rooms and the walk-up counter where a barkeep served drinks to two middle-aged gentlemen, and he entered the taproom. Agitated conversation and the scent of roast with a bitter thread of alcohol swirled in the space. From what he could tell through the cloud of sweet pipe smoke and the ripe press of bodies, only one seat remained, and that at a table for two. Like most of the clientele this evening, the man in the other chair was young. Probably in his early twenties, though his crumpled linen coat suggested his purse might be lighter than that of those sporting silk waistcoats and clocked stockings.

Ansel edged his way toward the spot by the window, removed his cocked hat, and addressed the stranger. "Pardon me. Mind if I share your table?"

Golden brows winged upward. "No, indeed." The man rose and indicated the chair opposite. "Please, join me."

3

"Thank you. Ansel Anderson." He put out his hand to shake his new acquaintance's.

"Jack Weaver." Resuming his seat, Jack picked up his knife and spoon. His pewter trencher held a generous slice of pork roast, potatoes, and buttered peas and bread.

Ansel's stomach growled, his lunch of an apple and cheese partaken on horseback long gone. "That looks appealing. How do you find it?"

"The food here is good, unlike at some taverns. You're new, aren't you?"

Even in a town the size of Savannah, he should expect to be pegged as a stranger. And viewed with some suspicion. Ansel scooted his chair closer to the table. "Just arrived to visit friends and conduct a bit of business." Hopefully, his companion wouldn't ask what that business was. He'd just as soon no one here knew he'd been brought in to join the Savannah guard of some twenty Georgia Rangers at the beck and call of the royal governor, James Wright. And despite his unexpected assignment, he'd no small aversion to deception.

Thankfully, a waitress arrived. She wore an apron over her shift and petticoat, her brownish-blond hair trailing from beneath her mob cap. He ordered a plate of roast and a cider.

When she hurried away, Jack looked up from chasing his peas with his spoon. "This is the most popular ordinary in Savannah. But you must already know that." His brown eyes fixed on Ansel.

Ah. He meant the password. "Yes, I've heard this is the gathering place for those of a certain persuasion. Though judging from the tenor of conversation, things did not go well today at the Commons House."

Not that he was privy to the inner workings of Georgia's Lower House of Assembly. Besides whatever news trickled over to Argyle, Ansel knew only what Judge Scott's letter had relayed —that the Commons House had endeavored to elect delegates to the Stamp Act Congress proposed by James Otis of the Massachusetts Assembly, which would be held in New York in October. The congress would seek to resist one of the latest in a series of unpopular laws Great Britain had enacted. The Stamp Act, passed by Parliament in March, required imprinted paper to be used for—or a small blue stamped paper to be affixed to —any legal, commercial, or official papers, as well as calendars, almanacs, newspapers, and even playing cards. The act would not go into effect until the first of November, giving ample time for the stamped paper to arrive from England and stamp agents to be appointed.

Jack snorted. "I'd say not."

When the waitress delivered Ansel's cider, he leaned back and took a sip, attempting a casual air as he surveyed the room.

His companion chewed and swallowed his last bite of bread. "Of course, many here tonight are representatives. Except for supporting their efforts to secure fair representation for our colony, I don't really move in their circles. I'm just a farmer's son from St. Paul Parish."

Ansel grinned. "Same as I, but from St. George's."

Jack nodded. "Well, here in Christ Church Parish, this is the best place to keep abreast of what's going on...long before the *Georgia Gazette* prints the news."

As was the case for most taverns.

Indeed, a voice rose from near the fireplace—unlit tonight, as the evening retained the balmy coastal heat of summer. The voice belonged to a man of about forty with dark hair and a slightly crooked nose, who addressed two younger men— gentleman, all, judging by the tailoring of their coats and the shine of their buckles and buttons. "I share your frustration, of course. But tell me what else we could have done, Clay. Wylly did his part. He set the meeting for us to elect delegates, but without Wright calling us into session..."

"Why do we need him to call us into session?" One of the

younger men glowered over his pewter tankard, though his earnest oval face, small mouth, and soft dark eyes negated any true appearance of ferocity.

"Be careful." The first speaker lifted his finger. "'Tis not wise to bite the hand that feeds you."

"My uncle's hand feeds us." The young man glanced at his other companion.

When his dinner arrived, Ansel thanked the barmaid but strained not to miss the rest of the conversation across the room.

"And your uncle's bounty flows from the benevolence of the royal governor. As does the license you and young Habersham enjoy as partners in your import business." The older man swigged his drink. "Let us rest easy. We will receive a full report from the recorder we send to the Stamp Act Congress. The missive we prepared will assure them of our support despite our governor's objections—and our determination to enact any legislation they pass."

Knifing a slice of pork to his mouth, Ansel chanced a glance at the man across the table. Did he share the speaker's confidence in a diplomatic approach, or was he more of a firebrand?

"You know who they are?" Jack tilted his head toward the men by the fireplace, seeming to channel Ansel's curiosity toward the others rather than himself.

Ansel shook his head. "Obviously, men of importance in the liberty movement."

"The one our age is Joseph Clay. As Lieutenant Jones said, he heads an import business with his cousin, James Habersham Jr."

Everyone in Georgia knew who the Habershams were. James Sr. not only oversaw the mercantile firm but a fifteen-thousand-acre rice plantation. It was the other name that made Ansel almost choke on his pork. "Jones?"

"Noble Wimberly Jones, physician and first lieutenant of the Second Troop of Georgia Rangers."

Ansel bolted down a generous swallow of cider.

Jack watched too closely as he wiped his mouth.

Judge Scott had said that Governor Wright did not know whom he could trust among his rangers and militia, but Ansel had not expected to find an officer of the very troop he'd be reporting to in the morning among the Liberty Boys at Machenry's Tavern.

"Would you like me to introduce you?"

"Er..." Heart thudding, Ansel glanced across the room.

Past the knot of men at the mantel, a pocket door slid open. A young woman peeked out, the hood of her dark cloak accenting the paleness of her oval face. "I'd probably better... find lodgings..." Her gaze seemed to latch onto him, and she gave a frantic little flutter of her hand.

"Is she waving at you?" Incredulity laced Jack's tone.

"Surely not. I have no idea who she is." Though never had a distraction proved timelier. Or lovelier. Even from this distance, the pink in the woman's cheeks and lips was visible, as was the snap of her dark eyes. She must be gesturing to someone past him. Ansel swiveled for his final swallow of cider, releasing a soft sigh of relief.

Playing along with Jack had been one thing. If he met First Lieutenant Jones tonight, Ansel would find himself locked into the role of a Liberty Boy when he needed to build relations and gather intelligence among the rangers without prejudice from either side. How careless he'd been.

"Well, I don't, either," Jack told him, "but I'd say she is definitely summoning you." His throaty tone hinted he wouldn't mind being the subject of the lady's attention.

Ansel peeked behind Jack again.

Again, the woman lifted her hand, but this time, she made a clear beckoning gesture.

He pointed at his own chest and mouthed, "Me?"

The dark head crowned with a mob cap under the hood nodded. The door slid closed.

Jack swiveled back from the glance he'd taken over his shoulder and chuckled. "Well, she is quite certain of her powers of persuasion, is she not?"

Ansel pulled coins from his pocket and placed them on the table. "This is an upstanding sort of establishment, correct?"

Jack's chuckle turned into a full laugh. "She is no tavern doxy, if that is what you mean. Yonder is the door to the ladies' parlor."

Of course. Except for barmaids and servants, women would not frequent the taproom. If this tavern made a special accommodation for the ladies, it offered more amenities than most.

His companion rubbed his golden-bristled chin. "Although I'm surprised to see any women here tonight."

"Me too. Perhaps she is in some sort of distress."

"And out of a room of men, she picks a perfect stranger to come to her aid?"

It was Ansel's turn to chuckle. "I own, that sounds fanciful. But I'm prepared to do my best to solve the mystery."

Jack arched a brow. "Need any help?"

"Will call if I do." Ansel winked. "Thank you for sharing your table and your insights. I hope to see you around town." Whatever this woman did or did not require, Ansel risked revealing too much if he continued his current conversation. And he needed to make his exit while Lieutenant Jones faced the fireplace.

Ansel threaded his way through the room on the side nearest the bar, then paused at the rolling door to knock quietly.

A feminine voice answered. "Come."

He entered, then slid the portal mostly closed behind him —not all the way, for he found himself alone in a small parlor with the lady, who faced the other way at a table with a mostly empty plate before her. She spoke before he could present himself.

"This is insupportable, Frankie. I can't hear a thing. Could you find me a spot in the corner..." Her voice trailed off as Ansel appeared before her and she looked up from picking chicken off a bone.

"Miss." Removing his hat, Ansel made a small bow.

Her fingers stilled, her eyes went wide, and her throat worked. "You are not Frankie."

~

*D*rat her weak eyes. How many times would they get her into trouble?

Temperance berated herself as she took in the man wearing the same color suit as her cousin, with the same shade of straight mahogany-brown hair tied with a silk ribbon beneath the black cocked hat he now held under his arm. There the resemblance ended. Where Frankie's skin bore the reminder of his childhood battle with smallpox, this man's was unmarked, unless one counted the dimples on either side of his mouth. Where her cousin's face was flat and of a weak chin, this man had high cheekbones, a thin nose, and a square, clean-shaven jaw. And instead of Frankie's almost-lashless brown eyes, she gazed into green jewels framed in a thick fringe of brown lashes.

A small chicken bone fell to the floor. She did not even try to go after it, for with her present luck, she'd mistake it for a crack, and her groping quest would further shame herself before this perfect specimen of manhood.

"Ansel Anderson, at your service. Although, am I to understand I was summoned by mistake?"

"No. Yes." Mercy, the clever words that usually vied for

attention in her head dried up like the chicken breast. Normally, she did everything in her power to steer away from males of Mr. Anderson's superior appearance and bearing, and here she'd unwittingly commanded him to her side. "I mean, from across the room, I thought you were my cousin. You are... similarly garbed." She waved her hand, avoiding his eyes.

His smile seemed to bestow compassion on her flusterment. "I thought as much. I could not imagine what good fortune would be smiling on me to be acknowledged by a lady such as yourself. And after I only just arrived in town."

He flattered her. What a poor impression she'd surely made on a newcomer to their city. All of this could've been avoided if her vanity had not prevented her from wearing her spectacles. "Please, I should—I mean, may I offer my apologies? And welcome you to Savannah?" After wiping her fingers on her handkerchief, Temperance attempted to rise, but apparently, she'd placed the chair leg on her petticoat when she'd last seated herself, and now, it pulled her back down.

In a flash, Mr. Anderson was behind her, taking hold of the top of her chair so he could assist with her second attempt at standing. "Allow me."

As he moved the chair, Temperance stepped around it and swung her petticoat free, but the motion brought her closer to the stranger. Ah, he smelled of leather and the outdoors. He'd traveled on horseback rather than by conveyance. "Thank you. I am very sorry to have troubled you, sir."

He gazed into her eyes. "No trouble at all. In fact, may I seek out your cousin for you? This might not be the best night for a lady to find herself unaccompanied in this tavern. The...er... passions of the men in the next room are rather high at the moment."

Indignation for her friends burned off Temperance's usual reserve. "I can promise you, only the finest, the most upstanding, of the city's gentlemen frequent Machenry's."

A CONFLICTED BETROTHAL

"I am sure that is true, but I cannot help but notice that you are still the only lady."

"Do you intimate my presence creates some sort of scandal...or temptation?"

Mr. Anderson blinked rapidly, taking a small step back. "I meant nothing untoward, miss."

"Good, because I share the 'passions' of the men in the next room. And they are precisely as elevated as any sensible colonist might expect, given recent events. That is why you are here, is it not?" She raised her brows.

"Uh, I understand. Forgive me." Again, a small bow. "I was only concerned for your comfort."

The faint red creeping up from Mr. Anderson's collar instantly cooled her dander. Her mother was right. When her patriotic ideals were challenged, she truly became another person. "Think nothing of it, sir. And rest assured, I am perfectly safe. I am well acquainted with most of the gentlemen here tonight. Only the silly rule about no women in the taproom keeps me in this parlor." She mustered a smile. "Frankie should return any moment. He only went to get some drinks. When I saw you with your back turned..."

The dimples reappeared. "You thought your cousin had abandoned you for another conversation."

"Precisely."

"In that case, I will bid you a good night." With a nod, he replaced his hat on his head and walked toward the door.

For the strangest moment, Temperance's heart ached, and she cast about for something to say that might justify bringing him back.

And then, with one hand on the frame, he turned, and she sucked in a breath.

He tipped his head. "Might I be bold enough to inquire of your name?"

Of course. He'd given his, but in her embarrassment, she

had not reciprocated. She opened her mouth to answer just before the door was flung wide behind him and someone else did.

"No, you may not. What are you doing in here with my cousin, sir?" Frankie pushed past Mr. Anderson, a glass of flip in one hand and a punch in the other. "Temperance, is this man bothering you?"

"No, indeed, Frankie." She hurried forward to place her hand on his arm. "In fact, I bothered *him*. I spied him across the room and thought he was you. See how similarly you are dressed? I beckoned him over, and he obliged. And now, we should let him take his leave in peace." With a gracious smile in Mr. Anderson's direction, she relieved Frankie of the cup of punch.

Surveying her with that proprietary air that made her squirm, Frankie stowed up one corner of his thin lips. "Dear cousin, what am I always telling you about...?"

She waved him to silence. She knew just where this was going and preferred not to visit that topic in front of this Adonis. She found the courage to face him again. "Good night, Mr. Anderson."

"Good night, miss..." He let the sentence hang, but if she judged rightly, whatever he saw in the taproom had more to do with its termination than a bid for her name. He turned back and glanced around the parlor. "Pardon me. I shall spare myself the trouble of elbowing through that crowd again and instead take the back exit."

Temperance moved to let him pass, her breath hitching as his arm brushed hers. But something in his manner had her sipping her punch and conjecturing after the door closed behind him. Somehow, as mannerly and obliging as he had been, he did not fit in here. And for some reason, she regretted that. Because that meant she'd probably never see him again.

CHAPTER 2

The most exciting part of Temperance's evening at Machenry's had occurred when the discussion about the Stamp Act Congress finally wound down and Frankie brought several of the leaders of the new Liberty Boys to speak with her in the back parlor. There, she had laid her idea before them. Her customary reticence had fallen away, as it always did when she spoke of the causes dearest to her. Not to mention, the men had responded to her sincerity and embraced her, figuratively, as a sister-in-arms. And now, the next afternoon following the meeting, she would put her idea to the ladies gathered in her family's parlor. Her heart beat faster than it had last night.

Except when she'd stood near Ansel Anderson.

His face had splashed across her mind's eye the minute she'd tucked into bed, expecting to plan all she'd say to her sewing circle friends today. Instead, all she could think about was the mysterious newcomer. What was his business in Savannah? Would he be here long enough that she might run into him again? Why hadn't she given him her name?

And what if she had? It wasn't as if he'd come calling on

her. She almost snorted, picturing explaining *that* to her father. *Oh, just a man I met at the tavern.* Indeed.

Why did she find Mr. Anderson so intriguing, anyway?

She knew why. He was the first impressive young man she'd spoken to in ages—because she was normally far too much of a mouse to look at one such as him, much less unstick her tongue from the roof of her mouth. And yet her own clumsiness last night had forced her into doing both. He must think her a ninny for it, too...waving down a perfect stranger in a pub.

Little did it matter. Something told her he would not share her ideals, and that was absolutely essential in a mate. She very much suspected she'd live out her years as a spinster, channeling her passion to her humanitarian causes.

Moving her teacup from her lap to the small table beside her, Temperance forced her attention back to the four ladies who were closer to her than her own mother or sister. She donned her dark horn glasses so she could actually see them. Her friends were used to her wearing them, so she minded doing so here less than she did in public, where their clunky appearance oft as not drew snide comments.

For two years, she and these women had shared secrets and burdens over needlework and scones—sometimes with laughter, sometimes with tears. They also shared their frustrations as women and colonists, for those two things bore marked similarities. Expected to marry and trust their husbands to represent their beliefs and desires in all things social and political, much as the colonists must defer to the separate entity of Parliament, this little group of Savannah ladies relied on one another for support. She could trust all of them...except perhaps Mary Mabry.

The girl sat on the blue wool-upholstered settee with a view of Governor Wright's mansion out the window behind her. To be fair, was it any wonder Mary shared in her older sister Katherine's excitement for patriot ideals but lacked her backbone? At only seventeen, she still lived in fear of her strict father's displeasure. But she would follow Katherine's example.

Golden light slid in from the west, dappling the live oaks draped with Spanish moss. Their meeting would soon be over and Temperance's opportunity lost.

She drew a breath and nudged her spectacles more securely in place. "Ladies, I would like to put a motion before you."

Lydia Harrison giggled. "Are we an official club now? Shall we draw up orders of incorporation?"

Cecily, Temperance's maidservant, met Temperance's gaze over the crystal jam dish she refilled. Her full lips turned up in the faintest of smiles. Temperance had talked everything over with her before her friends had arrived. Cecily's tiny nod restored her confidence.

"Actually, that is not far from what I'm proposing. I'd like our little sewing circle to become something more, if you are all amenable."

"Amenable to what?" Elizabeth Patterson, the only married woman among them, tilted her mass of dark brown curls.

If Elizabeth approved of her plan, the others would likely see the wisdom in it as well. Though the wife of a successful cotton and rice factor had yet to conceive any children, she was like a mother to them all. The advice they often sought from her had proved sage in both social and personal arenas.

Temperance folded her hands in her lap. "Last night, I spoke with some of our friends among the Liberty Boys." She practically whispered the last. Her parents thought Frankie had accompanied her to an evening of opera at Mr. Lyon's Long-Room. "They would be most pleased to find support in the form of a sister organization, the kind that women in more progressive colonies have already been forming this summer."

"A sister organization?" Katherine lifted her brows. "I'm intrigued."

"I'm not," Mary mumbled, picking a hangnail. "Sounds dangerous."

Elizabeth sat forward. "What would this club be called, Temperance?"

"Why, just as you might expect. Daughters of Liberty." Even the name sent a thrill through her. She practically shivered with it. With all the possibilities.

Lydia stifled another giggle behind her hand. "Liberty Girls!"

Mary sent up a moan. "Really, Lydia. I find no wit in this notion. 'Tis one thing to grumble in our private parlor against how little say we have over our lives and politics. 'Tis another entirely to brand ourselves with a name associated with a group of rebels the governor would love to throw out of the colony."

Katherine patted Mary's voluminous petticoats. "Let us hear Temperance out, sister. Then we will decide."

"You mean *you* will decide."

"No, you all must decide." Temperance spoke firmly, drawing Mary's gaze. "If none of you think this is a good idea, we won't go ahead. But if most of us do and anyone doesn't, that person should consider themselves free to leave with no ill feelings. But please, I ask only that, as always, everything said here be kept in confidence."

Her pink lips pursed, Mary nodded. She smoothed a blond hair behind her ear and lowered her lashes. "Go on, then."

Temperance reached for a newspaper lying on the table beside her. "As you know, I have an aunt and uncle living in Charlestown. They send their papers to us on a regular basis, which tell us more than the *Gazette* alone. Of course, the Sons of Liberty are much more active there. As part of our weekly meetings, I would provide a summary of any pertinent news. We would also report on anything of note we hear around town, since we all have different contacts."

Elizabeth dipped her chin. "Which we already do. Between your father on the Governor's Council and your cousin and my husband in the Commons House, we hear things earlier and more accurately than most."

"True. I also think one of us should represent our circle at the Sons of Liberty meetings. That way, we can learn how best to support them."

Mary let out a little squeak. "Attend their meetings? How are we to do that?"

"We could go in disguise." Lydia's blue eyes twinkled. Even when she wasn't up to mischief, her flaming red hair and pert smile made her look as though she must be.

Katherine flicked her hand in Lydia's direction. "As though anyone could disguise *you*."

Temperance reined the discussion back in. "I went last night and sat in the women's parlor of the tavern with the door cracked."

"By yourself?" Mary gasped.

Temperance pursed her lips. "Frankie was there, of course." And a new man, a mysterious stranger, whose face she recalled even now. *Stop that woolgathering at once, Temperance Scott.* She pressed on before she could lose her train of thought—or speech—again. "Since we are a sewing circle, we could help other Daughters of Liberty groups put pressure on the British merchants by making our own cloth."

Lydia brushed a crumb from her lavender-striped silk taffeta petticoat. "You know I never wear anything but silk." As a daughter of the superintendent of the filature house, she never had to.

Temperance had anticipated her response. "Of course. There's nothing wrong with wearing the silk produced here in Savannah or at Ebenezer." The Salzburgers, who had settled twenty miles north of Savannah in the 1730s, now surpassed the port city's silk production. "In fact, supporting local industry is exactly what we are about. But we all need other fabrics, don't we? For undergarments, bedding, and household items, if not for clothing? Why can't we bring in some spinning wheels and a loom and find someone to teach us how to produce our own linens, as they do on the frontier? Shouldn't we learn to be independent of the mother country in everything that we can? It can only help our economy."

Lydia gave a light shudder. "If not our skin."

Bearing a teapot, Cecily came to stand behind Temperance. "The cotton my mother makes for shifts and petticoats is soft as silk, if not as slick. She has a spinning wheel you ladies could borrow."

"Thank you, Cecily. That would be a great help. Perhaps she could teach us?" Temperance reached around to pat the servant's hand.

Cecily nodded and smiled. "She already agreed. She'd be happy to."

Elizabeth tapped the slight cleft in her chin. "That is wonderful, but what about a loom? Where are you going to find one of those, and how will you get it moved and set up here?"

"Right. And where would you hide it from your father?" Lydia raised her teacup for Cecily to top off her jasmine brew.

"I agree, that bears some thought. I don't have all the answers yet. I was hoping for your help in working out the details. But first, what do you think of the idea?" Temperance held her breath after asking.

"I love it." A brilliant smile broke across Katherine's face. "I agree with everything you said about independence. That begins with small steps, not big ones. If we can't support ourselves, we'll fall face-first when we finally have the chance to let go of Mother England's hand."

Temperance laughed. She could always trust her friends to buoy her ideals.

But Mary nibbled her lower lip, a furrow on her smooth brow.

"What is your concern, Mary?" Temperance asked.

"I'm not trying to be contrary..." She shot a glance at Lydia as if anticipating a quip and beat her to it. "*Contrary Mary*. But I'm not sure how making our own cloth has anything to do with stamped paper."

Temperance smiled. "It doesn't. Not directly. But we've witnessed this chain of repressive laws England is enforcing over the colonies. The Sugar Act. The Currency Act. Then the Stamp Act and the Quartering Act. While they may not all affect us personally, we have to grapple with the root question of whether Parliament has the right to tax us when we have no representatives there. We must make them see that only our colonial legislatures are properly informed and elected for that task. We have to stand up, or what will the next law demand? When will it finally be too much?"

Elizabeth chuckled, presumably at her fervency. "What Temperance is saying, Mary, is that we have to use whatever leverage we can to put pressure on England. We must refuse to purchase their goods. We can only do that by making things ourselves."

"Right. The Non-Importation Agreement the merchants are discussing supporting." The furrow deepened between Mary's brows. "It isn't fair that England should produce everything and not let us become self-reliant." She looked up. "I'm willing to learn."

A rush of relief loosened Temperance's shoulders. "Wonderful. So are we all in agreement? We shall henceforth be known as the Savannah Daughters of Liberty?"

Katherine popped off the sofa and held her hand out. Each woman came forward and placed her hands atop the others. Temperance removed her glasses before joining them, as she needed the lenses to see far away, but they blurred whatever was in close range. When Cecily hung back, Temperance tilted her head toward the center of the room. The servant put down her teapot and joined them, allowing her tan-colored hand to hover atop all the white ones. The beauty of it lodged in Temperance's throat.

As they surveyed each other with solemn eyes, her heart surged. The women understood the seriousness of this. And so they should. They were at the cusp of something big. Something that could eventually demand more of them than they could imagine in her cozy parlor lit by golden early-evening light.

Lydia snickered. "I feel as though we should perform a right-hand star. If only we had some music." As she swished her rustling petticoat, the ladies laughed and stepped back.

Leave it to her to lighten the mood. Temperance smiled and shook her head. "Ladies, for next time, think of things you'd like for us to accomplish or rules you feel we should put in place. Now, I hate to rush you out, but my father is receiving a caller in his study soon and prefers..." Gracious, must she always stumble into awkwardness?

"Prefers not to have a house full of women?" Lydia sent her a wink.

"Ahem...I believe that is the idea."

"Thank you, dear Temperance." Elizabeth kissed her cheek. "I so admire your idealism. I will give this deep thought, and we will speak more next week."

Temperance hugged her. "Your support means everything." Elizabeth's maturity would keep her grounded, their efforts practical and focused.

As the ladies chattered and gathered their wraps and hats, Temperance moved to the window that looked out on the front entry. Someone was dismounting at their hitching post, a man wearing the blue breeches and coat with red waistcoat of the Georgia Royal Rangers. Was this their father's guest, the arrival from Fort Argyle he'd told them about? She eased behind the blue-and-white toile curtain and peered around it for a better view as he came up the steps.

A gasp slipped from her lips. Oh, no.

The ranger was Ansel Anderson.

She hadn't officially met the man, and yet the evening prior, she'd announced to this man, who must be the loyalist son of her father's oldest friend, that she was an avid patriot.

CHAPTER 3

The house Ansel approached was of whitewashed wood, not brick, but that did not make it any less imposing. Two and a half stories in Georgian style with three dormers crowning the hipped roof, pedimented windows, and columns framing the entry, it provided a perfect counterpoint for the governor's mansion across fashionable St. James Square. How grand must Judge Scott's plantation house south of Savannah be?

Ansel swallowed his intimidation as he lifted the knocker. After all, his father and Bazel Scott had started out in the same law firm in Charlestown. Father had attempted to branch out to Augusta, Georgia's second-largest city farther north on the Savannah River, but the rough-and-tumble frontier town had not provided a good living for a lawyer. Judge Scott had encouraged Michael Anderson to apply for a grant when the Proclamation of 1763 opened new land south to the St. Mary's River and west to the Ogeechee.

Ansel's father had done well with his two hundred and fifty acres, supplementing crop income by serving as a justice of the peace and earning respect as a captain of militia. But Ansel's older brother, Martin, would inherit the farm. Ansel had to make his own way. One way men of good family did so was by serving in the military—and answering when a friend capable of granting favors called.

But he had to be honest regarding his uncertainty about his capability on that score. Last night had showed him how quickly he could blunder. And that could endanger not only himself, but his mentor as well.

A middle-aged black man answered his knock. "Yassir?"

"Lieutenant Ansel Anderson to see Judge Scott." That sounded strange to his own ears.

He'd thought the highest he'd rise would be the top rung of the ladder in Fort Argyle's quartermaster's store. He even minded not that he was to be *third* lieutenant.

The rangers' second lieutenant, Moses Nunee Rivers, supported Captain John Milledge back at Argyle. And the first lieutenant—well, he'd encountered Noble Wimberly Jones last night, though he wouldn't be telling Judge Scott that. Or Captain James Edward Powell. Something in Ansel nudged him to get to know the man first, especially after he'd met him this morning when he'd reported to Fort Halifax on the river. Jones and Captain Powell had both been so welcoming that he'd vowed to allow each to prove their own merit, patriot or loyalist. Besides, Judge Scott would not yet be anticipating any intelligence.

"He's expecting you, sir. This way." The somber servant led him through a foyer with a marble-topped table supporting an enormous vase of chrysanthemums. The blooms reminded Ansel of home, where his mother kept an extensive garden of both flowers and herbs.

To his left, upholstered walnut chairs surrounded a long dining table. The door on his right was closed, but low feminine voices and soft laughter hinted of the daughters his mother was so keen he meet.

They walked past columns flush with the walls that echoed those on the front stoop and turned right into a room in the rear of the house—Scott's study and library, with a desk and bookcase in mahogany and an additional impressive book press with curtained glass windows, none of which were unexpected in the home office of a judge and member of the Governor's Council. Likely, Scott kept his law books inside.

The man himself stood from behind his desk and strolled forward to meet Ansel with a hand extended. He wore a white curled wig over his graying hair. It had been almost black and worn unpowdered in a queue the last time Ansel had encountered him.

"Ansel. What a fine-looking man you have become. When last I saw you, you were about so tall." As the judge released the handshake, he indicated a spot around his own still-trim waistline.

"Before you left Charlestown." His father had since visited Judge Scott in Savannah, but Ansel had not accompanied him.

"I'm surprised you remember me."

"My father has always held you in the highest regard." A younger Bazel Scott and his wife had been frequent dinner guests, though it had been a long time since Ansel had seen his girls. "I admit, my memory of your daughters is fuzzy."

"A problem soon to be rectified...and I doubt it will be repeated." The man's eyes glowed with obvious pride in his offspring as he indicated a wingchair facing his desk. "Please sit. I only regret I cannot extend a supper invitation for tonight. I'm afraid I'm expected at my club."

Adjusting the saber that he'd worn for this meeting, Ansel took a seat. "I would not presume our acquaintance extended to socializing, sir. I understand that I am here in a military capacity, to fill a need."

His father had encouraged him to ingratiate himself to the judge while he served in Savannah and to remain alert for the ideal occasion to present his personal request. His mother had suggested one way to do so would be to win the favor of one of Scott's daughters.

Though he appreciated his mother's input—to a point—and understood that a wife—certainly the *right* wife—would enable Ansel to receive a larger land grant, he could earn his next position simply through doing his duty well in this one. He did not need to affiance himself to any willing miss. He had yet to meet a woman who held his interest past a second glance. Although, the one in the tavern last night—

"And yet, I fully intend that we will socialize." The judge settled in his leather chair. "The friendship between our families will provide a natural explanation for the time we spend together, time when you will keep me informed of all that you are learning."

"Of course, sir. So I will be reporting directly to you, not to Captain Powell?"

Judge Scott answered his unspoken question. "Governor Wright trusts that Captain Powell will respond to his orders and raise his troops when called. But he is taking the private allegiances of no man for granted. Besides, it would not be wise if you came to be seen as Powell's man. No, we will keep our intelligence-sharing outside the fort." He lifted a crystal decanter from the corner of his desk. When Ansel declined, he proceeded to pour himself a small glass.

"Allow me to take this opportunity to thank you for my new position," Ansel said.

"You can thank me by bringing me good information. The governor is relieved to have a man on the inside who is not embroiled in Savannah politics—one trained in a purely military environment."

Indeed, Fort Argyle had been its own bubble. Some men found the isolation unnerving, but Ansel thrived under routine, structure, and a clearly defined path to success. He'd also discovered an aptitude for the ways of the frontier. And that brought him 'round to his chief concern. "Sir, on that note, I must tell you ... I am no parlor warrior. Whatever my father may have told you out of a desire to assist both of us, I have no training or skills in the art of intrigue."

His mentor laughed. "I did not expect you did. Nor do I expect that you will need to be cracking any codes or sending any secret signals. All we are asking is that you make friends of officers and enlisted men alike. Attend the social functions your connection to me will provide. Mingle with the sons of society among whom most new ideas take root. If possible, gain entry to the meetings of these so-called Liberty Boys. It may be that you allow them to believe you are one of them, or at least amenable to their notions. But I would guess that would be as far as your deception would extend."

Ansel nodded slowly. "I have some ideas about how to do that."

Perhaps his attendance at Machenry's last night had not been a *faux pas*, after all. Despite his desire to enter the Second Troop with a clean slate, another surprise had awaited him when Captain Powell called a private into his office this morning to show Ansel to the barracks. The private was Jack Weaver, garbed in blue and red, just as Ansel was. They had stared at each other a moment before Jack proceeded with military protocol, tipping his hat and addressing him by his rank, giving no sign of recognition. If the man could keep a secret, he might offer a valuable entrée into the Sons of Liberty.

"I'm glad to hear it. Now..." Judge Scott clapped his hands and stood. "I must beg your pardon, but it's time for me to prepare for my evening engagement. Shall we say supper, here, next week, same time?"

Ansel rose and offered a bow. "It would be my pleasure."

His host showed him to the foyer. The parlor remained

closed off, though the buzz of chatter and laughter had ceased. The butler opened the front door and bowed him out.

That had gone better than expected. Judge Scott's expectations did not seem unreasonable. Perhaps Ansel could fulfill them, after all.

As he descended the steps, he took a deep breath of the salt-tinged air, muggy and warm in early September. Roses remained in bloom along the brick walkway, and palm trees lined the square. Even as far inland as Augusta, a tropical climate prevailed.

What would it be like to enjoy a marked change in seasons? Would he ever lay eyes on the mountains hunters and trappers praised, the autumn colors vivid on the slopes? Fresh streams and waterfalls? The herds of bison and deer and abundance of rabbits and turkeys?

If newcomers from Europe, the Carolinas, and Virginia were gobbling up the land from the last treaty with the Creek and Cherokee Indians as quickly as his father said, pioneers would soon press the boundary line west of the Appalachians. Should he be content to settle for a hundred acres this side of the Ogeechee?

An open carriage with a liveried African driver atop, drawn by two handsome white stallions, pulled up to the gate as Ansel reached the picket fence. His steps faltered, for inside, next to a distinguished-looking man with silver streaking his thick brown hair and yards of white lace at his cuffs and stock, sat the girl he'd encountered at Machenry's. Was this imposing man her husband? Were they friends of the Scotts?

The black boy standing at the rear of the carriage leapt to the ground and ran around to release the folding steps.

The stocky gentleman climbed down ahead of the young woman and extended his hand to help her alight.

She moved with a grace that belied her awkwardness of the night before, and she took Ansel's breath away in a ruched gown of deep-yellow silk held out on the sides with panniers, her almost-black hair captured beneath a flat straw hat.

The man kissed her hand and gazed at her with near adoration. "As usual, Miss Scott, your company was delightful."

Miss Scott? He'd met the judge's daughter last night at a Sons of Liberty meeting?

The lady gave a slight curtsy. "Thank you for the drive, Lord Riley."

"Henry, Miss Scott. Please. Just Henry."

Lord Riley's companion paid as little heed to his last statement as Ansel did to the man's title, freeing her hand and turning toward the house. Ansel stood back from the gate, frozen in place. Her gaze settled on him, and her brows rose. Strangely enough, admiration, not recognition, lit in her eyes—as though he'd been a peacock spreading his plumage in her yard. Was she that fond of men in uniform?

Jolted into action by the glare of Lord Riley, Ansel tucked his hat under his arm and hastened forward to open the gate.

Miss Scott flowed through it like a banner of liquid sunshine, smelling most appropriately of lemon verbena.

He bowed. "'Tis a pleasure to see you again so soon, Miss *Scott*."

Her brown eyes widened.

Did she expect him not to speak of their previous meeting? Ansel glanced around. Indeed, she might prefer her father remain unaware that she claimed Liberty Boys as bosom friends, but no one stood within hearing distance.

The next moment, understanding dawned on her features. "And a surprise as well, finding you here, at my home, after we met at...um..." A delicate frown quirking her brows, she snapped her fingers.

"Machenry's," he supplied.

Her pink lips pursed as she clutched her closed fan before her. A hint of displeasure?

He leaned closer. "Don't worry. Your secret is safe with me, as I trust mine is with you."

"Of course. But I hope I did not give you the wrong impression of the kind of company I keep and the places I frequent. I'm truly not in the habit of gallivanting to taverns."

"Oh, your cousin—Frankie, was it?—made it more than clear that your reputation was at no risk." And outside the shadowy interior of the tavern, without the dark cloak, her appearance in the sunshine made it more than evident why both Frankie and Lord Riley presented the demeanor of a pit bull.

"Yes. He would." A smirk danced about Miss Scott's lips. "Frankie does go to the oddest places and runs in some unusual sets. But *you* were also at Machenry's, Mr....?"

No surprise she did not recognize his rank, but the fact that she failed to recall even his name dented his ego a bit. "Lieutenant. Lieutenant Ansel Anderson. I realize the uniform is a bit of a surprise. Let's just say that as a newcomer, I wanted to get an accurate sense of the patriotic fervor in Savannah. I could hardly do so garbed thus."

"And did you? Get an accurate picture?"

"Oh yes. Most especially from yourself, Miss Scott."

The judge's daughter gave a peal of mirth and took a step back, her hand going to her bodice. "Oh dear. I do hope I did not say anything untoward, Lieutenant. Not being aware of your persuasion, I would, of course, wish to avoid drawing any ire in such a place."

"I understand. We were both merely observers." Ansel dipped his chin.

"And now, what brings you here?"

"Even today, you do not remember me?" He allowed a grin to play about his mouth.

She cocked her head, the silk ribbon on her hat dancing in the sultry breeze. "Should I?"

"It's all right. I did not remember you last night either. Our fathers are friends—were the best of friends back in Charlestown when we were young children."

"Anderson. Of course!" Her face lit up. "Father has mentioned the name recently, but I own I did not put it together when you said it. He told us the son of his friend would be coming to town. To accept a promotion, I believe?"

"Thanks to your father, yes. I am here to express my appreciation for his recommendation to the governor, though I confess, I find the prospect of living up to his expectations a bit daunting."

"Why is that? You appear perfectly capable."

Did he imagine it, or did her faint smirk carry a hint of approval as her gaze swept him? He cleared his throat. "I'm much more accustomed to the inside of a fort's storeroom than the intrigues of fine parlors."

She rolled her eyes. "If there's any intrigue, I'm unaware of it. But you might find a few more amusements here. And while there's not much society to speak of, what little there is forms a tight-knit group. Perhaps I can be of some assistance in navigating it." She tapped his arm with her fan.

"I would value that." Indeed, a savvy—and beautiful—lady at his side could prove a valuable resource as he gained entrée into the right circles.

She smiled and drew a circle in the air with her fan. "But let's not mention to anyone else where we first met, hm?"

"As I said, your secret is safe, miss."

The lady gave a pert nod and started to turn, but Ansel wasn't about to let an opportunity pass twice.

"Judge Scott has two daughters. May I ask, which are you?"

She swiveled to face him again. "Temperance—she is the one you'd meet in a tavern." Beneath her sheer tucker, her bosom heaved above her rather low-cut gown, and she tossed her head. "Make no mistake, Tabitha would never be that careless."

With a wiggle of her fingers, Miss Scott—Temperance?—left Ansel awash in confusion.

~

"What did you say to him?" Temperance accosted her sister the moment she entered the front door. Temperance had lingered in the parlor after the last of her ladies departed, helping Cecily set things to rights, waiting for her chance to waylay Ansel Anderson after his meeting with her father. She had to convince him not to mention to anyone in her family where she had been last night.

But then her mother had wandered downstairs following her afternoon nap and had bent her ear for half an hour about the importance of her taking dance lessons to help her find a suitor if she wouldn't consider Frankie. By the time Temperance had escaped, the young officer had left the house, and Tabitha had snared him on the front walk.

"What you should have but wouldn't have." With a huff, Tabitha unpinned her hat.

"What do you mean?"

"I mean, you already met Lieutenant Anderson. And not when we were five."

Words stuck in Temperance's throat.

"Right," her twin said. "What were you doing at Machenry's—a place malcontents are known to gather?" Tabitha spoke the name of the tavern on a hiss of a whisper.

Temperance went cold. "I...we...Frankie and I might have stopped there for supper last night."

"Stopped there? Or went there for a meeting and not to Mr. Lyon's Long-room at all? When will you cease to be so careless?

Even if you care nothing for your own reputation, you will ruin this family's. *My* reputation."

"Don't fret. Lord Riley will take you regardless."

Tabitha's piercing look made Temperance bite her tongue. "You may think yourself witty, but sarcasm is not wit, sister dear."

"I'm sorry, Tabitha." Temperance dropped her head. Truly, no one else prodded her to weaponize her words the way her sister did. But if anyone could sympathize with being pushed toward an unwanted suitor, she could. Tabitha's hunger for status and wealth might see her settle for a convenient match but did not make her undeserving of love. Or kindness. Even if Tabitha did not often return it. Did Temperance not strive to live her life by the example Jesus set in the Good Book?

"You don't need to explain anything when next you see Lieutenant Anderson. I know how you clam up around men besides our cousin. I gave the lieutenant to believe Frankie dragged you to Machenry's."

Temperance spoke softly. "Thank you." Though the task had been accomplished in her usual assuming manner, her sister had saved her what promised to be another awkward conversation with Lieutenant Anderson. So why wasn't she grateful? It must have to do with the way her sister so often stole her voice—and not anything about the lieutenant. She hardly knew him.

Tabitha released a little puff of air. "I don't know why I cover for you. Yes, I do. I do it for myself."

Temperance pressed her lips tight. At least Tabitha was honest enough to admit that.

Her twin cocked her head, folding the long, trailing ribbons of her hat inside the brim. "I like that Ansel Anderson. He cuts a fine figure in his uniform."

As Temperance's stomach plummeted, her chin rose. "You think him a potential replacement for Lord Riley."

"Perhaps." Tabitha shrugged. "We shall see. But I don't want him put off by a sister of mine sympathizing with the rebels. He is clearly a king's man."

Temperance narrowed her gaze on her sister. "Why do you say that?" Lieutenant Anderson's warning in the tavern, followed by the call made on their father in his uniform, would certainly make it seem so. Had he said something to Tabitha that confirmed it? If he had, whatever spark she'd felt in his presence must prove naught but a passing attraction.

"Besides being the son of father's best friend? And an officer in the rangers? Once I dug you out of the pit your visit to Machenry's put you in, he seemed eager to clarify that he was only there out of curiosity himself. And he indicated that our father was responsible for his promotion."

"You think he is in Father's pocket?"

"Wouldn't you be, if you owed him so much? Oh, wait. You do. Well, at least some of us recognize our good fortune and are smart enough to protect it. Yes...I'd imagine if there is one man Father would be willing to court me instead of Henry Gage, Lord Riley, it might be Ansel Anderson. Well..." She laid her hat on the side table and patted her hair, a tiny smile tugging up her mouth. "Once he figures out which one of us is which."

Temperance's mouth dropped open. "You let him think you were me?"

'Twould hardly be the first time. But with the last unwitting swap Tabitha had pulled on Temperance, their mother had finally dropped her mollycoddling of her firstborn. She'd railed at Tabitha for an hour and then canceled her engagements for a fortnight—an effective form of punishment for a social butterfly, as it turned out. Until now.

Tabitha gave a puff of a laugh. "How else was I to find out why he recognized you?"

"By clarifying that you were my sister and then asking him?"

"Where's the fun in that? Besides, I have to figure out why you allow our cousin to keep calling on you when you have even less interest in him than I have in Lord Riley." Tabitha surveyed her a moment, her brows drawn flat. Then she sailed toward the stairway, the long Watteau box pleat of her *robe à la francaise* trailing out behind her.

Temperance stifled a groan. Tabitha's deception had probably muddied the waters, which in the long run could lead to more questions—not fewer—from Lieutenant Anderson. And while Tabitha must not have known about the meeting at the tavern, her suspicions about Frankie meant Temperance needed to be more careful. Her twin would continue to watch and listen, and it would only be a matter of time until she used what she'd learned to her advantage.

CHAPTER 4

"And that concludes your tour of Savannah." Jack Weaver grinned at Ansel as he locked the door of the powder house on Reynolds Square.

Two days after Ansel's arrival, Lieutenant Jones had assigned the younger man to help familiarize him with the city, especially the places they might conduct military business. They had started at the King's Storehouse on River Street, then ridden to Market Square in the northwest corner of the grid of six squares, a straight shot from Fort Halifax west on Bryan Street. He'd already been to St. James Square when he'd visited the Scotts. The guardhouse sat on Wright Square, recently renamed to honor the latest governor. A pyramid of stones there marked the grave of Tomochichi, a Creek Indian leader who had helped James Oglethorpe found the colony. According to Jack, hangings were also conducted in that location.

They had ridden through Upper New Square on the southeastern edge of the city without stopping, merely admiring the homes of the former governor and Gerard De Brahm, a German geographer and engineer. He'd designed forts in the area as well as the town of Ebenezer and now worked from St. Augustine surveying the coast.

Ansel studied the silk filature house with its small dormers and triple chimneys. Beyond it sat the Council House, where the Commons Assembly met. Had Lieutenant Jones asked Jack to be Ansel's guide because Jack had told him he'd encountered Ansel at Machenry's? If so, Jack had yet to question or caution him—though the Council House provided an easy opening. He'd been friendly but all business.

"What about Johnson Square?" Ansel turned from the Council House and faced west. "The one that lies between here and Market Square." Jack had described the earliest neighborhood that had sprung up here, Derby Ward, with the first store, public well and oven, and house for strangers as they passed through, but the massive portico of Christ Church had beckoned.

Jack pocketed the powder house key and swiped the sweat from his brow. "What of it? 'Tis not a place we go often...unless you plan to attend Christ Church."

That was exactly what he intended. "I admit, I'd coveted a closer look. Such a fine building, the sanctuary must be magnificent."

Jack winked. "I won't be escorting you there, my friend. Though it is a beautiful place. A friend of mine, Peter Tondee, worked with the carpenter who built it."

Would Ansel see the Scotts there? His father had spoken of the family as God-fearing Anglicans like the Andersons. He'd take any opportunity to further satisfy his curiosity about the mysterious daughter. Temperance. He rubbed his chin. Tabitha?

He followed Jack to their mounts. His bay stallion, Oliver, rolled his eye at Ansel as if wondering how long until he could have a proper jaunt in the fields outside Argyle. Poor creature felt as cramped here as Ansel did. "So we're back to Halifax?" Huzzah.

"No hurry." Jack's saddle creaked as he mounted. "We have time to stop in for spruce beer at my favorite watering hole near the wharf."

"Perhaps I can take in the docks while you do that."

"Not a drinking man, are you?"

He'd honor the lack of challenge in Jack's question with simple honesty. "Afraid not. Back when I first joined up, when everyone got all bestirred about the Cherokees around sixty, sixty-one, the South Carolina boys saw all the action. The new recruits at Argyle—myself among them—spent too much time at the local tavern."

"Understandable. So what changed?" Jack headed his mount toward the river.

Ansel jerked his chin toward the house across the square where Jack had told him the famous Methodist minister John Wesley had lived. "A circuit-riding preacher showed up."

"Oh, no!" Jack made a face of mock horror as he maneuvered around a dark-skinned sailor in short pants, carrying his sea bag. "Those wild Methodists are worse than the Anglicans. But if you're rubbing shoulders with them, you might be more of a rule-breaker than I thought."

Ansel cut him a glance. "Actually, life is most rewarding when we honor God and country." How could people do that when they were constantly finding fault with the king and Parliament, the very government God had appointed over them?

"Even when the laws erode our God-given freedoms?"

"Most of the time, it's the ne'er-do-wells who complain the most." The statement slipped out without thought. When Jack stared at him, he shifted. His innate need to make others see truth warred with the agreement he'd struck with Judge Scott.

Deception went against his grain in every way, yet he needed to make a friend of this man. He waved his hand. "Forget it."

"No. Tell me. What were you going to say?" Jack's tone remained even, indicating potential open-mindedness.

"I was just thinking about the smugglers who railed against the Sugar Act, even though it actually *lowered* the tax to three pence a gallon on the molasses they used to make their rum. Is breaking the law worth saving a penny and a half?"

"No, but much has happened since the Sugar Act."

He weighed his response while waiting for a wagon loaded with canvas sacks to pass, then he urged Oliver to draw even with Jack's horse. "I'm aware of the principles behind the protests. And I don't disagree with them. But there are ways to work within the system." He could truthfully present himself as a moderate, a man open to patriotic ideals who still respected the authority he served under...much like Benjamin Franklin. The Philadelphia printer had represented the colonies before a committee of Parliament, working to find alternatives to the Stamp Act.

"Come to the tavern and tell me how. You can order soup and cider." Jack smirked over at him.

"On such a fine day, I prefer to avoid both vices—beer and politics." Better to make a joke than an enemy...or to behave disingenuously himself.

"And yet, I met you in a tavern full of politicians. Intriguing." Jack laughed, lifting himself in the stirrups. "Come. It's just up ahead."

He gestured to a row of frame buildings on their left, fronting the wharves on the right, where the high, sandy bluff met the wide mouth of the river. Seagulls cawed and circled the masts of tall sailing vessels visible from River Street. Ships, schooners, and sloops carried rice, lumber, and barreled beef and pork to the West Indies as well as indigo and raw silk to England. They returned with luxury goods and staples from the mother country. The activity of the docks drew Ansel, but something else captured his immediate notice—a slight figure in a tapestry bodice, laced stomacher, and blue petticoat, followed by a servant as she hurried along the boardwalk and inside a door.

Was that Miss Scott?

"What is that place?" Ansel pointed to the building the pair had just entered.

"The one next to Harris and Habersham?" Jack frowned, tilting his head. "A new store, I believe, in Johnson and Wylly's old place. The owner has a strange name." He scratched his chin. "Button something. Button Gwinnett."

"What does he sell?"

"Just about everything. Why?"

Best not to reveal his curiosity about Miss Scott. Jack could possibly confirm if she kept regular company with the Sons of Liberty, but then he'd want to know why Ansel asked. He hadn't seemed to have recognized her the other day, and if that was the case, Ansel should honor Miss Scott's request that he not discuss her presence at Machenry's.

His second encounter with Miss Scott had taunted him since the day prior. Not only had she seemed strangely resistive of giving him her name, but she'd contradicted everything she'd spoken with great conviction at the tavern.

Even her manner had been different. At Machenry's, she'd been endearingly awkward. Sincere. Outside her house, though, she'd been coy, almost flirtatious—as if she could charm him out of his discernment. He could only surmise that the reversal stemmed from fear of his association with her father rather than a change of heart. And that could only mean that Judge Scott might be harboring a subversive under his own roof.

"There are a few things I could stock up on after months on the frontier." Things required by a gentleman expected to mingle in society. Ansel offered his companion a conciliatory smile. "We can have that conversation some other time, can we not?"

"Of course."

"I look forward to it." He infused his tone with sincerity. Jack seemed a good sort. Ansel would figure out a way to win his trust without betraying his own conscience.

"See you back at the fort." Jack returned Ansel's smile with a fleeting one of his own, but his brow remained furrowed before he turned his horse toward a tavern with a gold-painted lion's head adorning its wooden sign.

Ansel secured Oliver outside Gwinnett's storehouse with a pat to his neck. "Sorry, old boy. This is better than the stable, though, right?"

Inside the building, he paused a moment for his eyes to adjust to the dimmer lighting. The plethora of goods would have taken him aback had he not been so intent on the two women facing away from him while speaking with another lady over a wooden table that held folded fabric. Ansel eased past tinware and ironmongery and a few other patrons until he drew within hearing range.

"You won't find finer Irish linens anywhere in town than these Mr. Gwinnett just got in." The young woman behind the counter nodded to a slightly portly man with brown hair who carried a large box out from a back room to a customer, then accompanied the older gentleman toward the street.

"'Tis lovely." Miss Scott's voice held a certain regret. "But some of us—at least, the ladies of my sewing circle—are abstaining from purchasing imported fabric. It's important that we learn to sustain ourselves here in the colonies as much as possible, don't you think? Though I did come in for some of your mold candles."

"Of course." The lady who must be Mrs. Gwinnett leaned forward to whisper, though her words still carried. "Just between us, I agree with you. I'm having a woman I met here make my winter woolens."

Miss Scott sucked in a breath. "I would love to learn more about that. A friend told me you might be of that mindset."

"I am, indeed."

"Then I'd like to invite you—"

Ansel's leg bumped a box of spoons, and it toppled to the floor before he could catch it. The crash and clatter drew the eye of everyone in the store, especially Miss Scott, who whirled. Her widened gaze latched onto him from behind rather adorable horn-rimmed spectacles.

~

Temperance snatched the awful glasses off. "Lieutenant Anderson! What are you doing sneaking up on me?"

He removed his hat and bowed. "Forgive me for startling you, Miss Scott. I saw you enter from the street and wanted to come in and say hello. And peruse this fine establishment, of course." Ansel extended his smile of greeting to Mrs. Gwinnett. She smiled back.

My. One would never peg this ranger for a country cracker. And yet, the man's demeanor held not a hint of flirtation. Somehow, Temperance could never imagine him using beguilement to get his way. He did not need to. His natural dignity would command admiration even if he dressed in the rough clothing of the frontier. Maybe especially then.

His gaze followed Temperance's efforts to conceal her frames beneath the embroidered linen that covered the contents of her basket. "I don't recall you wearing those when you were out for your ride with Lord Riley."

Temperance's breath froze in her throat. Thankfully, Cecily

saved her, diverting the lieutenant's focus as she ducked past him and started gathering spoons.

"Oh, no. Please don't do that. This was my fault. I will pick them up." He touched Cecily's shoulder, and she moved to the side. Ansel crouched and lifted the wooden box, and Cecily deposited her fistful of utensils into the bottom before he placed it back on the table.

Temperance's estimation of the man rose another notch. "What brings you to the waterfront today, Lieutenant?" she asked as he continued collecting spoons.

"Jack Weaver took me on a tour of the city." When he'd dumped the last spoon back into the box, he straightened and met her gaze. "You may know him?"

"I..." She swallowed. "The name sounds familiar." Frankie had mentioned the man as one of the rangers who often accompanied Lieutenant Noble Wimberly Jones to their meetings. Had he been present at Machenry's earlier that week? She'd basically declared her connection to all the Liberty Boys that evening to Lieutenant Anderson. Would she only compound the harm her sister had done by acting ignorant now?

"He is a private in the rangers. A friend of First Lieutenant Jones, I believe." His piercing stare made her seek a means of escape.

But when she turned toward Mrs. Gwinnett, another customer had approached to ask her a question. The shopkeeper's wife shot her an apologetic smile. Temperance waved her off. "We'll talk more another time."

Lieutenant Anderson's timing couldn't have been worse. And why did she have the distinct feeling he'd been standing there listening to their conversation before his blunder drew her notice?

Cecily stepped forward. "Miss Scott, Mr. Gwinnett is back. You want me to get them candle molds?"

"Er...of course. Thank you, Cecily." Since she could make no legitimate protest for her maid leaving her alone with the handsome loyalist ranger—three strikes against him as far as she was concerned—Temperance dug into her change purse for some coins and handed them to Cecily. She looked up to find the man staring at her, his expression strangely intense. A look that sent a tingle to her toes. "And, um, how do you find Fort Halifax, sir?"

"Depressing. I'm glad to be free of it, to tell the truth."

"Oh. Not as nice as Fort Argyle, then?"

"Not by half." His fingers drummed the table next to him. "I'd guess only two of its walls might withstand enemy fire. Did you know they constructed it from the log ruins of the previous fort?"

"Fort Oglethorpe?" She laughed. "Well, 'tis no surprise. It was used to store presents for Indian trade."

"As I have discovered. The whole place reeks of liquor and tobacco."

Temperance grimaced. "I doubt you will need to worry about actual cannonade. Fort George would provide the first line of defense." The newer palisade sat on Cockspur Island in the mouth of the river.

"Yes, I suppose we at Halifax bear little threat from foreign navies *or* the Indians. 'Tis an adjustment from the frontier." He offered a lopsided smile, summoning his dimples again. "Our presence here is mainly to support the governor, of course. In cases of civil unrest."

His continual assessment, friendly as it was, tied Temperance's stomach in a knot. Since Cecily was settling accounts with Mr. Gwinnett, Temperance moved past Lieutenant Anderson, her petticoats brushing his boots in the narrow aisle, and moseyed as casually as possible toward the door. Once he followed her outside, she could make her excuses, and he would return to his fort, whether he enjoyed its confines or not. Her next two errands must be completed in secrecy, but how could she make conversation until they parted? Small talk was not her forte.

She spoke over her shoulder. "Tell me about Fort Argyle."

"It's its own city, really. The brick barracks lie outside the fort, along with residences and some other businesses. Argyle serves as the entrenched main encampment and headquarters for both troops of rangers—our meeting location, our launching point for assignments."

"And you never came into Savannah while you were stationed there?"

"No. Only the smaller towns around it. When I had leave, I went home."

"And where is home?"

His straight brows knit together above those amazing eyes. "Did I not tell you that when we last spoke?"

A flush stole over Temperance's face. "I-I'm sorry. I don't recall." That must have been something he said to Tabitha. She had hoped to allow the incident to pass, avoiding any further questions it might raise, but as she had feared, her sister's interference had only made things more awkward for her. And that was noteworthy when she was so accomplished at it herself.

He held the door for her with a slight frown. What a ninny he must think her. "My family owns a farm in St. George's Parish. It was your father who encouraged mine to apply for a grant in 1763, when my father's law practice in Augusta failed to thrive as hoped."

"Of course. I'm sure you told me that. Well, here is Cecily, so we shall be on our way, as I'm certain you must be on yours." She dropped a little curtsy.

Before she could head for Bull Street, Ansel positioned himself in front of her. "Please. Allow me to escort you home."

Her heart sped up. He meant to question her, not express interest in her. She would do well to remember that. "Thank you, but I have a couple of errands that may take some time." Both of which would only increase his suspicions of her.

A wry smile played about the corners of his mouth. "As I confessed, I'm in no hurry to return to Fort Halifax. Where are you headed?"

"First? My dance mistress's house on Johnson Square."

"Perfect. I wanted a closer look at Johnson Square. Just let me get my horse."

She'd never met such a single-minded man. As he pivoted, she waved her hand. "There really is no need." Seizing the opportunity to make good her escape, she turned to step out into the street. Only, she'd forgotten about the boardwalk, and she stumbled and flailed to keep her balance with one foot on and one foot hanging off.

Lieutenant Anderson whirled and grabbed hold of her. Her fingers sank into the supple wool of his uniform and the thick muscles beneath. His widened eyes probed hers. "Are you all right?"

"I'm...fine." Again, that scent of leather and pine. This close, the tiny picks of dark hair he'd shaved that morning were visible on his jaw. She forced her fingers to relax their hold, but she couldn't look away.

Until Cecily clucked her tongue and said, "Miss Scott, why you not wearing your spectacles?" Ever so helpfully, she fished them from Temperance's basket and held them out.

Temperance sighed, took them, and put them on. Then she stared at Ansel Anderson with her owl eyes. Incredibly, he moved not an inch, and his expression did not change, so she confessed, "Lieutenant, you have been deceived." Perhaps the offer of a single puzzle piece would divert his focus from the larger picture.

He maintained his decorum. "In what way, Miss Scott?"

She laced her fingers in front of her. "The woman you met

outside my house yesterday afternoon was not me. I remained inside after hosting my sewing circle."

"Then..." Speculation lit his eyes as they narrowed on her.

"It was my twin, Tabitha. I'm sorry. She is quite a minx."

He shook his head. "You are not accountable for her actions." He pointed to her spectacles. "But you—"

"Yes. I, Temperance, wear glasses, accounting for my not seeing you properly the other day at the tavern or the curb today. 'Tis a source of some embarrassment for me." Her cheeks heated, but the confession came as something of a relief. Now, he could think of her whatever he would, and he wouldn't worry about the consequences. She wouldn't.

"They look fitting on you, Miss Scott."

Already braced for the expected offense, she drew back, but his aristocratic features softened into an indulgent smile. "Th-thank you?"

A chuckle rumbled from his chest. "I really do mean it as a compliment. And I would imagine that they would help a great deal in going about town. But what I started to say earlier was that it *was* you at Machenry's."

She took in a quick breath. She could hardly deny it now. "It was."

"May I ask why you chose that particular establishment on that particular night?"

She could see but one safe way to satisfy Lieutenant Anderson's curiosity. "As I believe my sister told you, my cousin took me to the tavern for dinner. Lord Riley is courting Tabitha. Frankie often calls on me."

"I see."

Temperance might have hoped for some small measure of chagrin—not because it was so unusual for cousins to marry, especially among upper-class families. But for her own admiration-starved vanity. However, he kept his voice surprisingly immaculate of emotion.

She forged on in the same business-like manner. "For the most part, I go along with his suggestions. Now, I really must beg your pardon. I will be late for my appointments."

Without waiting for him to come up with another reason to accompany her, she grabbed Cecily's arm and hurried them away. She glanced back to find him still watching her.

No matter. When he came for dinner next week, Tabitha would divert him. Temperance could count on it—and she wouldn't interfere. Some things were more important than unrequited and misplaced attractions.

A sudden inconsistency hit her with the force of a stamp mill. If Ansel was a loyalist informant, how had he gotten into the meeting at Machenry's? In the haste of self-protection, she'd just squandered her opportunity to turn his own question on him and find out.

CHAPTER 5

*A*nsel waited until Miss Scott and her servant turned the corner at Johnson Square, then mounted Oliver and followed. The imposing beauty of Christ Church was forgotten. All he could think about was the sensation in his gut that Temperance Scott was up to something.

Another possibility hit him as he scoured the square for a residence that could belong to the dance mistress. Perhaps she took his curiosity about her political leanings for romantic interest. If this cousin of hers was courting her, she might well find that objectionable. Perhaps that accounted for the strange impression he'd gotten from her. Just the same, he should rule out any suspicions.

He caught a glimpse of a figure in a flowered bodice down the street opening a gate in a picket fence and approaching a whitewashed plantation-style house. Ansel urged Oliver into an adjacent drive behind a massive live oak with Spanish moss almost brushing the ground.

Miss Scott and her maid proceeded along the walkway lined in boxwoods and up the steps. But rather than knock on the front door, Miss Scott looked around. She said something to her servant, and the woman—Cecily—moved behind her, blocking the view from the street. Miss Scott ducked, doing something on the porch, then straightened and hurried away, Cecily following.

Ansel remained concealed until the two women crossed the square and entered the gate of the churchyard.

When they were out of sight, he rode to the house next door, looping Oliver's reins around the fence, and sprinted up the walk. Urn planters with red, orange, and yellow marigolds basking in the sunlight bracketed either side of the steps. A sign by the door read, *J. Swinton, Lodging. Dance Instruction for Young Ladies and Children, Thursdays and Saturdays.* Rocking chairs lined the front porch. Flush with the house, a wooden box had been built in and painted white—presumably a parcel or grocery drop.

Ansel opened the lid. Empty. But this was just where he'd seen Miss Scott bend over. Perhaps she'd retrieved something?

A corner of a paper tucked behind one of the braces caught his eye. He tugged it out and unfolded the single crease. A list of French terms, unfamiliar to him, had been written in two columns. He blinked and frowned. *Cahiers. Feuilles—*

Steps sounded in the hallway of the house, and the door flew open so quickly Ansel barely had time to stuff the paper in his pocket—an urge which the narrowed gaze and downturned mouth of the middle-aged woman he found himself facing prevented him from examining. "Er...Mrs. Swinton?"

"Do I look like the missus to ye?" The woman indicated her clothing, clearly servant's attire. "I be her housekeeper."

"Is Mrs. Swinton in?" He really should deliver Miss Scott's message, though how would he explain why he had it? Especially when he didn't even know what it was?

"She is not. Can I help ye with something?"

"Um...I heard dance instruction was offered here."

"For ladies and children." The housekeeper pointed at the

sign. "For the instruction of gentlemen, you will be wantin' Mrs. Mary Smith on the new square. Monday, Wednesday, Friday."

"Thank you, madam." Ansel made a bow. "Please pardon the disturbance."

She gave a curt nod but remained in the open doorway, staring at him with one corner of her lips quirked up. And not in a smile. Under her watchful gaze, he could hardly put the paper back. And he could think of no natural way to ask her to deliver it to Mrs. Swinton. He'd have to return it later. After he'd studied it further.

Ansel made his way back to his horse and led Oliver around the square to the church.

Why would Miss Scott be here on a weekday? Was she meeting someone?

A wrought-iron gate in the brick wall opened to a courtyard. Chanting voices drew him to peer between the bars. Gathered on the grass beneath a grapevine arbor sat a couple dozen women and children. Their dark-skinned faces glowed in the early-evening light as they recited the words of the Twenty-third Psalm, reflecting an inner peace despite their faded, homespun clothing and the puckered brands borne by some on their flesh. An older man in the dark suit of a rector sat on a bench before them, shifting slowly to one side as though his back pained him. He spoke loudly and with a German accent. And standing at his side, holding a Bible, was Miss Temperance Scott.

She wasn't conducting clandestine meetings. She was helping her minister teach slaves.

∼

Temperance slid her finger down the latest issue of the *Georgia Gazette* at the next weekly meeting of the Daughters of Liberty. "It seems that the eleventh of

October is the date set for the colonial representatives to meet in New York, to petition his majesty and Parliament for relief under 'the insupportable grievance of the Stamp Act,' as it says here." She looked at the ladies crowded into her parlor.

A few heads nodded, but their faces were too blurry to discern expressions.

"While our Georgia delegates were denied the opportunity to attend, we will look forward to the report of what occurs. And next week, we will meet as discussed in Gwinnett's storeroom." After folding the paper, she laid it aside and slid on her glasses.

Ah, yes. Most of the women turned to Ann Gwinnett, smiling—except for Mary Mabry. Little worry dimples appeared on her smooth cheeks.

"Are you certain your husband approves?" Temperance asked their new member.

Not the newest, for Ann had brought two friends, Mrs. Jenny McKenzie, who had recently moved to Savannah from the backcountry, and Mrs. Emmaline Dash, who had brought her maid with her. Temperance had been obliged to ask their butler, Jonas, to bring in more chairs. What a wonderful problem to have. Thankfully, the shop on the wharf would offer plenty of room for future growth.

"Oh, yes. My Button is a patriot at heart. He just has yet to fully realize it." Ann winked at Mary, and she relaxed a bit. "Mrs. McKenzie has already had her loom delivered."

Temperance rose with a rustle of her petticoat. "We are thankful you offered your space to house it, and Mrs. McKenzie, your skill to teach us how to use it."

The middle-aged Scottish woman bobbed her head. "My pleasure, miss. Although we will start with spinning lessons, o' course. 'Tis pleased I am to be included."

"We are delighted you joined us, Mrs. McKenzie. And you,

Mrs. Dash. And please, if you have friends of the same persuasion, bring them next week."

The ladies followed Temperance's lead, standing and gathering their belongings. They chatted a few moments while Cecily and Mrs. Dash's servant, Rhoda, cleared dishes.

Temperance took the opportunity to surreptitiously remove the lace tucker she'd worn with her deep-amber taffeta. She'd anticipated that she'd lack sufficient time for a full change before dinner, but was her gown elegant enough? No doubt Tabitha would dress herself to the hilt, as their mother always did. But what did that matter? Hadn't she already determined that her sister was welcome to Lieutenant Anderson?

When the Mabry sisters made their way to the door, Temperance stepped into the hallway with them. Jonas saw them out while Temperance bid Elizabeth and Lydia farewell.

Elizabeth took a moment to hug her and murmur in her ear, "I'm so proud of what you're doing."

"Not just me." Temperance drew back and squeezed her hands. "All of us. Together, we will make a difference."

As her friend moved past her, Temperance froze, for standing at the door of the study were her father and Lieutenant Anderson. Had they heard? She recovered her equilibrium enough to offer adequate parting comments to the newer members of their circle. When the door shut behind them, Father and his companion came forward.

"Temperance, our guest is here early. Your sister is not down yet, so I thought perhaps you could take Lieutenant Anderson for a turn in the garden." Oblivious to the breath Temperance held, Father patted the man on the arm. "I shall be back down shortly."

"Of course." Ansel's gaze swept Temperance—perceptive, as always. "Although, I do not wish to force my company upon Miss Scott." Hat in hand, he offered her a slight bow. "I can entertain myself with a book if you need time before supper as well."

"Thank you, but I'm fine." Did she look as though she needed the time? Temperance gave a discreet pat to her hair, and her fingers brushed the tip of her spectacles over her ears. Rats. Just because the lieutenant had seen her in them and had pretended to like them did not mean she wanted to make that image of her a lasting one. She hastened to remove them, tucking them into the pocket tied beneath her petticoat.

Father waved his hand. "Temperance does not fuss over appearances like my wife and older daughter—older only by a matter of minutes, naturally. You will find this one an eminently practical girl. You don't have plans, do you, Temperance?"

"No, Father."

"Very well, then. 'Tis a meet time to renew your acquaintance. Enjoy the garden." Father turned and headed up the stairs.

Temperance faced Lieutenant Anderson with a hesitant smile. She'd determined to avoid his scrutiny, but neither did she want him to think her rude. In fact, she'd struggled to not think about him all week. She tilted her head toward the door, which Jonas opened. "Shall we?"

He glanced into the parlor. "Should your maid accompany us?"

Temperance flushed. She should have thought of that herself. "Of course." She leaned into the next room to summon Cecily, who relegated carrying trays to the kitchen staff and trailed them onto the porch.

Ansel offered Temperance his arm as they descended the steps. To avoid any further mishaps in his presence, she took it. He placed his free hand over hers, the little gesture so unexpectedly thoughtful that she narrowly refrained from shooting him a look of astonishment.

"You had quite a group for your sewing circle today."

She found enough breath to answer. "Yes, we are growing."

"I had no idea sewing circles were so popular. And you seem very inclusive."

Temperance ventured a glance at him. Had he noticed Mrs. McKenzie's homespun clothing? "We will take all the help we can get. We do a good bit of charity work, especially for Bethesda."

"The orphanage south of the city started by Reverend George Whitefield?"

"The same. Reverend Whitefield travels a good bit to preach and raise money for Bethesda. He hopes to one day make it into a college. We do our best to support his efforts."

"Laudable. There would seem to be no end to your benevolence, Miss Scott." Lieutenant Anderson paused on the tabby walkway and turned to her. "If it's all hands on deck, do your servants take part?"

"Pardon me?" She was having trouble getting past wondering what he'd meant by his comment about her benevolence—not to mention, the intense scrutiny of his green eyes.

"In the sewing. Your maid." The lieutenant tilted his head toward Cecily, who had taken a seat on a wrought-iron bench visible through a break in the boxwoods. "And the servant who came with one of the other ladies today. Do they sew with you?"

"Oh. No. Generally, they…serve." A hot flush stole over her face, and she dropped her hand from his arm, staring into a patch of lavender. "You shame me, Lieutenant."

He stiffened slightly. "I'm sure that was not my intent."

"And yet, I *should* be shamed. For all my ideals about equality, I have overlooked something so obvious that you took it for granted." She lifted her chin, blinking in the bright light. "But I will rectify that omission at the next opportunity—the next meeting. If Rhoda and Cecily wish it, I will put it before the ladies."

One of his eyebrows lifted. "And if they decline to admit servants as members?"

Temperance's mouth opened, then closed. What *would* she do? Should she risk her larger goal of starting a Daughters of Liberty group just when it was gaining momentum? Which principle was the greater? Finally, she concluded, "Then I shall have some persuading to do."

Lieutenant Anderson's shadow fell over her as he took a step closer. "Miss Scott, I am glad we have this moment to speak alone. I confess, I had hoped for it." His fingers brushed her arm. "You have made quite an impression on me."

Her heart fluttered and panic surged. What was he about? And how was she to handle it? Any wit that might flow from her pen or her lips in support of a noble cause never translated into beguilement. Modesty, however, she did not have to manufacture. "Why, Lieutenant—"

"I promise"—he lifted his hand—"I mean nothing untoward."

"Oh, of course not." Temperance curled her fingers against her palms. Why did she keep mistaking his sincerity, his unsettling intensity, for personal interest? Because she secretly wished it so?

"What I meant was that I see that you are a woman of deeply held principles. Admirable ones. At first, I thought—"

"Temperance?"

She startled at the voice calling her name and squinted as a shape appeared around the corner of the house. "Frankie?" Relief warred with irritation. What was he doing here? Hadn't he gotten her message to stay away? Today, of all days?

Lieutenant Anderson straightened, though he still spoke in low, quick tones for her ears alone. "Miss Scott, if you need to use your spectacles, I have already told you 'tis no matter to me."

Because he would never give a second thought to her appearance? "Lieutenant Anderson," she snapped, "I hardly need your permission. And I think I know my own cousin."

He blinked and moved back. "Forgive me. I meant no offense."

And yet she seemed to keep offending him. How did she explain that it had been naught but her embarrassment talking? Her pride again. She dropped her chin, but Frankie strode up before she could speak.

"Sir." He acknowledged their guest with the most abrupt bow she had ever witnessed, then turned his broiling brown eyes on her. "Cousin. Once again, I find you alone in this man's company, although this evening, I see he wears his true colors." His disdainful gaze swept Lieutenant Anderson's blue-and-red uniform with its polished brass buttons.

Temperance winced. Frankie must have failed to note the butts of both pistol and carbine beneath that uniform coat. He should have a care, and indeed, Lieutenant Anderson bristled. Before he could respond, she pressed her lips together and indicated Cecily on the bench.

Frankie followed her gesture. "Ah. I see." At least he had the grace to sound contrite.

"Frankie, this is Lieutenant Ansel Anderson. It turns out, he is the son of a good friend of my father's. Lieutenant Anderson, my cousin, Mr. Franklin Scott. I don't believe you were introduced when last you met."

One of Frankie's thin brows arched upward. "No, as I recall, the lieutenant was in great haste to leave."

Lieutenant Anderson pasted on an overly polite smile. "Good news. I'm invited to supper, so we'll have ample time to get acquainted."

"Oh, I doubt Frankie will be staying." Temperance slid her

fingers around her cousin's arm and squeezed meaningfully. "He probably just dropped by to give me some message or another. Isn't that right?"

What Frankie gave her was a blank stare and a shake of his head. "No. I am here at your mother's invitation. To make an even number for your supper party."

Of course he was. Mother would not have overlooked an opportunity to throw her into Frankie's company. It was Mother's approval that usually overrode Father's reticence for Frankie to squire her about of an evening—though that had suited Temperance's purposes thus far. She swallowed the sigh that wanted to break free and instead painted on a smile. "How lovely. Why don't we all go into the parlor? Father should be ready to join us."

With his mouth set firmly, Lieutenant Anderson extended his arm to indicate they should precede him toward the house. He must share her exasperation over her cousin's arrival—but for an entirely different reason. Given his serious demeanor coupled with his disavowal of romantic intentions, she should be glad to escape whatever topic he'd been about to introduce.

When Father met them at the door and ushered the lieutenant into the parlor, offering a drink—which Ansel declined—Temperance leaned close to Frankie. "Did you not receive my message?"

"What message?" His breath smelled of tobacco.

She widened her eyes. "The one I left at Swinton's, telling you to stay away for a while because Tabitha and our guest tonight are both asking too many questions. My father arranged Lieutenant Anderson's transfer and promotion, and I have my suspicions as to why."

"He wants loyalist eyes and ears in the rangers. I knew I disliked the chap." Frankie's brows pinched together. "What has he been asking you?"

"Why I was at Machenry's—he and my sister both were. Why we are so often in company."

Her cousin straightened, smoothing the lapel of his striped silk coat. "Then 'tis providential I did come, Temperance, for there is but one explanation that can satisfy. Only a clear demonstration of my devotion will provide the needed protection from this unsolicited speculation."

Oh no. She had just handed her cousin the justification he needed to press his suit. He reached for her hand, bowed over it, and brushed her knuckles with a kiss. His lips were cold and firm, like the leather on the sidesaddle she almost never used.

Her gaze shot to the open door of the parlor. Indeed, while taking the chair her father indicated, Ansel looked their way. And her hand jerked back as if of its own accord.

However was she to play along with Frankie's plan when this man was near?

CHAPTER 6

Did Ansel imagine it, or did a slight shudder wrack Temperance's slender frame when her cousin kissed her hand? Perhaps not, or if it did, the man paid no heed. He merely regained the hand she pulled away and tucked it through his arm, drawing her into the parlor.

The cousin's arrival had proved as inopportune as it had in the tavern, both times interrupting Ansel's chance to measure Temperance's loyalties. Mrs. Gwinnett's presence at the sewing circle after her conversation with Temperance seemed to confirm the members entertained some notions of colonial dissent. Yet holding a private opinion hardly constituted a crime, as he had just pointed out to Judge Scott.

The other things he'd learned about Temperance—helping with the religious instruction of slaves, using her sewing circle to work for the orphanage while including those of lower classes in the endeavor—indicated her causes leaned toward the humanitarian. The paper stuffed in the side of Mrs. Swinton's delivery box still raised questions, but by all appearances, it had contained naught but a list of dance movements. He might not have recognized some of the strange French terms had it not been for the word, *minuet*, written at the bottom and underlined.

His spying and removal of the paper had nagged his conscience ever since. He would have to look for another opportunity for private conversation with the young lady—if possible, to discern what she'd been up to in leaving it where she did.

He'd just risen to acknowledge her entrance when another pair swept through the door and cut off the approach of Temperance and Frankie—the mother and the other daughter. Both women wore bright silks with embroidered, vining patterns and copious lace at the elbows. While unpowdered, their hair was piled high on their heads and accented with tiny flowers. They halted before him and affected elegant curtsies.

An indulgent smile lit Judge Scott's face. "Lieutenant Anderson, may I present my wife, Mrs. Marjorie Scott, and my older daughter, Miss Tabitha Scott."

"It is an honor, madam." Ansel bowed first over Mrs. Scott's hand, then Tabitha's. "Miss."

Her dark eyes shone while her lips twitched with suppressed mirth. A minx, indeed. Likely, she'd expected his jaw to drop when he beheld her and her sister together, their differences so obvious in each other's company. He was not sorry to disappoint her.

He smirked back. "Your older daughter and I have met before as well."

Out of view of her parents, Tabitha gave him a quick wink. She was flirting with him, when she had a lord courting her? The girls back home had been too shy to speak when he left for Fort Argyle, and the few women at the fort had been officers' or merchants' wives. He might lack experience with females, but an innate sense of self-preservation told Ansel he'd be wise to keep this one at arm's length.

Perhaps it would help if he reminded her where her interest

should lie. "I am surprised your friend, Lord Riley, is not joining us tonight."

"Why, then, I could not be your supper partner." Tabitha aligned herself with him, facing her mother. "And supper is ready, is it not?"

"It is, indeed. We may go in." Following the order of those of highest standing leading into a supper or social event, Mrs. Scott took her husband's arm and allowed him to escort her to the mahogany table Ansel had previously glimpsed in the next room.

Tabitha wasted no time claiming him and tugging him after them, leaving her sister and cousin to bring up the rear.

The table glittered with crystal glasses, a silver candelabra, a silver centerpiece of roses and sugared fruit, and an assortment of utensils more daunting than all the supplies in the storeroom of Fort Argyle combined. Once they were seated, servants brought warm china bowls and a tureen of clam chowder.

As this was a private function, Mrs. Scott was free to initiate the conversation. "Please tell us, how is your family, Lieutenant Anderson?"

"My parents and brother are well, ma'am, and send their regards." At least, his father had relayed such news about the others when he last came alone to visit Ansel at Fort Argyle. Judge Scott's invitation had merited a private conference between father and son.

"If I remember correctly," Mrs. Scott said, "your mother was quite the musician. Does she still play the harp and sing?"

"Most beautifully." It had been far too long since he'd heard his mother's soothing music of an evening. She had always known just when to employ her gift to bring peace to their home.

"You should hear my Tabitha at the spinet." Mrs. Scott fluttered her lashes with as much coyness as if she praised herself.

61

"I am sure she is very accomplished."

Was that a hiccup—or a snort—from Temperance? He couldn't tell, as she buried it in her sleeve.

After a narrowed glance across the table at her sister, Tabitha lifted her chin. "I would be happy to play for you after dinner, Lieutenant." A tinge of defiance definitely edged her offer. "Then you can judge for yourself."

"I would be honored, miss. Though I'm sure I would not be qualified to judge." When her eyes widened, Ansel hastened to add, "Only to enjoy."

Tabitha's expression resolved into satisfaction, and he attempted to return to his soup.

"And your brother, is he married yet?" Mrs. Scott tilted her head. The motion caused her hair—which might not all be her own—to wobble slightly. Was that dot near her mouth a true mole, or a *mouchet*, the small patch he'd heard fashionable ladies favored? 'Twas hard to tell, what with the fine layer of powder that covered her skin. Would the woman even look the same without her cosmetics?

As for the daughters, while she exuded freshness now, Tabitha seemed the sort to increasingly cover aging with such falsities, whereas Temperance...

He redirected his thoughts to the question his hostess had asked. Ah, yes. His brother. "He is courting." Ansel paused in lifting his spoon to offer a smile. "The daughter of a physician we knew in Augusta. As you can imagine, the distance has provided some challenges, but we expect a betrothal by Christmas."

"How sweet." Mrs. Scott tittered, then cast a subtle glance at Tabitha. "Who knows? With all the eligible young women in Savannah, you could beat your brother to the altar."

Surely, she would prefer a lord for her firstborn. Perhaps she simply relived through Tabitha the challenge of luring naïve young men.

"Oh, Mother, you made him blush." Tabitha giggled and leaned toward Ansel until her shoulder bumped his. Ansel dared not look. Her bodice...must it be so low? "The poor man has hardly set foot in our city and already you'd assign him a match."

Mrs. Scott affected a pout. "I don't know why I should hope to, when I've been so unsuccessful where my own children are concerned."

"Perhaps you just have not found us the right person." Tabitha's response was practically a purr. At least she did not look at him, though awareness practically hummed from her person.

Ansel shifted in his chair and resisted loosening his stock.

"Pray, do not lose heart, Aunt." Frankie sent a proprietary smile Temperance's direction—which she did not return. "Affections can take time to grow. And they can flourish from the most unexpected quarters."

Tabitha's brows rose, as did her glass. "I couldn't agree more, Frankie, dear." As if toasting him, she took a sip of the amber liquid in the crystal goblet.

"Besides, we can be assured the lieutenant has been busy learning his new duties. He won't have had time to call on the ladies. Isn't that right, Anderson?" Frankie peered around a servant bringing a mackerel with a lemon in its mouth. Another set a ham on the opposite end of the table. Bowls of green beans, yellow squash with red peppers, and cornbread appeared on the massive sideboard.

Ansel allowed a rueful chuckle. "I perform drills and take my stint at guard duty, much as I did at Fort Argyle, though there's not much to watch out for except passing schooners and seagulls. But you are correct—apart from tonight, I have yet to make time for social calls."

As the servants moved silently around the table serving the main course, Tabitha patted the tablecloth with her dainty hand. "You must remember my offer to make your introductions when you do. There are music evenings, lectures, horse races, dinners, sometimes dances."

Ansel's glance to gauge the judge's reaction intercepted the faint tightening around Temperance's mouth. Did her sister's forwardness make her as uncomfortable as it did him? And yet, Judge Scott gave him a faint nod. Perhaps he'd even encouraged his older daughter to help Ansel break into society.

"Thank you, Miss Scott." Hopefully, his tone conveyed no more than politeness. "I will bear that in mind."

After a servant slid a slice of ham onto her plate, Tabitha picked up her fork. "And I will keep *you* in mind when certain invitations come."

Frankie chuckled. "Oh, but Lord Riley won't like that one whit. You shall have a proposal out of him before the first frost."

"I'm not looking for a proposal," Tabitha snapped. Oblivious to her father's lowered brows, she gave the dark ringlets over her one shoulder a little toss. "At least, not from him."

"Then we can make a merry foursome, can we not, Temperance?" When Frankie patted Temperance's free hand, her throat worked as though a piece of cornbread she'd just swallowed had gotten lodged there.

Ansel sought to draw out the voice she seemed to have lost tonight. "Where do you spend your free time, Miss Scott... Temperance?" He added her first name tentatively. Perhaps his tone would convey he meant to distinguish her from her sister, not take a liberty. Still, it rolled off his tongue with a softness he hadn't expected.

She straightened abruptly at the sound. "Um...I..." She looked from her mother to her sister, as if expecting one of them to supply her answer. "I spend a lot of time at church."

"And do you take part in any special activities there?" He watched her carefully. Would she talk about her weekday ministry?

What appeared to be thinly veiled panic flitted across her features. She shot him an intense look, then dropped her gaze. "Mainly just the regular services."

Ansel gathered a bite of mackerel onto his fork. "Will you tell me more? 'Twould help me know what to expect before attending."

When she hesitated again, Judge Scott joined the conversation. "The Reverend Bartholomew Zouberbuhler of Switzerland is the rector. Trained in South Carolina in the Anglican tradition. A fair enough preacher, though he isn't the equal of his predecessors."

"Oh, Mr. Scott, 'tis a bit unfair to compare anyone to John Wesley and George Whitefield, is it not?" His wife cast him a chiding smirk.

He tilted his head back and forth. "I suppose. His accent makes him hard to understand."

"Not for the French and Germans in the city." Finally, Temperance felt strongly enough about something to interject.

Ansel offered her a smile, but she pretended not to notice, moving her beans around on her plate. He forked a bite of squash. Although the dinner proved a sight better than what the cook served back at the barracks, the exotic imported spices made everything taste too strong, unlike the fresh but familiar flavors that burst from his mother's garden back home.

"The slaves don't seem to mind him either. In fact, they love him." Tabitha turned to Ansel. She must have taken his frown as a need for explanation rather than surprise at her awareness. Was she aware her sister served the slaves? "You may as well know, Father doesn't approve of how he has the black people worship alongside the whites."

"They should have their own service—that is all." Did the imposing man's averted gaze and gruff tone signal some defensiveness?

"That is not all." The disagreement, bold as it was, came

from Temperance, so softly that Ansel had barely heard it. He had to look at her to be certain she was the one speaking. Indeed, she continued, though she did not raise her gaze from her plate. "You wouldn't permit his assistant starting a mission on our plantation, either...like the ones I told you about at Wild Heron and Great Ogeechee."

And that explained why she had tensed when Ansel had almost asked about her service work at the church.

Judge Scott's fist thudded on the table. "That will be quite enough on that topic."

Temperance jumped, but Tabitha stared back at him with defiance in her eyes. And yet, which one of them actually defied him in principle? In action? Something stirred in Ansel's chest. Awareness. Admiration?

"Indeed." Mrs. Scott sucked in a soft breath, followed by a swallow of liquor. "Whatever one may think of his policies regarding the slaves, the Reverend Zouberbuhler is a good man, Lieutenant Anderson, who walks the streets of our city ministering to the poor and sick, whatever race or religion they may be. We are fortunate to sit under his teaching, and we would be pleased if you would join us any Sunday of your choosing."

Ansel smiled, his tight shoulders relaxing at the reprieve. If nothing else, Mrs. Scott was an accomplished hostess. "I would like that very much. Thank you, ma'am. I will join you this coming Sunday." Perhaps an invitation to dinner might follow? A chance to speak with Temperance again? He could only hope his hunch that Frankie wasn't the church-going sort would prove correct.

Tabitha tapped the table, leaning toward Ansel again. "You must also put our Twelfth Night Ball on your calendar."

He stiffened. "Your family hosts a ball?" The most he'd attended in the country were outdoor dances—no doubt completely unlike a holiday ball in the capital city.

"Indeed." Tabitha's eyes sparkled. "The week between Christmas and the New Year is the most exciting of all. After Advent, the whole city celebrates. Well, at least, we Anglicans do. There are hunts and dinners and balls every day. And ours is the biggest. Why, did you not know, our whole top floor is a ballroom? I can show it to you after supper."

He blinked at her as a white-gloved servant cleared his plate. Another replaced a vegetable platter with one displaying spiced peaches in brandy.

Frankie cackled at Ansel's reaction. "Why, cousin, you managed to scare him spitless. I bet he never looked like that when facing a band of Cherokee warriors."

Ansel wasn't about to tell him he'd never faced Cherokee warriors. Or that his tactless pronouncement was also perfectly accurate. He had no idea how to perform most of the country dances, with their delicate, leaping steps and complex movements up and down the line, much less a minuet, the showpiece of any European or colonial ball.

Temperance caught his gaze across the table. She offered an understanding smile. "I can advise you on dance instructors, if you recall."

His heart squeezed. "Thank you, Miss Temperance." He wouldn't tell her until they were alone that he'd already gathered that information—when he'd followed her to Mrs. Swinton's.

Frankie brushed off her kindness. "Lieutenant Anderson will be too busy with his ranger duties for dance lessons, Temperance. Why, you probably already identified all the dangerous insurrectionists among their ranks to my uncle, have you not, Lieutenant?"

At the unexpectedness of the bold query, Ansel froze.

A servant slid a chess tart onto his dessert plate.

Frankie assumed a tone of jest, but behind it...yes, something glinted in his eyes. Fear?

Ansel sent up a quick prayer for wisdom before speaking. "I will tell you what I told your uncle, sir, that in any emergency, the rangers would answer the governor's call."

He'd had the conversation he owed Jack, and the man's reasoning held water. He'd countered Ansel's arguments supporting the governor with unyielding but calmly stated arguments and facts—some of which had not been fairly represented at Argyle. On many issues, they had seen fit to compromise. Ansel was still mulling over the ranger's ideas, but he knew enough to speak firmly now.

"They are among the finest men I've ever met," Ansel continued. "They would lay down their lives to defend our city against any foe, from without...or from within."

"You truly think they are all loyal to Wright?" Though his tone teased, Frankie's sharp features bore a distinct edge of challenge. He knew the answers to his own questions. He merely gauged whether Ansel would guard his secrets.

If he did not, at least for now, he would blow his own assignment in the rangers.

"I would not be prepared to guess at this point." The same thing he'd told Scott earlier that day. Thankfully, the judge had not pressed him, agreeing that he should deepen his relationships and merely monitor the mood of the military so long as no particular threat loomed. "What each man believes in the sanctity of his heart is between him and God. Whether or not he will act on his sworn duty is the true test of his honor."

CHAPTER 7

On the Sunday afternoon following Ansel's dinner at her home, Temperance sat in the garden with Cecily with the latest edition of the *Georgia Gazette* across her lap. She often read from it to her servant, who absorbed the news as eagerly as Temperance herself.

A soft, balmy breeze stirred the leaves of the hardwoods and the Spanish moss in the live oaks. Hummingbirds buzzed among the lavender spires of the false dragonhead and blue mist flowers, gorging themselves on an end-of-season meal. The sun draped Temperance's shoulders with the weight and warmth of a light cloak. Not many days like this remained before October's chill. They should make the most of it.

And yet, Temperance was forced to constantly wrangle her thoughts and emotions back from the house. Or more accurately, the man inside it. Ansel had attended church with them this morning. His polished appearance in his uniform and his deep baritone as he reverently sang "A Mighty Fortress is Our God" had drawn many an admiring and speculative glance. Afterward, he'd accepted her mother's invitation to a cold dinner, as they never asked the servants to cook on Sundays.

Then he'd gone into the study with Father while Mother and Tabitha plied their needlework in the parlor. When he emerged, there was little chance he'd escape their feminine ambush. But she couldn't stop glancing toward the window of the study.

Was that a curtain moving? A flash of blue behind it?

Temperance ducked her head and resumed her reading aloud. "'When the power which should naturally protect and defend us is employed to oppress us in our dearest rights, and deprive us of that liberty which the constitution of England entitles us to, which God himself has established in the very frame of our natures...'" She paused and looked up at Cecily, who sat with her basket of mending in the shade of the arbor.

Cecily's needle slowed as she returned Temperance's gaze. "Something wrong, miss?"

"I was just thinking, we're all looking at this article reprinted from the *New York Gazette* and thinking about our colonial rights, but we don't extend those rights to all our citizens."

One reason for this realization was Ansel Anderson. Her father had told her that Captain Michael Anderson, Ansel's father, did not hold with owning slaves. Because of that, he relied on the income from his militia and civil offices to supplement his farming. She had so many questions. But right now, she needed to ask one of her own maidservant.

Temperance lowered the paper. "I can't change that for the whole country, and I can't even change it for my family, but what I *can* do, I will."

Cecily's full lips twitched. She was well-accustomed to Temperance's rambling diatribes. "I'm not following you, miss."

"Cecily, would you like to join our sewing circle?"

She cocked her turbaned head. "I'm already in your sewing circle."

"No, I mean, would you like to be a member? A true..."

Temperance leaned forward and whispered. "Daughter of Liberty?"

Cecily's eyes rounded as the words took effect. "You mean...I would get to be a part of whatever you do to help the Liberty Boys?"

Temperance nodded and reached for her hand. "You and Rhoda, too, if she wishes." She had not yet presented the idea to Mrs. Dash, or even to the other ladies, but first, she needed Cecily's permission. "I cannot imagine a more appropriate member." She squeezed her maid's hand, then released it as a new thought sobered her. "Although..."

"What is it?" Her brow furrowing, Cecily fingered the torn petticoat she was mending.

"At this time, we support them more in principle than action. But there may come a day, if England fails to repeal the Stamp Act, when more is required of us. I cannot mislead you, Cecily. A slave participating in such activity might well assume more risk than her mistress."

"Oh." Cecily blinked, then lowered her gaze for a moment. She took a tremulous breath. "Miss Temperance, I'm not sure as I should say what I'm thinking."

"I'm asking you to, Cecily. You know I don't look on you as a slave, but as a friend."

"That doesn't change facts, miss."

"No, but we have not always shared honesty between us?" Yes, her relationship with her maid was unique. And not one she talked about. But Temperance found in Cecily more of a kindred spirit than in any of the young society women, many of who were more interested in imitating the stylish British courtesan Kitty Fisher and snaring a husband than addressing society's ills.

"Yes'm."

"Then, please." Temperance motioned upward. "Look at me and tell me what you truly think."

Slowly, Cecily lifted her gaze to meet Temperance's. "My heart tells me that what you just read in that paper is God's truth. Every person has a voice, and the king and Parliament should hear us over in England. If I have a chance to help with that, I oughta be brave enough to take it."

The smile that spread across Temperance's face overflowed from the warmth in her heart. "I'm so glad, Cecily. We will tell the ladies next week." And she would pray for no resistance. Because this was one small way she could give Cecily a voice.

The crunch of a step on the crushed-shell walkway drew their notice.

Ansel approached, removing his hat as Cecily rose and tucked her chin.

Temperance's heartbeat sped, but in excitement, not fear. She *should* be afraid, hesitant to expose herself to his piercing questions. And yet, she found herself wanting to trust him. She'd already decided that if she was again caught alone with him, she'd offer him as much truth as she could. The way he'd handled her sister and Frankie at supper this past week had demonstrated discernment.

"Pray, do not allow me to interrupt." He waved his hand out. "I can take a turn about the garden while you finish your conversation."

Temperance almost gaped at him. What white man showed such deference to a slave? "Thank you, but that will not be necessary. Cecily and I were just finishing up."

Cecily folded the petticoat, leaving the needle and thread secured through the material on top. "Would you like me to bring you some lemonade, miss?"

"That would be lovely." It would leave her alone with Ansel —as she thought of him now that she knew him better—but only for a brief time. And the proximity to her father's presence in the study lent the visit propriety. In fact, as she glanced toward the window, he waved at them. She waved back. As

Cecily scurried off, Temperance indicated the lieutenant should take the maid's vacated seat. "I'm surprised you did not join my mother and sister in the parlor for tea."

"I don't want tea." Smile lines bracketed his mouth. Oh, heaven preserve her. And that direct gaze... "Lemonade in the garden with you sounds...*lovely*." He directed her own words back at her with a wink that threatened to discombobulate her entirely. "I snuck out the back way."

She fiddled with the edges of the newspaper. "I am honored by your company, but you would find Mother and Tabitha much more entertaining."

"'Tis not entertainment I seek." He rested his cocked hat on his knee.

"What *do* you seek?" Her pulse galloped at her temerity in even asking the question. Information, no doubt. Certainly, not to know her.

As usual, she'd withdrawn into herself when her mother and sister monopolized the supper conversation the other night. When Tabitha had whisked Ansel upstairs to show him the ballroom after the meal and Frankie had taken his leave, Temperance had retreated to her room, cringing at the peals of laughter from above. She could just imagine Tabitha skip-stepping around up there, Ansel's gaze following her lithe figure. How could he not be entranced?

Tabitha always got what she wanted.

Ansel tapped a blunt forefinger on his hat. "For now? A good and honest conversation. What are you reading?" He leaned forward. "The *Gazette*?"

"Y-yes." She resisted the urge to hide the headline. "A reprint of an article from New York."

"What does it say?" One of his dark brows winged upward.

"That...when our rights are overlooked..." She searched for the paragraph she'd been reading to Cecily and placed her finger on the text. "'Should we bear our wrongs in silence?

Should we suffer the cruel violation without complaining, and remonstrating, and using every effort to awaken the latent principles of justice and compassion, in those who have the power in their hands?'"

The other brow joined the first one near his even hairline. "What do you think 'every effort' should look like, Miss Temperance?"

"Why, asking for the repeal of unjust acts, of course. Asking for our own representatives to settle these matters." Such went without saying.

Ansel sat up straight. "What about hanging a stamp master in effigy? Burning it?"

She tilted her head. "Well, that would certainly make a point. The stamp masters may not be the ultimate target of protest—that being the king and the English Parliament—but they will have to agree to their office. Besides the governors, that makes them the most visible representatives of King George this side of the Atlantic."

"A handy visual aid, then."

"In essence." Temperance lifted her shoulder. "Though I can see where it could lead to unnecessary violence."

He frowned. "Such as storming the stamp officer's property, pulling down his fences, and entering his residence to destroy his furniture?"

Temperance drew herself up at the unexpected heat in Ansel's question. "Where is this coming from?"

"From the account your father just shared with me of what happened back in August in Boston." He gestured to her newspaper. "That issue might not include it yet, but a paper he had from Charlestown did. Unfortunately, these demonstrations rarely remain within the law."

Temperance suppressed a shiver. Hadn't she just warned Cecily of the very thing? "Of course, I would not countenance breaking the law, but you cannot believe our king and Parliament have always treated the colonies fairly, Lieutenant."

"In what way have they not, Miss Temperance?" He sat back and crossed his arms.

At the threat of confrontation, her heart thudded. She folded the newspaper. "You asked for genuine conversation, yet your posture invites debate. I have no interest in ruining the peace of my Sunday afternoon." She started to rise, but he leaned forward and touched her arm.

"Forgive me. I've spent too long at a military fort among military men. We often speak without tact. But since coming here, I'm learning there are different ways to go about things. I would be your pupil if you would teach me."

Her pupil? A shiver went down Temperance's spine, and she pulled her arm close against her side. "Are you sincere, sir?"

He placed his hand over his heart. "I swear it. How about if you give me your view, and I will give you mine? Each stated simply, without passion." His teasing smile told her he already grasped her struggle on that score. "Then we can decide for ourselves which arguments are stronger. Does that sound acceptable?"

"Very well." Temperance laid the newspaper at her feet and clasped her hands in her lap. Loosely. She forced her fingers to relax. "The first big blow England dealt us, apart from the Sugar Act, which only affected some, was when they outlawed printing our own currency. The items we are forced to buy from England already cost more than the materials we provide to them. Then they removed the old bills from circulation, and the cost of everything went sky high."

"It made things difficult for now," Ansel countered, "but in the long run, the Currency Act will protect the value of money if we all use pounds sterling. The denominations were different across the colonies. And some bills could be used for public debt, some only for private. The system was far too confusing."

True to his agreement, Ansel spoke in calm, measured tones. "The act will restore the confidence of British merchants. And help pay for the ten thousand troops stationed in America after the French and Indian War."

"The troops they are forcing us to house and feed with the Quartering Act?" That sounded a little bitterer than she'd intended. She sweetened her statement with a smile.

"Those troops protect the frontiers from Indian raids. Many have been requested by the colonial governors. Why shouldn't civilians give them quarter if there is not public accommodation?" He sat forward, splaying the fingers of one hand.

Temperance scoffed, arranging the pleats of her petticoat. "Backwoodsmen are more than capable of guarding their own borders. They've been doing so for years with colonial militia and rangers, as you should know." She shot him a glance. "They hardly need sons of British nobility who don't want to give up their commissions now that the war is over."

One corner of Ansel's mouth raised. "With that, I do agree. At least the royal rangers pull from the local population, those skilled in scouting and tracking and native relations."

She couldn't resist a smile of satisfaction.

"Now, what of the Stamp Act?" He leaned back, but he rested his hands on his knees this time. "I suppose you're going to talk about taxation without representation. Would it surprise you that I agree with the principle?"

"Well...yes." She blinked at him. "I thought you would be one who subscribed to the laughable notion of virtual representation, when truly, we all know that the legislators in England know or care nothing about our concerns here."

"That is why we should have representatives in Parliament."

Temperance spluttered. "They would never allow it. And even if they did, those men would be outnumbered and ostracized. Of course, no one is saying we shouldn't pay taxes at all.

But only a colonial legislature could fairly assess and rule on taxes for the colonies."

"Think of it from the other side. Why allow a separate legislature? Do we not have English blood running through our veins? Have the king and the governor not given us opportunities, land, and jobs? Would a colonial parliament truly look to the good of the whole empire, or only to their own good?"

"Yes." Until the last question, she'd mentally scrambled to counter his very logical—she had to admit it—arguments. But here she could anchor her defense. She lifted her chin. "We are more than capable of seeing the big picture. Of working in cooperation with the mother country. As I said earlier, 'tis not as though we are trying to get out of anything. We only want the same rights the citizens of England enjoy. Do you find us so small-minded that we would fail to elect qualified men? Or do you think the men we would choose would be so selfish or rebellious it would render them incapable of supporting both king and colony?"

"No." The warm smile that lit Ansel's face completely absolved all her tension. "I do not think that. I see your point about a colonial legislature, although I fear England would be less likely to allow that than giving up seats in Parliament."

"Then you think we are without hope for ever achieving equality?"

"On the contrary, I believe there is great hope. I'm thankful for diplomats like Benjamin Franklin and Isaac Barré, who bring our needs before Parliament in person."

Temperance nodded. While many thought Franklin had not done enough to represent the colonies, Barré, an Irish politician who had served in the colonies during the Seven Years' War, as they preferred to call it in England, had actually coined the term "sons of liberty."

"There is always hope for a compromise. We reached some in our conversation just now, did we not?" Ansel stood to remove his coat, then laid it over the bench and sat back down. He wiped his forehead with the back of his sleeve. "Bit hot out here."

"Yes, to both your points." She glanced toward the house. "I wonder what's taking Cecily so long." If conversation moved in a more personal direction, her words would dry up as fast as her parched throat.

Ansel tilted his dark head as he studied her, the sun bringing out the mahogany highlights in his hair. "You know, a friend of mine in the rangers made some of the same arguments for greater colonial autonomy, but you made them with much more moving language. You're a genuine orator, Miss Temperance."

"T-truly, I am not. I only manage to find words when the need for justice...*forces* them out of me." She made the accompanying gesture, bringing her hand up from her chest as she grimaced.

"'Tis the mark of a true statesman—or woman. A belief in a cause that is so pure, it overrides their natural reticence."

At the unsolicited praise, Temperance ducked her chin. "If only my family shared your opinion. I'm afraid they find my crusading an embarrassment."

"Such as you teaching the slaves?"

She sucked in a breath, looking up. "How do you know about that?"

"I'm glad your maid isn't back...because I need to make a confession. I followed you from the riverfront the other day."

"You did?" The heat intensified, sweat breaking out on her brow. "Why?" If he knew about her work at Christ Church, he'd also witnessed her clandestine stop at Swinton's. Had he taken the list that Frankie had never received?

His gaze held hers, forthrightly, yielding no evidence of regret. "You were in such a hurry to get away, especially when I mentioned Machenry's. You weren't there just to eat, were you?"

She nibbled the inside of her lip. How much should she tell him? "Frankie knows I like to hear what is said on such nights. But a healthy political curiosity or even holding certain beliefs does not make me liable to storm a stamp agent's house."

"I know that now." A grin blazed forth. "That is, after I followed you to what I thought was surely a secret meeting and found you leading Africans in the Lord's Prayer. You know my family does not hold with slavery."

"I...might have heard that. Can I count on you not to tell my father what I'm about?" She offered what she hoped to be a coquettish smile. She hardly knew how to employ such wiles, short of copying her sister. But if it would divert Ansel from bringing up her other errand, she would jump up and dance a hornpipe. "You saw how he was at supper the other night."

Drawing his lower lip up in a regretful grimace, he nodded. "I know what it is to be in the minority on that issue. I won't tell him. But I'm still not certain what to make of this." He fished a scrap of paper from his waistcoat pocket and unfolded it with one finger.

"My list of dance steps!" She attempted to snatch it, but he drew it back, skimming the columns as though for the first time. Perhaps an explanation would induce him to surrender it. She couldn't risk him examining it more closely—if he hadn't already. "I have a number of steps to learn before the Twelfth Night Ball. I have requested Mrs. Swinton drill me on these so that I can perform them without my spectacles."

Ansel's brow furrowed. "And why would you want to do that?"

"Because Frankie will undoubtedly be my partner, and while he fancies himself accomplished, well, let's just say I cannot count on him to alleviate my clumsiness." Temperance made a little face.

"Wearing your spectacles would help, it seems."

Temperance fought down panic. "I must know the steps

well enough to dance with my eyes closed. Please don't ask me more." She fanned herself with her hand. A man like Ansel would never understand the damaging power of hushed whispers and tittering laughter.

"What if I learned them also?"

"What?" The word barely squeaked out.

"What if I took this list to Mrs. Mary Smith and asked her to teach me as well? For I daresay I am in greater need of tutelage than you, country ruffian that I am." He drummed his fingers on his knee. "If I'm to attend the ball, I might as well learn a few dances so I can rescue you from your cousin."

"I—you...you don't have to do that." Temperance blinked as she fought her inner battle with confusion. He *wanted* to dance with her? Surely, he had some ulterior motive. And how did he know Mary Smith gave lessons to men? Had she told him that?

"I have no more wish to be a laughingstock than you. You can remember these steps to tell Mrs. Swinton so I can keep the list, can you not?" He folded the paper and stuffed it back into his waistcoat. Temperance swallowed a protest as he continued. "I must ask your forgiveness for taking the message you left her."

She waved her hand. "Oh, please, think nothing of it." *Please.*

"I'm afraid her housekeeper caught me in the rather awkward act of reading it. Although, I doubt Mrs. Swinton would have found it, the way you'd stuffed it—"

"Ah!" Temperance shot to her feet. "There is Cecily at last."

CHAPTER 8

Not the cousin this time, but the maid.

Ansel pressed his lips together. He'd retained the message, although why the need impressed him, he couldn't say. 'Twas nothing but a list of dance steps. Perhaps something in her reaction to his possession of it aroused his suspicion. She'd portrayed more alarm at the sight of that paper in his hand than at his revelation he'd followed her to Christ Church.

No. She'd explained herself. Been open about her beliefs. And he'd heard the ring of truth in them. Maybe he should stop being so guarded and accept that she was exactly as she appeared.

What made him so uncomfortable about trusting this girl?

Ansel shifted in his chair as Cecily placed the tray of cookies and fresh lemonade on the table between him and Temperance, then stepped back.

Temperance smiled up at her. "Aren't you going to join us?"

"Got me some lemonade on the back porch, miss. I'll take my mending there."

Was that panic in Temperance's eyes as Cecily retreated

along the tabby walkway? Panic akin to what sat in Ansel's gut. And why?

He wouldn't be afraid of trusting her if he did not admire her. A lot. Like her, even. Unease washed him in a cold deluge more bracing than any lemonade, though he palmed the perspiring glass and took a long drink. He'd never met a girl who intrigued him as Temperance did. As unusual as her behavior over the list had been, her relationship with Cecily was even more remarkable.

"You treat her no differently than you would a white woman."

"Pardon me?" Temperance's brows shot up.

"I don't know another lady, slave-owning or otherwise, who would invite a black woman to have lemonade with her. Or join her sewing circle. Or read the newspaper to her. That was what you were doing when I walked up, was it not?"

"Yes." Temperance ducked her head and nibbled the edge of a sugar cookie. "Yet you were the one who suggested I ask her to join the sewing circle."

"She was already going, though, right? Why not just let her keep coming without saying anything?" He tilted his head. "Because I would lay odds you're going to say something."

"Of course. I told you I would, did I not?" She shot him a quelling look. "Serving tea is one thing. Sitting down to sew with us is another."

"I inherited my views on slavery from my parents. Where did you come by yours?"

Temperance brushed cookie crumbs from the petticoat of the light-blue silk dress she'd worn to church. Along with her dark hair and the color so wont to rise in her cheeks, it gave her complexion the look of a china doll. A matching blue ribbon supporting a black-and-white cameo at her delicate throat completed the impression.

"From the very best teacher, first-hand experience." When

she sighed, he dipped his head, prompting her to continue. "Father never let us go to the slave auction with him. He shielded us from the ugliest parts of slavery, and he treated his people with kindness. But he has always believed Africans are of inferior intelligence. And that they are better off here, away from violent tribal warfare, where they can receive care for their souls and bodies."

Ansel scoffed. "In a land of such opportunity...for all but them."

Her fingers clenched in her lap. "We're on the same side of this, remember? Do you want to hear the rest of my story?"

She disliked confrontation, clearly, but he couldn't concede quite yet. "I do, of course, but I cannot reconcile your father wanting slaves to receive spiritual teaching with forbidding you to teach them."

"He would say that is not my place. He believes they should have their own pastor, like Reverend Zouberbuhler's assistant, Joseph Ottolenghe."

"If he has this help, then why do you volunteer?" When her lips pursed, he opened his hands. "I'm not criticizing. I just want to understand."

She let out a little breath. "Your questions frequently put me on the spot." She looked away a moment. "Ottolenghe no longer works with the reverend. He is at the filature house now. He wasn't...successful as a minister to the slaves. They did not trust him. I think they picked up on his own prejudices."

"I see."

"Besides, you may have noticed that I only meet with the women and children. I find it helps them when a woman is there." She picked at a fold in her dress.

"That makes sense. Please, go on with your story."

"One day when I was around eleven, Father took me to the wharf with him on some business. A slaver had just arrived, and they led the human cargo right past us, bound in their

83

clanking chains. Father tried to turn me away, but I broke free of him. I was aghast to see people treated in such a way. I felt my heart break, right on that wharf." Temperance squeezed her hands together above her chest, her gaze becoming unfocused, looking beyond him and the bright garden around them, into the past. The anguish that twisted her features also twisted Ansel's gut. "And then I saw her."

"Who?"

"This raggedy little girl with fuzzy pigtails, trying to cling to her mama's dress even though the chains kept jerking her away. She looked at me, and we locked eyes. In that instant, I *knew*. She felt everything as keenly as I would have. The terror. The humiliation. The panic. It was as if, for a moment, God allowed me to *become* her." Tears rose and flowed from Temperance's eyes.

Ansel fished out a clean handkerchief and handed it to her.

She blotted her face. "I'm sorry. I cannot speak of it without reliving it."

"Please, don't apologize." He started to reach for her hand, wanting only to comfort her, but just before their fingers touched, she jerked hers away. The expression that flashed over her features—it wasn't alarm. Or indignation. No, more like anxiety. Was she so frightened of all men...or only him? He shouldn't have distracted her. He slid his hand back. "What did you do?"

"I went and got Father and told him he had to save the little girl. Of course, I wanted him to set her free." She choked out a self-recriminating laugh. "I thought she and her mother could start their own life in Savannah. I did not understand that he would buy her and become her new owner for life. But I wouldn't leave him alone until he did something."

Ansel clutched his hat brim. "And what was that?"

Temperance puffed out a little breath, her gaze still distant. "We followed that slave trader to the market and made an offer for mother and daughter on the spot. Darcy and Cecily never got on the auction block. They came home with us, Darcy to our kitchen and Cecily to be trained as maid to me and Tabitha. Eventually, Darcy became housekeeper for our place here in town. Of course, we have another mammy who runs the plantation house."

"Of course." How many slaves did Judge Scott own? Did Ansel want to know? "And Cecily has been with you ever since, whether here or there?"

"Yes." Affection swelled the small word.

Ansel glanced at the young woman calmly sewing on the back porch. "The bond between you is easy to see."

A sad smile flitted over Temperance's face. "I determined from the first day that I would treat her like my friend, not my maid. Probably because I needed a friend so much." A shy smile quirked her lips. Had her words embarrassed her? "I taught her to look me in the eye. I took her everywhere with me. I talked with her like a confidant, and I was right—she was the smartest girl I knew. We discuss everything that women—certainly slaves—are told they shouldn't discuss." Her chin lifted. "But I can do that in the privacy of my own home. I'm trusting you with it now."

"Thank you for that, Miss Temperance." Ansel did reach for her hand then, as if touch would seal their bargain. He'd never handled anything so soft and delicate. "Your kindness to her is commendable."

She did not pull away this time, though she tilted her head. "'Tis kind of you to say so, but I did not share this seeking your praise. I wanted you to understand where my convictions come from. I believe that each of us bear the image of our Creator. Each of us were designed to be free. So when I see a government taking away that right—either of the colonists or of the slaves—well, 'tis like the prophet Jeremiah said, 'a fire shut up in my bones.'"

85

Ansel released her hand. "What say you to the passage in Romans thirteen that reminds us that every soul should be subject to the higher powers, for they are ordained by God?"

She laughed heartily. "Oh, if I but had a pound sterling for every time that has been quoted to me." She sobered. "I believe other places in the Good Book show us that when governments abuse their powers, we are within our rights to protest. Psalm 9 tells us God ministers in uprightness. He is a refuge to the oppressed. Galatians 5:1 says, 'Stand fast therefore in the liberty wherewith Christ hath made us free, and be not entangled again with the yoke of bondage.'"

Impressive. A woman who knew her Scriptures. His mother's reminder to look for such a woman, for she would be worth far more than gold, sprang to mind. Ansel patted his hat against his leg. "You are saying we should hold our own government to the example and standard of our Lord."

"Exactly." Temperance's eyes lit. "When a government keeps taking more and more of your freedoms, when you do say enough?"

"Each man must surely answer that for himself, with his conscience as his guide. And it stands to reason that different people may come to a point of speaking out, or acting out, at various times."

"Indeed. I would never favor violent protests. I hope you know that now."

"I do."

"Good." Tipping her straw hat to keep the sun out of her eyes, Temperance studied him, pursing her lips a moment before speaking again. "I'm glad we had this conversation. I've never known a man to listen like you. To be open to new ideas."

"I've always been sure of what I believe. But I've been confined to a fort for a long time now. Being in a new place, among new people, can teach a person a lot if he's willing to learn. My father showed me that. We've had to adapt to new places more than once. Therefore, I vow to go into unfamiliar situations with caution—and my eyes and ears open—before I make judgments...or decisions."

"That is commendable too." She lowered her dark lashes—not as thick as her sister's, to be sure, but clumped together now with the remnants of her tears. "And I do not really deserve your admiration. Cecily is still my slave. Well, technically, my father's. I have hopes that I might free her one day if I marry, but since she serves Tabitha and me both, I don't know if that will ever be possible."

Ansel dared the lightest touch to her chin. When he caught her startled gaze, he smiled. "I have a feeling you will make a way."

She stared at him.

Indeed, why was he so drawn to touch her? And from where did the familiarity come to act on the impulse? Her sister would have answered with a quip. A coy smile. But Temperance did not break her serious demeanor. "I have given you a confidence. Now will you give me one?"

His heart skipped a beat. What would she ask? And why did he want to oblige so much? "If I am able."

"How did you get into Machenry's? We both know there was a password that evening. Did someone give it to you and send you there?"

He sat back. Did she think her father had prepared him? How much did she correctly assume about his mission to monitor the liberty movement? Thank heavens, he could answer without giving any of that away. "No one sent me there. I had heard through the grapevine about the Liberty Boys and where they met."

"Frankie had to know the password to get in. But you'd just arrived from Fort Argyle. So how did you manage?"

My, she was persistent. He threw the truth out there. "I guessed."

"You guessed the password?" She blinked and shook her head. "How?"

"I'd learned they called themselves the Amicable Society. Given the questions posed by the innkeeper to myself and the man before me, I took a stab at it, and providence was with me. *Amicable* was the password."

She smirked. "Well, you might be lucky, but don't get too cocky. They change it every meeting."

He narrowed his eyes. "And how would you know that?"

Temperance's hand fluttered to her mouth, then she dropped it and let out a sigh. "Frankie, of course." She opened one hand toward him, her brows knit. "You'd be surprised how many sons of prominent loyalists get their thrills from clandestine meetings and political wrangling. Still...we're both hoping you won't feel the need to tell my father about the friends he keeps. He only likes the excitement, truly. He would never do anything alarming."

Wouldn't he? He seemed the sort to test a theory with action, especially if it would put him in a position of power. But Ansel held his tongue. He'd almost forgotten Frankie was more than her cousin. Did she care for him, that she would defend him so, despite her comments and reactions that hinted to the contrary?

Temperance took his silence for reticence to answer her original question. "Can we agree to keep between us that we were all at the tavern that night? Now that we've reached an understanding of what we believe and that we don't intend to burn down the town over it?"

He found the hint of a smile playing about her lips far more entrancing than her sister's "accidental" touches and alluring glances. The dulcet tones of that very young lady broke into the close space between them, petulant and demanding.

"So this is where you have been all afternoon, when I thought you were still in Father's study." She sashayed past

Cecily and down the porch steps, her hat ribbon and silken petticoat fluttering in the breeze. "Shame on you, Lieutenant Anderson! Hiding out here with my sister while Mother and I waited inside."

Regret flashed over Temperance's countenance before she schooled her expression.

Ansel experienced the same emotion. He leaned forward to murmur a response before Tabitha drew too near. "I think we can forget about Machenry's."

If there was any true cause for concern, even over Frankie, time would lay it bare.

A smile danced over Temperance's face, warming him from the inside out. He'd do all he could to maintain and grow her trust. But he had enough leverage to impose one small condition, did he not?

Tabitha came and stood next to them, a hand on her hip. "Now, just what secrets are you telling? Rest assured, no one can keep a confidence from me for long."

"We were speaking of dances." Ansel raised his face if not his eyes to her. "I believe your sister had just agreed to attend your Twelfth Night Ball with me." He leaned forward to whisper to Temperance, "And wear her spectacles."

He didn't even try to contain his grin as her mouth dropped open.

89

CHAPTER 9

Friday, October 25, 1765, marked the fifth anniversary of King George III's ascension to the throne. The occasion called for all troops of Georgia militia, horse, and rangers to muster in Savannah. Those who did not faced the threat of being fined or discharged.

Following the drills on the parade ground outside Fort Halifax, Ansel gave Oliver's reins to a cadet inside the fort and joined the color guard assembled beside the flagpole. As third lieutenant, he bore the responsibility of presenting the King's Colours, a duty previously assigned to the cornet—a junior rank since dispensed with. At Fort Argyle, Second Lieutenant Rivers would be performing the same honor.

The drummer beat a cadence as Ansel raised the flag near the caponiére facing the river. He squinted against the glare of the sun off the water, and a streak of pride ran through him at the red, white, and blue standard rippling in the salty breeze. At how many forts the world over was this flag even now waving?

He stood back at attention with Captain Powell as First Lieutenant Jones called out, "Make ready!" The crews of the big guns at opposite ends of the fort awaited the next command.

A CONFLICTED BETROTHAL

"Load." They powdered and primed the cannons, then returned to attention. "Fire!"

Smoke and fire bellowed forth as the bells at Christ Church and Independent Presbyterian began to toll noon. Between the volleys, a surge of voices grew—shouts and jeers from the crowd that had gathered around the parade ground, where the mounted rangers still held their horses in check. And were some of the citizens throwing things? Ansel strained to make out what was happening from the corners of his eyes. Yes, something small and round flew from the crowd, and one of the mounts sidestepped. After the fifth volley, a strange silence fell when there should be cheers. Only a few shouts and disgruntled murmurs pierced the quiet.

The notes of the fife warbled with ironic brightness. *God save great George our king, long live our noble king...*

Ansel startled when Captain Powell broke with tradition on the second stanza and sang out. "'O Lord our God arise, scatter his enemies, and make them fall.'" Other voices joined in—from soldiers, not civilians. "'Confound their politics, frustrate their knavish tricks. On Him our hope we fix. O save us all.'"

After he led them in three cheers for King George, the captain dismissed the soldiers. He stormed off to his quarters as if personally affronted by the disrespect of the dissenters, but Lieutenant Jones turned to Ansel with his dark brows raised. "'Twould seem we rangers no longer enjoy the status we once did." His wry tone offered more acceptance of the inevitable than offense.

"Indeed. At Fort Argyle, the anniversaries of the king's birthday and ascension to the throne were met with patriotism and picnics." Ansel surveyed the unusually small crowd, now trickling back toward the city as the rangers returned to the fort. "October has been so calm. I did not expect trouble today."

"Calm like a pitcher of flip before the red-hot iron is inserted." The voice behind them made them turn. Face set in grim lines, Jack Weaver drew even with Ansel, leading his stallion.

"An apt comparison." Lieutenant Jones removed his cocked hat and ran his hand over his face as if to relieve the glare of the sun. Or the tension behind his eyes. "People are on edge, not knowing who will be appointed stamp master here or when the papers will arrive in port. When either occurs, I fear the foaming and burning will begin in earnest."

Ansel frowned at Jack. "What were they throwing at you?"

His friend moved back to point at his horse's side, where scarlet mush and seeds streaked the blue roan's coat. "Moonshine got a tomato. I'm just grateful it was rotten...and not the potato someone else hurled. Thankfully, that one missed."

"Disgusting." Why did people allow the weight of their grievances to diminish their integrity? There were better ways to deal with problems. Ansel shook his head as Jack fished a bandana from his pocket and wiped away the pulp.

Lieutenant Jones resettled his hat above his queue. "Twas all Captain Powell could do to restrain himself. I'm sure he felt the need to avoid confrontation. But with the people in so ill a mood, I wouldn't be surprised if he doesn't order guards posted around the city tonight."

"Not a bad idea. Perhaps they were expecting more from the assembly yesterday, when Alexander Wylly presented the documents from the Stamp Act Congress."

The congress in New York had ended their session by producing the fourteen-point Declaration of Rights and Grievances, which they had forwarded to all thirteen colonies to adopt and post signed copies to England.

"Georgia lacks a Patrick Henry." Lieutenant Jones referenced the fiery orator who had persuaded his House of Burgesses to pass the Virginia Resolves protesting the Stamp Act back in May. "But if the majority of colonies respond, 'twill be the first time we have united in protest against England."

He did not disguise the awe that tinged his voice. He and Jack had become less guarded in front of Ansel over the past few weeks, probably owing to his friendship with Temperance.

Jack shot Ansel a glance. "Temperance told you that all they instructed Wylly to do was publish the documents in the *Gazette*?"

"That was it."

"Temperance, is it?" Lieutenant Jones surveyed Ansel with a crooked grin.

"Oh, don't you start too." He put up with enough ribbing from Jack—ever since he'd started seeing the young lady on a regular basis. Had she even realized he'd been attempting to court her? Tabitha certainly had not seemed to, inserting herself whenever possible.

In fact, Tabitha had been the one with the idea of taking him for a drive to their plantation. Judge Scott had accompanied them in the open carriage, proudly explaining rice cultivation as they passed acre upon acre of recently harvested fields. A handsome white plantation-plain house had presided over a score of outbuildings, including a winnowing shed where dozens of slaves had been hard at work, fanning the threshed grain in wide, flat baskets. A household staff completely separate from the one in Savannah had served them dinner.

Ansel had come away from the tour convinced that, despite Temperance's condemnation of slavery and his growing understanding of her political sentiments, he was out of his element. Judge Scott would never approve a match between a landless third lieutenant and either of his daughters. But he hadn't been able to stay away from the younger one. How could he, when she challenged his thinking and emotions in ways he'd never experienced? It was as though he wasn't fully alive apart from her.

He frowned, facing the first lieutenant. "Do you really think there will be more trouble today?"

"We would be wise to be prepared. Why?"

"Temperance will be at the church this evening. If overnight watches are posted, could I be assigned to the governor's residence?" Wright's house lay directly across from the Scotts', whereas the powder magazine and guardhouse—two other likely targets of the citizens' ire—fronted different squares. "I could escort her home on my way."

"I remember young love." Lieutenant Jones grinned, no doubt thinking of his wife, Sarah, with whom he had thirteen children. "Let me see what I can do for you."

Ansel flushed. Young love? His mother would certainly approve that aspiration, but his parents hadn't seen how wealthy and influential the Scotts had become. Such a goal did not line up with reality. But helping Judge Scott to protect her, even from herself? That he could do.

～

In the courtyard of Christ Church, Temperance drew a deep, satisfied breath. Today's catechism class had gone remarkably well. She inhaled heady scents of autumn—wood smoke and the decay of changing leaves. A yellow-orange poplar leaf fluttered to the hem of her woolen petticoat as she inserted a wooden spoon into a bowl of soup.

Bright, dark eyes glowed up at her. Nicholas, her favorite student, accepted the meal she handed him. "I do good today, Miss Scott?"

Temperance beamed and bent down to the ten-year-old boy's level. "Nicholas, if I had just a little more time with you, you'd have the whole prayer book memorized." If only she could teach the slaves to read and write so they could study their own copies of the Scriptures, but that was against the law. She'd been tempted with Cecily, but her maid had protested that she'd do nothing to put Temperance in danger.

Nicholas grinned. "I like the prayers. They stick in my head." His finger sank into his curly dark hair as he tapped his temple. Then he whispered, "You got a verse for me today?"

"Of course. Just for you." Temperance wet her lips as she glanced around. The other female volunteer was carrying on the soup line without her, no doubt accustomed to Temperance's little conferences with the students most eager to learn. But neither she nor Reverend Zouberbuhler knew Temperance selected personalized Scriptures for them to memorize. This one was particularly suited for Nicholas, who had been separated from his parents upon his arrival in Savannah. "Psalm 68:5-6. 'A father of the fatherless, and a judge of the widows, is God in his holy habitation.'" She waited for him to repeat it before she continued. "'God setteth the solitary in families: he bringeth out those which are bound with chains.'"

Nicholas's eyes widened. He wasn't the only one who would be stunned by Temperance presenting such a verse. But she did not doubt he'd heard the ones about slaves honoring their masters ad nauseam. Wasn't it only right they learned *all* of what God had to say on the subject?

She squeezed his arm. "Say it back to me, dear boy. 'God setteth…'" Slowly, almost inaudibly, the boy spoke the words with her. His dazed expression indicated he'd received something completely new to mull over. As she'd intended. "Remember, God has a plan for you."

Reverend Zouberbuhler was approaching, so she stood, sending Nicholas on his way with his steaming stew. She greeted the reverend with a smile, but his knit brow made her stomach surge. "Is everything all right, Reverend?"

"Ya, ya." The minister waved his hand. "We thank you for your service, as always. I can only wish I had a half dozen volunteers as dedicated as you. But 'tis best you be getting home, Miss Scott. The streets rumble with discontent tonight."

Which was exactly the reason Frankie had escorted her

here rather than Temperance coming in Cecily's company. And wouldn't the good reverend be alarmed to learn it was toward any action rather than away from it that Frankie would escort her when they left? He'd told her to expect a protest—Savannah's first.

"Pray, do not concern yourself, sir. My cousin will take me home. I only need wait for him."

"He is here." Reverend Zouberbuhler gestured. "By the gate."

Temperance fished her spectacles from her pocket and slid them on. Sure enough, a familiar figure in a cocked hat, a half cloak, and knee breeches waited on the other side of the wrought iron bars. "Ah." She smiled as excitement purled in her midsection. What would her cousin have learned this afternoon from the other Liberty Boys? "Then I had best be going. I will see you next week."

"Ya, ya. God go with you."

The gate squeaked as Temperance swung it open. From the moment Frankie turned to her, the tension in his posture and intensity on his face revealed that his anticipation exceeded even hers.

"I thought you would never come out." He grabbed her hand and pressed a kiss to the back of her glove, as though it had been weeks rather than hours since he'd seen her.

Temperance withdrew. Why couldn't her cousin grasp that her enthusiasm focused on their shared cause, not their relationship? "Then why did you not come inside?"

"And have all those raggedy slaves crowding around, looking for a handout?" He convulsed in an expressive shudder. "No, thank you."

"Frankie, your philanthropic ideals don't extend past your own haughty nose." At least their familial relation gave her the right to speak to him with the blunt honesty he deserved.

"One step at a time, my little crusader." He patted Temperance's cheek. "First, we must look to our fellow white man."

"And woman." She drew her lips flat.

"And woman. Whose idea my friends at Machenry's liked very much."

She lifted her brows. "You told them about the letters?"

No one knew for certain when or how the stamped paper had arrived, or even if it had, or who had been appointed to oversee it, but people had begun to speculate. Temperance and Frankie had compiled a list of names of prominent Savannah men likely to act in support of the distribution of the stamps.

Why not write and ask them? Temperance had meant the words as a joke.

Frankie had not laughed. He'd said that sending an ultimatum might actually apply enough pressure to solicit a response.

And so Temperance had begun penning sample letters to the suspects for the Liberty Boys to review—all a little different depending on the evidence and the role each loyalist was believed to have played in support of the Stamp Act. The Liberty Boys could alter them as they saw fit and deliver them in whatever manner they chose. Such correspondence coming from them would add a level of legitimacy.

"They want me to bring them as soon as possible. We must get ahead of this. Stamp agents in other colonies are resigning rather than enforce a tax so abhorrent to the people. Did you hear what happened in Virginia?"

"No, but, Frankie—"

"They invited the new stamp master to a ball the day he arrived and treated him with the utmost politeness, then informed him his baggage had been loaded onto a vessel to sail the next morning to London. And that he'd best accompany it, for his life would be in danger if he stayed another day." Frankie tipped his head back and cackled with delight.

She snagged her fingers in the lace on his sleeve. "But I'm not finished with the letters." Before speaking again, Temperance waited until the lamplighter at the nearby post completed his business and moved on. "And they are meant to be only an example, mind. An idea for what the Sons of Liberty might do."

"Of course. But they cannot come to a decision without reading the samples, now, can they?" Impatience tinged his voice.

Temperance pressed further. "We agreed, we need more information on the identities of the Stamp Act conspirators before taking action. I'm not certain they are correct about the two suspected of being stamp master."

"Whom do you suspect?" Frankie lifted one brow.

"From listening to my father talk about the Governor's Council, Wright trusts none more than Habersham." She sealed her lips immediately after speaking the name, almost wanting to take it back. Indicting the president of the council, partner in the import firm Harris and Habersham, and owner of a fifteen-thousand-acre rice plantation could get her into the equivalent of a vat of boiling oil. Especially if she was wrong.

Frankie let out a low whistle. At least he recognized the danger. "We may hear more tonight. I can feel out the possibility with his son and nephew."

She nodded. "The Josephs." She'd seen Joseph Habersham and Joseph Clay at Liberty Boys meetings, even though the older brother of Joseph Habersham, James Habersham Jr. remained, by all appearances, a loyalist like his father. Frankie swore he'd one day come out on the right end of things.

"Our people are gathering at Machenry's now. Some went to gather materials."

"Materials for what?" Temperance blinked as a group of young men blundered past, smelling of alcohol. One swung a lantern just above the cobblestones while another led forth in a bawdy ballad.

Frankie ignored the indelicate lyrics and Temperance's blush, though he did wait until the tune faded around the corner to ask, "What do you think?"

At his snappish tone, she drew a step back. An effigy? After what had happened in Boston... "Is it safe?"

"Is revolution ever? Now put up your hood and come along, or we'll miss what could be an important night." Frankie lifted the folds of her cloak to drape about her face. His eyes glowed as he studied her, and for a moment, she held her breath. He wouldn't kiss her, would he? He'd never taken such a liberty, but she'd never seen him this inflamed with passion either.

Instead, he closed his fingers around the bridge of her spectacles, pulled them off, and handed them to her. "You don't need these with me to guide you."

Temperance put the glasses away, but something flared in her chest. "I promised Ansel we didn't intend to start trouble."

Frankie's expression soured. "You're worried what that sycophant of a soldier thinks?"

"Father said the governor may post guards tonight after people were so disgruntled at the ceremony. If things go poorly and Ansel finds out we were there, it could be hard to explain for both of us."

Frankie's brows slashed down into the space between his eyes. His hands encircled her arms and pulled her closer. "Make up your mind, little cousin. The time for sitting the fence is over."

"Temperance!" Her name cut through the twilight.

She jerked back to face none but Ansel himself, riding toward them on his horse. "Is anything amiss?" He swung his leg over the saddle before the stallion even stopped moving, then led the animal abreast of them. His gaze sought hers. Though she tried for a casual smile, her eyes must have been wider than normal, for he added, "Are you well?"

"She is perfectly well. She's with me." Frankie kept one hand on her arm and drew her beside him.

"I assume you are here to escort her home? There's a crowd gathering on the next square. Talk of a protest. It isn't safe."

"Maybe not safe for you." Frankie sneered at Ansel's bright uniform.

"Do you have some quarrel with me, sir?" Ansel stepped into her cousin's space, his shoulder edging between them. "For this is not the first time I've borne your snide comments."

Temperance fought the urge to cheer.

"Perhaps if you did not keep showing up where you're not wanted, you would not have to."

"Gentlemen, please." Breaking free from Frankie, Temperance placed her hand on Ansel's firm upper arm. "My cousin did come to escort me, and he is right that I feel no threat. But if you think caution is in order, Lieutenant"—best not to further antagonize Frankie by using Ansel's given name—"I will yield to your counsel and go directly home."

Ansel's gaze softened as he took her in. "I am going that way, as I am assigned to cover the governor's residence. You can get there more quickly and securely if you ride with me."

"Ride with you…" Frankie spluttered, and Temperance could guess why. The notion of finding herself in such close proximity to Ansel Anderson so liquefied her knees that she'd never be able to get up on his horse.

But she put up a hand to silence her cousin even as she gave him a look of warning. Better that she yield on this small point than arouse Ansel's suspicions.

Frankie could attend the protest and tell her later what happened.

"Thank you, Lieutenant." She spoke calmly. "'Tis very thoughtful of you."

Ansel led her to his stallion with a glance over his shoulder at Frankie, then he faced her. "Oliver will stand in place while I lift you up. Put your hands on my shoulders."

She had but a moment to grasp that he meant for her to sit properly, with both legs on one side of the horse, though on a regular saddle. His hands enclosed her waist, and her hands fluttered to his shoulders as he raised her.

True to Ansel's word, Oliver did not move.

She angled herself forward, grasping the reins Ansel handed her, but not before she glimpsed Frankie watching, his hands balled into fists. The next moment, Ansel mounted behind her and reached around her to take the reins.

"Good evening, Mr. Scott." Did she imagine it, or did Ansel's voice hold a hint of smugness?

Oliver's hooves clipped on the cobblestones as they turned toward St. James Square. Ansel grasped her waist firmly with one arm, securing her rather precarious position. "Don't worry. We'll go slowly."

A shiver—or a thrill?—passed through her at that gravelly promise. "Did you just happen by Christ Church as I was leaving?"

"Now, what do you think?"

Definitely a thrill. She lowered her hood so she could turn her head and peek at him. A mistake, for his warm breath fanned her cheek. "I really would have been fine."

"That is not what I observed. Your cousin takes his familial liberties too far." Ansel's jaw hardened as he stared past her.

"Sometimes he has to be reminded not to be too familiar. Given my lack of brothers, though, he is a convenient escort...if a bit too willing."

"And are you?" His gaze swung back to her.

"Am I what?"

"Willing?"

Facing front, Temperance sighed. "Frankie has his faults,

but we share a number of things in common. He offers me an alternative to the lonely life of a spinster." She tightened her fingers in Oliver's dark mane. "Suitors have never lined up for me as they have for my sister."

Ansel wove them around a lumbering cart filled with barrels. A bunch of boys bearing torches burst past them on the other side and ran, whooping, up the street, no doubt bound for mischief. "Perhaps her suitors hope for a chance to inherit your father's estates."

"Instead of Frankie?" Temperance blew out a small puff of a breath. "Unlikely. And don't tell me you failed to notice Tabitha's many charms." She glanced back to gauge his reaction.

His mouth was twisted to one side, his brow quirking as if he had not even heard her question. "So he is your father's heir?"

"He thinks so, though none of us know the true contents of Father's will—except Mother, of course." She shrugged. "And she pushes me toward Frankie."

"I suppose your sister would be after him if not for the more rewarding prize of Lord Riley."

Temperance laughed with an odd relief that Ansel was on guard against the schemes of her mother and sister. She relaxed her posture, his chest against her back offering a reassuring support. "She would find someone else. Tabitha thinks Frankie a buffoon. But it makes sense he would inherit. The two hundred acres that belonged to his father adjoin our plantation."

"How did he lose his parents?"

"In a cholera outbreak. He was away at university. He has been like part of our immediate family ever since."

Ansel made a rumbling sound behind her. "And yet, you have not answered my question. Are you willing to be his bride?"

The ready answer that came to her was a question. Her heart thundered in her ears when she contemplated speaking it. Yet somehow, she did. "Is there another option?"

CHAPTER 10

The next evening, Temperance sat at the mahogany desk in her bedroom and attempted to concentrate on the missive before her while Cecily cleaned up the tea service. The other letters Temperance had written remained tucked away in the secret compartment that could be exposed by removing the long bottom drawer and pulling on the sides that extended along the dividers between the long and short drawers.

So far, she and Frankie had identified four potential men involved with the stamps.

George Bailley, a landowner, merchant, and the commissary of the Governor's Council, had opportunity to bring in the stamps with the recent arrival of one of his ships. He also possessed the storehouses to conceal them.

Thomas Moodie, a former Scottish laird who served as the Council's deputy secretary, could have assisted in the endeavor.

The intelligence gathered by the Liberty Boys pointed to either Simon Munro or Dennis Rolls being appointed the stamp master. Rolls was a member of Parliament living in

A CONFLICTED BETROTHAL

Savannah, while the merchant Munro owned extensive holdings in St. Andrew's Parish.

She finished the letter to George Bailley with the ultimatum for a confession Frankie had suggested. *You must advertise at the exchange, the market, and the pump, or otherwise, we shall suspect you have it in your stores, and the fatal consequences that may arise from this you may judge.* Her quill trembled a bit as she wrote the threat.

Words, that was all. She would insist on meeting with the Liberty Boys in person to present her sample letters. They would read them before her, and then she would take them back and destroy them. The patriots could do as they wished with her ideas. Ideas were not criminal.

We are, sir, your humble servants, The Townsman.

The signature emboldened her. Included her. A singular signature representing a plural, ever-growing constituency. A voice crying out for a city. Wasn't it right to be part of something so important?

Temperance replaced the quill in its holder, but she couldn't get it out of her head that James Habersham Sr. could be involved. Should she compose a letter accordingly? Did she dare? What had Frankie learned last night?

At horse hooves slowing before the house, she leapt up and scurried to the window. She pulled aside the curtain and scanned the street and the square, but she lacked a good view of the front walkway. The rider had probably stopped at another residence.

Cecily glanced up from laying out Temperance's supper dress. "Who're you looking for?"

"Frankie?" He might still be stewing that she'd ridden away yesterday with Ansel. "Ansel?" Neither had appeared today. She would settle for either—for completely different reasons.

"Seems to me you've seen a good bit of both lately."

"I'm dying to know what happened last night. You know I stay in touch with Frankie because he keeps me informed."

"I heard on the grapevine about people marching through the streets to protest. And of course, I know you and Mister Frankie share an interest in such things." Cecily selected a choker from Temperance's jewelry box. "But you don't look at him the way you look at the lieutenant." Her voice had gone soft and sweet, like the swirls of cinnamon in the scone Temperance had just savored.

She sighed. "I've never met a man like him, but I don't know how he feels. Therefore, I don't know if my own feelings should enter into the matter."

"They always enter into the matter. Especially when he looks at you the same way." Cecily paused to smile at her before hoisting the tea tray and making her way to the door.

Could she be correct? Temperance turned back to the window with a sigh and swept another glance over the square with a yearning she couldn't deny. After the prior day's events, she'd expected Ansel to stop by to discuss the current state of unrest with her father. If he did, would she have the courage to seek Ansel out? Her desire to affirm their connection warred with the logical reasons she should remain guarded.

Ansel had held his peace when he'd bid her farewell the night before. When she'd questioned if there was another option for her besides Frankie, he'd asked if she wanted there to be. The way he'd put it back on her had frozen her. *Fear* had frozen her. How could she confess her growing feelings for him? Her desire to be loved for herself, flaws and all? That would make her the most vulnerable she'd ever been.

Ansel had admired her compassion, her intellect, her faith, and her humanitarian projects, but that did not mean he harbored romantic feelings for her. Had his questions about Frankie also revealed a more personal interest in her family estate? Father had warned both his daughters about suitors with ulterior motives. Surely, Ansel was too honest to be one of those.

But there was also the question of his loyalties. While his openness attracted her, it was far from agreement with her principles. As long as he was in the rangers—

A crinkle of paper had Temperance whirling around.

Her sister stood over her desk, the letter to George Bailey clutched in her hand. She must have slipped into the room right after Cecily departed.

Temperance's heart dropped into her stomach,

Tabitha held up the paper, her eyes wide. "What is this?"

"It is nothing." Temperance hurried forward and snatched it from her. How much had she read? Not much in that amount of time, surely. "A business question for George Bailey."

"What kind of business?" Tabitha cocked her head, her curls spilling loose over the shoulder of her flowered cotton bodice.

"The kind that is not yours." The ink had yet to dry, so she couldn't fold the letter or even hold it against her. She settled for replacing it on her desk and lowering the top. She'd move it later. Tabitha could have no idea of the secret compartment. For now, she turned the little key in the lock and then slid the key into her pocket.

"And not yours, either, apparently, as you did not sign your own name. What are you up to that requires an anonymous signature?"

She turned to face her sister with her hands behind her on the desk and her heart pounding. All her ready words failed her. Finally, she squeaked out an untruth. "Nothing."

Tabitha's eyes narrowed. "Last night, the so-called patriots hanged and burned an effigy of a stamp officer. What do you think they would do if they knew who the man really was?"

Temperance lifted her chin. "I would never be involved with anything violent."

"Oh, no. You would just stir others to it with words you scratch out while hiding behind your quill. Under normal circumstances, I would tell you to stop being such a meek little mouse. To act on what you believe. But these are not normal circumstances. And if you do anything to jeopardize this family, I will turn you over to the Governor's Council myself. Is that clear?"

Temperance swallowed hard. "'Tis only your own manipulative mind that makes you so suspicious. Now, please leave my room." She didn't even want to know why Tabitha had come in to begin with. Guilt at her deception pinched her heart, but she had no answers that would satisfy her sister. Especially since what she was saying was correct.

Tabitha swiveled and strode away. She slammed the door behind her.

Temperance sank onto the chair in front of her desk. What was she doing? The only result her plotting had wrought was to alienate those closest to her. She was playing a false game with her whole family—and Ansel. She even used her co-conspirator, her cousin, to her own ends.

With shaking hands, she unlocked the top of the desk. There would be no missive to Habersham. She moved the Bailley letter to the secret compartment and slid the drawer back into place. When she mustered the courage to open it again, it would be to burn the letters.

~

*A*s the day after the first Stamp Act protest in Savannah dwindled into an orange twilight, Ansel leaned against a building in an alley across from Machenry's Tavern. He drew his cloak closer against a chilly breeze that swirled drying leaves about his boots.

Ansel had missed all the excitement last night while he'd

been consigned to guarding the governor's mansion, but chances were good that some of the conspirators would trickle into the popular watering hole this evening to plot their course of action. With the public shift from verbal to physical threats, Judge Scott would likely require names. While Jones and Weaver and several other rangers subscribed to the ideals of the patriot cause, they, like Ansel, had been on duty last night. He needed the identities of the more activist Sons of Liberty he could give his benefactor before calling on him again—some leading away from men who were fast becoming friends.

And Temperance? Was he avoiding her as much as he was avoiding her father?

She'd taken him off guard, asking if she had another option to marrying her cousin. How many women wanted to spend their lives alone, never marrying, never finding love? Some, perhaps. Temperance certainly could pour her passion into her projects, but the very way she'd questioned him told him that wouldn't be enough. There'd been longing in her voice. She had turned halfway, as if afraid to look at him. She wanted more yet feared it. But when he'd given her the opportunity to voice her desires, she'd gone silent, withdrawn. Become almost cool.

Perhaps he'd assumed too much. Those "common interests" she shared with Frankie might join them more tightly than Ansel had thought. Controlling men often bound women to them in ways he would never understand. Maybe Temperance disliked him pointing out those deficiencies, those dangers.

He'd been sure when he'd come upon Temperance in Frankie's clutches last night that the man had been pressuring her to go someplace other than home.

And there might be more danger than he'd even assumed, for Frankie Scott approached the tavern now, coming up the side from the rear of the adjacent alley. Standing below the window, he reached up and rapped on the glass.

Ansel ducked into the shadows and only peeked out again when two men exited the front door and circled around the side. Both had been in the tavern the day of Ansel's arrival. Frankie stepped forward and exchanged an unusual, extended handshake with them in turn. A few words were murmured, inaudible from across the street. Then Frankie handed an envelope to each of them. He gestured, and they split up, going three different ways.

Ansel did not have to ponder which one to follow.

~

The summons from Judge Scott came in the middle of the next week.

Ansel had sat in the rangers' pew rather than with the family on Sunday. Several times, he'd sensed a set of eyes on him and glanced up to find they belonged to Temperance. She'd quickly looked away. What did she want from him? Surely, she'd been so vague when he'd taken her home because she, too, recognized the impossible gulf between them. Yet when she looked at him like that...

At the moment, he was more concerned about telling her father what he'd witnessed outside Machenry's. He'd weighed the matter and concluded that he owed Frankie no special loyalty. In fact, if the man was up to something harmful, the rest of the family would be best served by Ansel revealing it.

As the congregants streamed from the sanctuary, he'd hastened to give his regards to the Scotts, then drawn the judge aside to ask when they might speak again privately.

Temperance had regarded the exchange with her usual sobriety, not hiding her interest.

However, Judge Scott was off to the plantation for some business that required his immediate attention. He would be gone several days.

Ansel had had no choice but to wait. Then, he'd received a message at Halifax requesting his presence in the judge's study Wednesday afternoon.

Rather than sit behind his desk as he usually did, Judge Scott joined Ansel in one of the two chairs facing it. He indicated Ansel should take the other. Today, he did not offer a drink. His thick brows drew flat over his eyes.

"We have a situation." He spoke in a low tone. "One that requires special vigilance."

Ansel nodded. "I was assigned to guard duty the night of last week's protest, but—"

"Not the protest. A handful of our prominent citizens have received threatening letters. The governor takes this very seriously and has asked that we do the same. We must find out who sent them."

Ansel pictured what he'd seen when he'd followed Frankie the night after the protest. The man had drawn his cloak up to hide his face, then dropped an envelope through Dennis Rolls's mail slot. Doubtless, it had not contained an invitation to sup.

Ansel uncrossed his leg and sat back. "What did the letters say?"

"They accused Dennis Rolls, Simon Munro, and James Habersham of being stamp master and Thomas Moodie and George Bailley of bringing in and hiding the papers. They instructed each of them to advertise the falsity of these claims in three public places or risk harm."

Ansel's eyes went wide. One did not threaten such men without severe repercussions. "The letters were sent anonymously?"

"Signed 'the Townsman.' But plurals were used in the final comments of some, and Habersham's closed with the term 'free people.' So either this is an individual who fancies that he speaks on behalf of the whole city, or this is a group of people. And if that is the case, we have even greater cause for caution."

"A group such as the Liberty Boys."

"Naturally, that is where one's mind goes. But we need evidence." Judge Scott reached into his pocket and withdrew a small silver snuffbox. He took a pinch of the dried powder onto his thumb, held it to his nose, and sharply inhaled. "Basil. Clears the head."

"Seems to me, the senders of the letter don't know who is involved with the stamps and are seeking to weed out suspects." Ansel drummed his fingers on his knee as the judge put away his snuffbox. At a creak, he looked toward the door, expecting to see someone there. But the door remained closed. "They aren't correct in any of their assumptions, are they?"

Would the judge tell him if they were?

Judge Scott chortled, setting him more at ease. "Indeed not. The stamps have not even arrived yet, and someone from outside the colony will be stamp master. A man named George Angus. Your troop will be called upon to protect him."

Ansel digested this new information with no small amount of dread. As an outsider being brought in, the stamp master would likely face similar treatment to those in the other colonies. Which might make for an interesting winter. "What will these men do in response to the letters? Will they advertise their innocence as instructed?"

"Some will. But Habersham is hopping mad. Who knows what he will decide."

This situation had to be defused and quickly. The loyalists needed somewhere to pin their ire. "I know of someone who bears watching." Frankie had been wrong about the stamp master once. Left to his own devices, he could bring further danger upon the Scott family. Upon Temperance. "Someone you might be able to bring to heel before he does more damage."

"Who?" A hand on his desk, Judge Scott sat forward.

A shadow shifted under the door. Ansel held up a finger

and hurried across the room with quick but furtive steps. The rug helped muffle any noise. And yet, when he flung the door open, only dust motes floating in the late-October sunshine met his expectant gaze. He stepped out into the hallway, but there was no one there. Shaking his head, he returned to the study and closed the door.

Judge Scott had come to his feet and assumed a frown. "Surely, you did not think someone in my own household would eavesdrop on us."

"Just wanted to make certain. I thought I saw someone go past." Ansel waited for his host to resume his seat, then he sank back down into his as well.

The older man tugged at his stock, loosening it as a sigh escaped. "You may be right to be so cautious. My Temperance is a good girl, but she asks more questions than is proper for a young lady. I blame it on my nephew. He stirs her up with information from the Commons House. Not that she would ever throw her lot in with the baser element we are discussing."

"Yes, well, regarding your nephew..." How would the judge take the concern he was about to share? The man had already indicated he harbored some suspicion, so Ansel swallowed and pressed on. But he lowered his voice to a whisper. "The night after the protest..."

~

Temperance fled to her room as swiftly and silently as her shaking legs would allow. She leaned on the door she'd closed behind her and stared at her desk. She hadn't touched it since Tabitha's warning had induced her to abandon the letters in the secret compartment. But her father had just told Ansel that someone had sent correspondence to the very people she and Frankie had named—and signed them in a way only she should know.

She forced herself to cross the rug and pull out the bottom drawer. It did not lock, but the desk had been in her room ever since her mother had bought it for her around the same time she'd taken Cecily as a maid. Temperance had been so excited to discover a hiding spot in the piece of furniture that she'd almost told Cecily. But she hadn't. She hadn't told anyone.

Now, she manipulated the partition to reveal the compartment.

Empty.

CHAPTER 11

'Twas all Temperance could do not to spill her angst over the missing letters to her sewing circle friends the next afternoon. No, not just sewing circle friends. They were true Daughters of Liberty now.

Mrs. McKenzie oversaw Elizabeth's progress on the loom, while Rhoda helped Ann at the spinning wheel. The other women stood around a big table in the middle of Button Gwinnett's back storeroom, stitching on a red-and-white-striped flag while the window behind them showed a tall-masted ship slipping out to the harbor.

Temperance drew a deep breath and focused on the thrill over her fears. "Ladies, this really is working. The paper from South Carolina said that over two hundred New York City merchants have signed the non-importation agreement. Those in other towns are following suit."

Ann looked up from untangling a thread. "Button says that British merchants are starting to feel the pinch. Bills are going unpaid. New orders aren't coming in. They are having to let workers go. Soon, they will be pressuring Parliament."

Temperance pushed her spectacles up on her nose as she

faced her. "How is business, Ann?" The store's shelves had looked empty on their way in today. As the previous stock thinned and income slowed, would her new friend regret her patriotic commitments?

Ann grimaced. "Not the best, admittedly, but 'tis a price we are willing to pay. Button is reaching out to some new local artisans."

"An endeavor I'm sure we will all support." Temperance scanned the room and received assurance in the form of nods and murmurs.

"Thank you. If that should fail, we might have to look at other options. Button is talking about trying his hand at farming."

Elizabeth looked up from passing the shuttle through the threads stretched taut on the loom. "Oh, we would hate to see you go. I do hope it doesn't come to that."

"Me too. Whatever happens, we will stay in touch." Ann offered a brave smile.

"Where else could we safely meet to make our fabric?" Mary laid her needle down to reach back and rub her neck. "Although I'm afraid I don't see the purpose of this flag. Where are we going to fly it?"

Conviction stabbed beneath Temperance's breastbone. *Would* they ever have the courage to fly it? Thankfully, Katherine rescued her from answering.

"I told you it's like the flags they are making in other colonies. The stripes represent those that sent representatives to the Stamp Act Congress. In Boston, they have a special elm they call a liberty tree. They display their flag there, where the Sons of Liberty meet."

Lydia cocked her head. "Perhaps we should see if Mr. Machenry will hang it out."

"Or Button," Ann suggested. "That would finish off his business for sure."

The ripple of laughter almost covered the knock on the door. When it repeated, Ann jumped up and went to answer, no doubt expecting her husband. But it was Frankie, face flushed, who peered inside and searched the room.

"I must see my cousin." His gaze latched onto Temperance's. "Come. I must speak with you on a matter of some urgency."

The initial relief that had washed over her turned as chilly as sea spray exposed to a salty wind. On her way to Christ Church later today, she'd planned to leave a note at their dead drop asking him to come talk to her about the missing letters, but what brought him here now? After removing her spectacles, she tipped her head toward the back door. They could have privacy on the bluff. "Join me out here."

Murmuring his excuses, he wove across the storeroom in his high-heeled boots, his mincing steps resembling a minuet, a newspaper clutched under his arm. As soon as the door closed behind them, he snapped the paper open. The strong wind from the river nearly ripped it from his hands. He steadied it, turning to shield the pages with his body. "Have you seen this?"

She angled closer. "What?"

"Your letters. The loyalists we sent them to had them printed in the paper."

Her mouth dropped open. "Frankie, I did not send any letters."

"Of course you did." His intense brown eyes flashed up to hers. "You put them in the dead drop for me."

Temperance shook her head. "I was going to send you a message to tell you the letters were stolen from a secret compartment in my desk."

"*Who?*" He gaped at her.

She raised her hand, palm up. "It could only be Tabitha. She walked in while I was writing one. I don't think she saw much, but she threatened me. I told you she was growing suspicious. She must have come back and examined the desk more closely, although she denied it when I finally managed to corner her." Temperance gulped. "Although even if she is guilty, how did they get from there...to here?" She pinched a corner of the newspaper.

Frankie's throat worked. "I sent them out for delivery. Naturally, I assumed if they were in the dead drop, you had to have put them there."

"Even if I had, that did not mean I wanted them mailed verbatim! I told you they were to be examples for the Liberty Boys. To discuss. To consider. Then to write their own correspondence or newspaper article or broadsheet."

He shrugged. Shook his head. "They liked them as they were. Said I should handle it."

"Oh, Frankie." Temperance covered her face and drew her shoulders forward, as if she could block out the dangerous chain of events their carelessness had set into motion. "And the recipients turned them in to the paper? What does it say? How bad it is?" She dropped her hands as Frankie flattened the paper to better secure it against the wind.

"They denied involvement and are offering a fifty-pound reward."

"For me?" The question squeaked out of her ever-constricting chest.

"For whomever provided this false information, as they claim." He followed a particular line with his finger, reading aloud. "'We have great reason to believe that some malicious person must have given this false information. We do hereby offer a reward of fifty pounds sterling to the Townsmen, if he will discover the author of this report.'"

Temperance wrapped her arms around her body. Strands of hair blew loose from her bun and whipped across her face. "So they want me to tattle on myself."

"It gets worse. I have it on good authority that the governor has been sent copies of the letters."

Her chin snapped up. "What will he do?"

"I don't know. But listen..." Frankie folded the paper, stuffed it inside his coat, and took hold of her by the forearms. "We're not letting you hang out to dry over this. I think I have the answer that will resolve everything."

"What's that?" Dare she hope that her cousin might take responsibility for his own miscalculations?Cover for her in some way?

"Those men are denying the charges because they are not true. At least, where Rolls and Munro are concerned. You were right about Habersham, Temperance. I delivered a letter to him myself, a couple days after the others, and he has not responded."

"*You* delivered a letter to him?" She blinked as moisture flooded her eyes. "My father said that someone had, but I never thought you'd have taken it upon yourself to write him."

"Why wouldn't I?" He gently shook her arms as if trying to wake her. "We'd agreed he was involved. And now we'll make that public. Once everyone realizes he is the stamp master, whomever is behind the letters will be vindicated."

"No." Temperance broke free and swiped an escaping tear.

"What do you mean, 'no'? Why are you crying?"

"I'm crying because I overheard my father tell Ansel the name of the stamp master." Her cousin sucked in a sharp breath, but she pressed on. "We were wrong—about all of them. And now these letters have gotten published, and a furor is about to break loose on our heads."

"Who is it?" Frankie's eyes became slits.

Temperance nibbled the inside of her lip. She couldn't let the patriots accuse and threaten another person falsely. But would it lead to violence if she named the man? "I need your word that he won't be harmed."

"You have my word." Frankie leaned into her space. "What is his name?"

Despite the flare of fear at his vehemence, she would not step back. She lifted her head and looked him in the eye. However well-meaning his actions, Frankie had broken her trust. Acted too rashly. He'd placed them in an impossible position, one from which they might not be able to extricate themselves. She could no longer depend on her cousin as her go-between. "That is something I will only tell the Liberty Boys in person."

~

The day following his conference with Judge Scott, Ansel helped unload a wagon of supplies into the commissary. Technically, he could have continued cleaning his rifle and let the privates deal with the delivery. But if he polished that gun one more time, the mere glare off it would be enough to slay any protestors where they stood. He sure wasn't liable to sight any Indians down its length. And anyway, the physical activity felt good. Far better than skulking around in alleys or trying to decipher a certain young lady's glances.

Jack passed him as Ansel trod to the commissary with a sack of flour. He patted Ansel's arm and slid something into his waistcoat. "Found a chap who agrees with you about representation in Parliament. James Otis. A Massachusetts lawyer. Should make for some nice light reading."

After Ansel reached the storeroom and plunked his load onto a shelf, he pulled out the pamphlet. *Rights of the British Colonies Asserted and Proved.* He grunted. If only Jack knew Ansel had just pointed the finger at the man he suspected of distributing—if not writing—the Townsman letters. When his friend wheeled a barrel of salt pork in, Ansel tipped the paper in his direction before tucking it back away. "Thanks for the pamphlet."

Jack nodded and cast a glance around. As Ansel had

already ascertained, they were alone. Still, his friend lowered his voice. "Meeting at Machenry's Monday night." No doubt, because the Stamp Act would go into effect tomorrow. "You should come."

"I would love to." Well...if Frankie Scott wouldn't call him out as a spy and drag him into the street for tarring and feathering. He'd have to find some believable excuse to offer Jack and bow out. The sad thing was, he actually wanted to hear what the Liberty Boys had to say. If they sounded like Temperance, he'd soon find himself agreeing with them on many points. "If I can't make it, I know I can count on you to tell me what transpires."

"Just come." Jack clapped his shoulder as they stepped back into the brisk evening.

And there Ansel stopped, for coming toward them atop a bay mare was Temperance herself. But was it? He adjusted his hat for a better view of the woman in the smart burgundy riding ensemble. He still wasn't sure as Jack let out a low whistle and Ansel went forward to help the lady dismount. The scent of lemon verbena settled any question of identity even before Tabitha's eyes—filled with tears—rose to his.

"Miss Scott. What is it?" He glanced toward the fort's entrance, but no servant or family member trailed her.

She held her mare's reins in one gloved hand and wiped her face with the other. "I'm afraid I find myself in need of your assistance, Lieutenant Anderson. I only wanted to visit Gregory and Stuart's new shop near the Exchange. You see, they are straight from Great Britain and promise to make the smartest habits this side of the Atlantic."

"And...how did you come to be here...alone?" He took hold of her horse's bridle and smoothed the animal's nose. Behind him, he could practically feel Jack's grin boring into his back as he and another private wrestled a barrel of apples down from

121

the wagon. "Why are you not in the carriage?" With Cecily...or her mother or sister?

Tabitha fluttered her damp lashes his way. "I always ride with my groom. I like to take a circuit around the city. Have you ever been to the burying ground for Christ Church?"

"I can't say that I have." Ansel frowned. "Seems a strange place for a young lady to want to go."

"Oh, no. I love to walk there. 'Tis beautiful, with the Spanish moss waving over the headstones." She made a floating gesture with her fingers. "One thinks of all the experiences, the joys and triumphs and sorrows, buried in those few walled acres. I find it full of life, not death."

Why was she going on about life and death? Ansel couldn't figure it out fast enough to dispel his frown and offer a response, even when she paused and searched his face expectantly.

"Oh, Lieutenant." Tabitha gave a light laugh. "It reminds me to not let opportunity slip through my fingers." When she trailed those very fingers down his chest, uncomfortable awareness tingled through him.

As the frazzling sensation dissipated into suspicion, he dipped his head. "So where is the groom, Miss Scott?"

"Tabitha. I seem to have lost him in the crowds on the wharf, Lieutenant. Or may I call you Ansel? Anyway..." She let loose a gusty sigh. "He is lost, and as I was so close to the fort, I thought I might prevail upon you to escort me home. If Father saw me ride in alone, there would be—" She stopped herself and covered a giggle with her hand.

Ansel's eyes went wide. Had this fine Savannah lady been about to utter a word even a man shouldn't say in polite company?

She resumed with a smile lingering about her lips. "Well, shall we just say it wouldn't end well for me?"

"I can see your dilemma." Any way it had unfolded, Tabitha

now stood before him unescorted. "I can saddle up and accompany you home."

"I would be ever so grateful."

Ansel sent the private helping with the unloading to saddle Oliver, then he caught Jack's eye. "Can you tell Lieutenant Jones where I've gone?"

"Oh, I certainly will." Jack's generous grin and wry tone promised Ansel should expect plenty of harassment about his involvement with the Scott twins.

Holding in a disgusted huff, Ansel turned back to help Tabitha onto her mare.

She waited until Ansel had mounted Oliver and they rode toward the gate to ask, "Do you think we could go down Bryan Street? I need to stop at the market."

Market Square was not out of the way to St. James Square if they took Bryan Street west, but the smirk lighting Tabitha's face hinted the detour she'd planned all along had been her stop at Fort Halifax. Even if her visit was contrived, Ansel could hardly refuse to accompany Judge Scott's daughter safely home—as well she knew. But he wouldn't be played for a fool.

"Miss Scott, I'm on duty. I do not have time for shopping."

"Only a quick stop?" She pushed her lips into a pout. "I'm in desperate need of foolscap, thanks to Temperance. How can I justify going back out when we can pass right by it?"

Ansel cut her a sharp glance. "So as not to worry your family?"

"Why?" She shrugged. "They know I'm out for a ride."

"Because if the groom returns before you do—"

"Oh, he wouldn't dare." She let out a peal of laughter. "He'd be far too frightened for that. Imagine him coming home to tell my father he'd lost me." They rode in silence a couple of minutes. "No, he'll probably look for me and when he can't find me, skulk about until after dark in hopes that someone rescued me. Which they did." She flashed him a bright smile as she drew up at the corner of the market.

"You should allow your rescuer to do his duty."

Ansel swung down from Oliver, then assisted Tabitha in dismounting. He trailed her while she admired baskets woven in the African tradition, boxes of French chocolates, and strands of Indian beads.

"Maybe you should rescue me more often." She sniffed the air. "You can start by getting me a cup of coffee on such a chilly day." Tabitha punctuated her imperial pronouncement with an expressive shiver.

It wasn't that chilly, but Ansel dug in his pocket for a coin and gave it to the vendor who kept a kettle over his fire near his stand of baked bread. While the German man prepared the brew, Tabitha examined a nearby table of books.

"I can't picture you as much of a reader."

She shot him a scolding look. "I should be insulted, and I would be, if I did not know us both to be people of action rather than words. No, I was thinking of my sister."

Ansel's brows shot up at the unexpectedly thoughtful notion. He nodded to the book Tabitha held. "I imagine she would enjoy a copy of *Pilgrim's Progress*."

Tabitha snickered. "Mother read it to us when we were children. Temperance liked it, but not I. Maybe I would have if the adventures had come without all the pious moralizing." She snapped the book closed and returned it to the table. "No, as promised, all I need is some of this foolscap. Temperance used all of ours, writing those letters."

Letters? The vendor was handing Ansel the coffee in a pottery mug. He grabbed it and turned so fast that some of the hot liquid sloshed onto his ungloved hand.

"Watch yourself." Tabitha brushed drops from his knuckles as she took her drink.

"Temperance has been writing a lot of letters?" When she nodded, he added, "To whom?"

A one-shoulder shrug and Tabitha sipped her coffee. "How would I know? What I do know, Ansel, is that you would be wise to be cautious where my sister is concerned. She doesn't think like we do. We know our duty and we do it. But she is not as she appears."

His heart slowed to a heavy, thudding rhythm. "What do you mean?"

"I mean...she keeps secrets."

~

Ansel returned to the barracks that night without stopping by the mess hall. Tabitha's warning about Temperance had stolen his appetite, as had her unadulterated flirtations. She'd focused more on charming him than answering his questions. He'd never met a woman more adept at turning a conversation. He'd been unable to get anything else about Temperance from her.

The bedstraw of his narrow cot crinkled as he threw himself on it and stared at the brick wall. Would Tabitha stoop so low as to smear her sister simply to capture Ansel's attention? She'd made it clear Lord Riley's wealth and status held little appeal for her. If the way she'd leaned into Ansel and kissed his cheek as she thanked him for "saving" her gave any indication...

He could only pray Temperance hadn't been looking out the window.

But what if Tabitha was right? Had she been hinting that Temperance had something to do with the Townsman letters? Had she passed them to Frankie?

Ansel shot upright and opened the drawer of the small table beside his bed. He laid the scrap of paper he'd saved there on the surface and lit a candle from the tin sconce on the wall. He stared again at the list of dances. In the flickering light, something caught his eye. A lighter swirl, like a watery brushstroke, between two of the French words.

He sat in the rush-back chair and held the paper to the light. Words formed between every term in both columns. Slowly, he spoke the phrases aloud. "Must...not...meet. People...asking...questions."

Ansel's hand dropped to the table as his gut hollowed out. This message had not been for Mrs. Swinton, unless the dance mistress was a party to something nefarious. Then who? Did Temperance have a secret amour? And if this was a romantic warning, why was it written in secret ink?

CHAPTER 12

Following Frankie's revelation about the printing of the Townsman letters, Temperance waited for the other shoe to drop—as it inevitably must. It happened the next afternoon when a wide-eyed Cecily came to tell her that her father requested her presence in his study. Temperance undergirded herself with a prayer and few slow, deep breaths, then descended the stairs.

As expected, her father presided behind his massive desk. But her sister's presence on the other side made Temperance's steps falter.

Father tapped his fingers together. "Come in, Temperance, and shut the door."

She did so, assessing her sister's expression as she took the vacant chair. Calm, but not smug. Perhaps Tabitha had not revealed whatever she knew about Temperance's letter-writing. Her heartbeat slowed a fraction. "What is this about, Father?"

"I will come right to the point." When did he not? "An anonymous source has informed me that one of you was seen entering Button Gwinnett's storeroom for a meeting of women suspected to be involved with the Sons of Liberty. Perhaps even a sister group. Now, I have my own inclination as to which of you that might have been, but in the interest of fairness, I brought you both here to give whomever may be guilty the chance to confess."

Temperance's pulse raced. The evidence of her rushing blood must surely stain her cheeks. She daren't look at her sister. Amazingly, Tabitha remained as silent as she. The clock on the mantel ticked a loud and extended ellipsis.

Father shot up in his seat. "Well, I'm waiting!"

Tabitha gave a sultry, unruffled laugh. "It certainly wasn't me." She flapped a dismissive hand. "You can ask the groom. He accompanied me to the riverfront yesterday, but I called on the habit-makers."

"I can and will confirm that." Father's gaze swung to Temperance.

She should have spoken before Tabitha did. Temperance swallowed. "I also went to the riverfront, with Cecily, and we did go to Mr. Gwinnett's shop, but that is because our sewing circle meets there now." To which her maid and Rhoda had just been voted in by a majority. Would Temperance land them in trouble after their very first meeting as members?

Father scowled at her. "Why would you want to meet in a drafty storeroom rather than in our comfortable parlor?"

"For more space, of course. Our group has been growing, as you know." She tightened her interwoven fingers in her lap. *Please, please don't ask me anything else.* Now that questions were being posed, her future involvement threatened, lines of honesty blurred as never before.

"If I ask Cecily if all you attended was a sewing circle and nothing more, what would she say?"

"She..." Temperance struggled to get a breath all the way into her lungs. Her father had unknowingly given her a narrow opening to wriggle past the deeper truth, but on the other end lay a cliff. "She would probably also tell you that I went to Christ Church."

"For what purpose?"

She let it all out on a single exhale. "To aid the reverend with the religious education of the slaves."

"And why would he need your help with that?" Father's neck bulged as he sat forward. "Especially when you well know how I feel about it?"

"Yes, I do know, Father." She twisted her cotton petticoat between her fingers. "I only help him with the women and children. He needs me since he lost his assistant. We're not breaking any laws. In fact, I'd dare to say we are upholding God's laws."

"Do not presume to lecture me on God's laws, young lady, while you not only failed to honor your father's wishes but lied to him as well. You can consider your volunteering with the good rector at an end." Temperance had no chance to protest before her father's focus shifted, unexpectedly, to Tabitha. "Should I also brace myself for an interesting report from the groom?"

Tabitha covered her face as though she might cry, fanned herself, and squared her shoulders. "I must plead that you go gently on him, Father."

He popped out of his chair as though the angst of this interview had suddenly become too much to bear. "Whatever do you mean?"

"The poor boy took a wrong turn at the wharf and lost sight of me. It wasn't his fault, I'm sure. You know how I am forever riding ahead." She leaned forward, her eyes suddenly widening as if in appeal to their common nature. "I can't help myself. I just get so eager—"

"Come to the point. Where did you go?"

"When I couldn't find him, I could only think of one place *to* go. Fort Halifax."

Temperance gaped at Tabitha just as her father did.

"You rode unescorted into a fort full of rangers?" He threw out his hand.

"I rode to your trusted friend, Lieutenant Anderson."

Of all the gall. Temperance couldn't stop the scoffing sound that escaped from her throat. Was she mistaken, or did one corner of Tabitha's lips curl up just a fraction?

Her sister continued. "He was ever so kind and rode home with me. We had a most pleasant evening."

"I don't care how pleasant it was. You are being courted by a peer of the realm and will do nothing to discourage his interest. Are we clear?"

At the volume he spoke and the manner in which he enunciated every syllable, Tabitha had no choice but to nod.

Father grasped the side of his silvering head for a moment. "Given the perilous times and your shared inclination for rebellion, for now, both of you are to remain at home unless accompanied by your mother or given permission to go somewhere by me. I trust you understand this is for your own well-being."

This time they did not wait to answer, saying in unison, "Yes, Father."

"That is all. You may go."

Tabitha rose and flounced to the door.

Temperance followed more circumspectly. Considering what could have happened, she had gotten off easy. But her heart weighed heavily in her chest. How was she to help anyone, slaves or patriots, when she'd just been placed under house arrest?

In the hallway, she caught Tabitha's arm before her sister mounted the stairs. For the first time in as long as she could remember, a sense of kinship stirred in Temperance's chest. If Tabitha had stolen the Townsman letters, surely, she would have told their father about them. And clearly, he had not known. "Who do you think made that report?"

"How should I know?" Tabitha jerked her chin up. "If you wouldn't persist in befriending traitors, we wouldn't be in this situation."

She'd overlook that for a chance to ask what she really wanted to. "Do you think it was Ansel?" Even putting the worry to words made her queasy.

"Given that he was busy at the fort when I arrived, I doubt it. Father has many more spies and connections across the city than a low-ranking ranger officer."

Temperance's relief flared into an inexplicable need to defend Ansel. "If he is so low-ranking, why are you interested in him?"

Tabitha's eyebrows shot up. "Have you *seen* the man? A sight more life in him than what's left in Lord Riley. If I could convince Father to open a few doors for Ansel and favor a match, I'd have everything I ever wanted."

Why had she thought for a moment that Tabitha would consider her feelings—or her safety? She'd do anything to get what she wanted. Temperance put a hand on her hip. "You did go through my desk, did you not? How did you know where to send the letters?"

"I have no idea what you're talking about." Tabitha started up the steps, then turned back and spoke in a low, fervent tone. "But I will admit, I warned Ansel about you. He deserves someone who shares his values. And we both know that isn't you."

~

Temperance stood by her window on Monday night and waited for the signal Frankie was to use to let her know when to sneak out. 'Twas all she could do not to pace, for if she paced, she might miss it. But oh, how her legs did ache. After three days shut up in her room, she longed to run, to breathe fresh air, and then to keep running...

But where could she go?

And of course, her own decisions had added to her confinement. Father had asked her to go to church with the family on Sunday, but she'd been determined to make her point. If he wanted to make her a prisoner, a prisoner she would be. She'd taken only tea and toast since Friday. But then, her stomach had threatened to devour the rest of her and she'd given in and chowed down a mutton chop and a sweet potato and a whole loaf of bread this afternoon. Thus, the energy to run.

If she were honest, her avoidance of church had more to do with avoiding Ansel. 'Twas bad enough the way she'd left him hanging after he brought her home the night of the protest, over a week ago now. But then he'd come presumably at her father's summons over the Townsman letters. While he'd asked more questions than he'd answered, his mere presence had made its own statement, had it not? And he'd been about to give Father some key information when she'd thought she heard someone approaching and had to flee back upstairs.

As if that was not enough, Tabitha had poisoned Ansel against Temperance on her obviously contrived visit to Halifax. And when he'd brought Tabitha home, she'd further sweetened the betrayal with a kiss to his cheek. This, according to Cecily's mother, who'd spied them out the kitchen window. And Darcy never lied.

A badge of honor Temperance had stripped off her own chest only recently.

The one thing that had gone right was Temperance sending Cecily out the back door before her father emerged from his study the day he'd confronted Temperance and Tabitha. Cecily had warned the Gwinnetts to put the storeroom back to rights in case of any surprise inspections. Ann also knew to contact the other women to arrange their next meeting elsewhere.

A CONFLICTED BETROTHAL

Then, Cecily had left a note at Mrs. Swinton's for Frankie, instructing him to summon Temperance for the Liberty Boys meeting using two flashes of his lantern from across the street on Monday night.

Temperance reached for a glass of water on the nearby table and gulped down several swallows. Where was he? Of course, if he came too early, his lantern would look ridiculous.

Sliding on her spectacles, she pulled back the curtain. A cloaked figure moved from the shadows of the neighbor's garden shed. And there was the signal. Temperance took up the candle she'd left burning on the table, cupped her hand around the flame, and held it to the wavy glass. She proceeded to move her hand twice back and forth, indicating that she was coming, then set the holder back down.

Temperance tiptoed to the door. She cracked it open and ascertained no one was in the hall and the door to her parents' room was closed. She made it to the landing. From there, she peered into the lower hall. By some grace of God, she reached the back door undetected.

The cool swell of air in the yard invigorated her, and she drew up her hood. She kept to the shadows until she reached the fence that encircled their home.

Frankie met her at the rear gate. He grabbed her arm and drew her near. "All this signaling is titillating, but what is it about? Why couldn't I collect you at the front door?" At least he grasped the expediency of the moment and refrained from commenting on her spectacles, as he often did when she wore them.

"Someone told Father of my involvement with the Liberty Boys. Come, we must away from here quickly." She did not squabble when he took her hand rather than offering his arm, allowing him to pull her down Whitaker Street until they reached the corner—where a formidable form wielding a walking stick stepped into view.

133

Temperance's heart fluttered. "Father." Her exclamation carried the same hopelessness as the hollow call of a mourning dove.

"Why, good evening, Uncle." Frankie released her and made a leg, his typical obsequious bow, proving his lack of awareness of their current situation.

Father addressed Temperance without a glance at his nephew. "What part of 'do not leave the house without my permission' did you fail to understand, Temperance?"

"Surely, you cannot have meant that to include me seeing Frankie."

"We were just going to sup—"

Father sliced into Frankie's explanation with a raised hand. "I have no wish to know. What will happen now is that that you, daughter, will tell your cousin goodnight and return to your room. He will leave and not call again unless *I* request him to."

"Yes, Father." Temperance tamped down the desire to protest and instead used the moment she'd been handed, hanging her head and then turning to Frankie. Raising herself on her tiptoes, she brushed her lips against his cheek as if in a kiss. But when his eyes went wide, she whispered as low and yet as distinctly as she could, *"George Angus."*

The tip of her father's walking stick intruded before she'd even quit speaking. He edged between them with a growl. "I don't think either of you understand how serious this is." He gave Frankie a light shove, then pointed at him as he stumbled to retain his footing. "The only reason you have not already been called before the Governor's Council is that you are my nephew and I convinced them we have nothing more than circumstantial evidence to tie you to the sending of the Townsman letters."

"But, sir—"

"Shut your bone box! You would do well to choose your words and actions very carefully from now on, my boy. For you will be watched. Anything else against you—and I do mean *anything*—and I won't be able to save you." Father's face twisted. "As it is, consider your...*courtship* of my daughter at an end."

And that might have been welcome news if it hadn't also meant that Ansel had betrayed Frankie.

Temperance swallowed her panic as she turned toward the house. Had Ansel betrayed her as well?

CHAPTER 13

Ansel angled his hat against the drizzle and fog swirling in from the river as he rode back to Fort Halifax on Friday, November eighth. With the point facing forward, the droplets just came in from the sides. The headgear's double-cocked design might be practical for firing a musket but not so much when on patrol.

It had not been a good week.

Tuesday, a group of sailors had decided Guy Fawkes Day, the anniversary of the Gunpowder Plot against Parliament, a fit occasion to act out the capture of the stamp master. Six of them had carried another all over town on a scaffold with a rope around his neck and a paper in his hand, calling out, "No stamps, no riot act, gentlemen." When Captain Powell got wind of it, he'd sent Ansel and several others—in plain clothes, so as not to invite the very riot the governor had recently passed a law against—to monitor the situation and, if need be, ensure peace.

Of course, the crew of sailors ended up at Machenry's, where they had pretended to beat the fellow with a cudgel. His pitiful cries had drawn great amusement from the crowd.

A CONFLICTED BETROTHAL

Finally, they had given it up and gone inside for drinks. Since no property had been damaged, no arrests were made.

Thursday, the *Gazette* reported the resignation of the South Carolina stamp master and the identity of Georgia's. George Angus and the stamps were said to be in Charlestown aboard the *Speedwell*. The Sons of Liberty had determined in their Monday meeting that they would meet the man upon his arrival, acquaint him with the sentiments of the people, and demand he step down. "Very bad consequences" were promised if he failed to comply. So there was that to look forward to.

All of this while Ansel passed a stint of duty at the damp, chilly guardhouse on Wright Square. The management of prisoners fell to the rangers, as did the unsavory task of apprehending runaway slaves. This morning, a man and a woman had been caught on the docks, seeking to sneak aboard a ship bound for Jamaica. Placing shackles on their wrists despite their tale of escape from a cruel master had wracked Ansel's conscience. He'd far rather face the threat of painted warriors. He had not signed up to enforce laws that stripped other humans of their most basic rights. Yet he was bound by the terms of his enlistment through next fall.

The irony of it sat heavily on him as he rode into the riverside fort and turned Oliver's care over to a cadet.

"Captain Powell would like to see you in his quarters, sir," the fresh-faced young man said.

What now? Ansel thanked him and made his way to the small log cabin adjacent to the rear wall. A thin plume of smoke spiraled from its brick chimney, the scent hanging on the moisture-heavy air. He cleaned his boots at the scrape beside the stoop, then knocked and entered when bid. Not only Captain Powell but Judge Scott looked up at his arrival. What was *he* doing here? Ansel saluted his commander and offered Temperance's father a slight bow.

"Come in, Ansel. You must be chilled to the bone." The captain rose and indicated the table near the low-burning fire. "I know better than to offer you whiskey, but would you care for mulled cider?"

"Thank you, sir. I would not refuse. I can pour it." In the absence of a servant, Ansel stepped over to the hearth. He handled the pot of cider staying warm in the embers with a rag, pouring the spice-scented amber liquid into a pewter tankard. The apple-based drink warmed him all the way down. He lowered the cup to ask, "How can I be of service, sir?"

The captain remained standing. "Ansel, how would you like to get away from here for a time?"

He blinked. "Sir?" As appealing as that sounded, did the force not need him now more than ever?

"I have some letters and dispatches I need delivered to Fort Augusta and various militia commanders in the countryside. The governor plans to bolster the guard here in Savannah. You're to deliver the correspondence in a timely manner and not linger at the fort."

"Of course, sir. I will ride there directly and then hasten back here."

"No need for that." Captain Powell waved a dismissive hand. "You shall be near your home in St. George's Parish. Ride out from there to visit the militia commanders. They are not being summoned, merely put on alert. Take the opportunity between calls to spend some time with your family."

Consigned to the countryside, in the middle of a potential insurrection? His midsection tightening, Ansel slowly lowered the tankard to the table at his side. "Did...I do something wrong?"

Powell laughed. "No, Lieutenant. On the contrary. What I've related is the official version of your orders. And now, I will step out, and Judge Scott will give you the unofficial version. You have my guarantee of privacy."

A CONFLICTED BETROTHAL

Ansel saluted again but couldn't quite keep his jaw firm as the captain left the cabin. He turned to the older man, who'd remained seated and silent throughout the previous exchange. "Sir? What is this about?"

Judge Scott sighed. He indicated the other chair. "Sit down, Ansel." When he complied, the judge shifted toward him, the ruby ring on his hand clutching his walking stick winking in the firelight. "I find myself in need of your assistance in a personal matter."

"Anything, sir."

The corners of the man's mouth lifted briefly. "I appreciate your loyalty on behalf of your father, but you might want to wait and weigh the assignment first."

His heart thudded. What was this about? "You have my full attention."

"Have you heard of the Daughters of Liberty here in Savannah?"

Ansel shook his head.

"Certain rumors have come to my attention of such a group. I fear my own daughter is involved."

"Temperance?"

Judge Scott merely smiled, a bit sadly. "I do not have proof, but her ideals and her close association with her cousin, whom you yourself fingered in the Townsman debacle, give me cause for concern. Someone told me last week they had seen one of the girls entering the back of Button Gwinnett's store with other women of a traitorous persuasion. Turns out, they were all members of Temperance's supposed sewing circle. Now, I am no fool."

Ansel swallowed. "No sir." Did the judge believe he was withholding information?

"I went to investigate the location but found nothing amiss. Yet in the interest of caution, I consigned Temperance to the house."

139

"You are keeping her under guard?" That would certainly not go well.

Judge Scott frowned as though incensed Ansel would question his judgment. "Not only for that. She has been lying to me about volunteering with the slaves. I don't know what has become of my daughter. She was once a humble and dutiful girl."

"Temperance feels strongly about the plight of the slaves." The images of the couple he'd just clamped back in chains rose in his mind like accusing specters. Out of respect for his father's friend, he wouldn't challenge Judge Scott on this score, but neither would he fail to defend Temperance's convictions, should the conversation require.

Her father turned the discussion with a soft snort. "However she may feel, her defiance of my wishes is but one more sign of her newly rebellious spirit. Perhaps you will understand the gravity when I also tell you that I caught her sneaking out to meet her cousin Monday night."

Ansel sat back in his chair, a breath expelling from his lungs. "The night of the Liberty Boys' meeting."

"Tell me in all honesty you do not suspect her of conspiring." Judge Scott's gaze locked on him.

The encoded list of dances forbade him to argue. His face twisted. "I cannot disagree."

"And you are not surprised."

He was not ready to offer his own accusations. He settled for a generalization. "Such seems common among the young adult children of prominent loyalist leaders. If you want to know your enemy, you would do well to look close to home."

"Thank you for your honesty, even though I can tell it pains you."

Ansel shifted, clasping the leg he crossed over the other. "I've grown to care about some of these who call themselves patriots. Even consider them friends."

A CONFLICTED BETROTHAL

"What we have asked of you has not been easy. You have warned me of my own nephew. I still will not require other names unless violence or unlawfulness are threatened. Of all people, I understand the value of ambiguity at times." Judge Scott sighed again and gestured with one hand. "And that brings me back to Temperance. Despite the difficulty she has caused of late, she is dear to me. I would even admit—my favorite. I would do all I can to protect her."

"Of course, sir." Ansel reached for his tankard. Maybe he should have accepted that whiskey.

"You said some of these patriots, you call friends. Is she among that number?"

After swallowing a drink of cider, Ansel lowered the cup. "I would say so." Even if Temperance did not find enough commonality with him to engender deeper affection, certainly, they shared a mutual admiration.

Gently, softly, Judge Scott tapped the butt of his walking stick on the swept-dirt floor. "Could you ever care for her as more than a friend?"

He almost choked on his sip. The judge offered him a patient smile as Ansel wiped his mouth and set the tankard aside again. "Your daughter has many pleasing qualities, sir. But we do not always see eye to eye. Even if I were willing, I doubt she would be."

"Then we should make her willing." The older man's definitive statement brought Ansel up short. Judge Scott tamped the ground with his stick again, firmly now. "An agreement between you and her provides the clearest answer to everything."

"I'm sorry, sir...an agreement?" What was he missing?

"A betrothal."

Ansel's legs stiffened of their own accord. Before he could unfold to his full height, the judge had whisked the stick out and nudged his thigh.

"Sit back down. Hear me out."

Ansel sank slowly back onto the chair. The room seemed to narrow around him.

"I need to get my daughter out of this boiling cauldron of discontent. James Habersham is on the warpath. Did you know that he offered a reward of fifty pounds sterling to anyone who turns in the sender of the Townsman letters?"

Ansel swallowed, remembering Tabitha's insinuations. "I did not."

"It was in the latest issue of the *Gazette*."

"I suppose I missed that." Not surprising, with the week he'd had. "Surely, you don't believe Temperance was involved in that as well?"

Judge Scott pressed his lips tight and tilted his head at Ansel.

"It *must* have been the Sons of Liberty."

"And who do we suppose is in collusion with them? With Temperance accused of leading a Daughters of Liberty group, I am unwilling to risk her safety. No, she must be removed from the situation." The judge drummed his fingers on the head of his walking stick. "I have already removed her cousin. He made a grave miscalculation when he supposed word of his plotting would not reach my ears. If he thinks he can defy me and still be handed my daughter and my estate...bah!"

Ansel waited for Judge Scott to collect himself before offering a necessary assurance. "I should clarify to you, I did not indict your nephew to make room for myself."

"I know that." With an abrupt gesture, the judge waved off his concern. "You are too direct for such machinations. That is why I trust you. That's why I'm here—and why you've been given this assignment. Take Temperance to your family's estate. Association with you will help allay suspicions. In a different environment, I believe she will listen to reason. And if you happen to return in a month engaged, so much the better."

The surge of excitement Ansel experienced was not only startling—it was surely premature. "Sir...you cannot mean for this to be an honest betrothal." He could understand a farce. A temporary alliance to remove Temperance from public notice until tensions in Savannah eased. More than that, Judge Scott couldn't intend.

But the man's smile was actually apologetic. "I understand what I'm asking. Temperance's ideals must be managed, no easy task for a man. She is far too opinionated. Not to mention, you risk your own future on her behalf. I know that soldiers such as yourself look to commendations from an untarnished career for advancement. I'm prepared to make this worth your while. There is still some good land from the 1763 treaty. I can see to it that you're fairly compensated, especially with Temperance as your bride. I will even give you that maid she is so fond of, and a young buck to marry the girl. With three extra people, you should qualify—"

"Sir, please." Ansel waved his hand to accentuate the words. He'd never presume to cut off Judge Scott, but further clarity was in order.

The man might as well have been speaking in Cherokee. Surely, he was not offering Ansel everything his parents had wished for him—and more than he dared wish for himself.

Well, apart from the slaves.

"Judge, what I meant to say was that I could not imagine you would consider me as a suitor for your daughter. When you set me beside someone like Lord Riley and all that he brings to the table..." He couldn't bring himself to finish his statement and cut his gaze to the floor.

"Ah, but we do have Lord Riley. For Tabitha." Judge Scott laughed and patted Ansel's leg. "Your modesty does you proud. Do not take this the wrong way, Ansel, but for Temperance, there were no suitors waiting in line behind Frankie. After what she's gotten herself into? Well, I would count it an opportunity on both sides if you and she could come to an understanding. Wouldn't you?"

Ansel sat back as his throat closed up. No. Not an opportunity. That sounded like a business transaction. And what he felt about Temperance Scott was so much more than that. But would she share his sense that God might be bringing something wonderful out of this mess? Or would she merely feel like a commodity being traded to one man instead of another?

~

Late the next evening, Ansel balanced three copper mugs of cider as he slid open the door behind the taproom in Abercorn's only tavern, a day's ride north of Savannah. The lusty fourth stanza of a German ballad followed him into the private parlor. The town—and the tavern—had seen better days. Mostly thirty years ago, when the newly arrived Lutherans had settled here while waiting for the road to be built to their permanent residence farther north, Ebenezer. But at least this small room offered relief from the appraising eyes of the men and the gossip of citizens who stopped for the Saturday night mail, a service offered by most taverns along main roads.

Relief, Temperance did seem much in need of. As he closed the door with his foot, she looked up with eyes more red-rimmed than when they had set out that morning. She must've been crying in the coach as he rode Oliver alongside. His chest constricting, he placed the mugs on the table between her and Cecily. "The barmaid is right behind me with supper, though as late as we are, all she could rustle up was some bubble and squeak."

Temperance reached for her drink without response, but Cecily turned her attention from a window into the alley, where it appeared two men were racing their pigs. "Thank you, Lieutenant."

Taking the seat next to Temperance, he winced as a chorus of squeals and cheers temporarily drowned out the singing. "Doesn't bode well for a restful night, I'm afraid. Hopefully, they will settle down. I've procured a private room for you." No small thing, given the fact that most people would roll onto a lumpy—and often bedbug-ridden—mattress with their fellow travelers, strangers though they be.

This time, Cecily waited for her mistress to reply.

Temperance lifted her gaze briefly to him. "Where will you sleep?"

"Outside your door." He wouldn't risk leaving the women unguarded while he slumbered in a separate chamber. Bowing his head, he almost missed the flutter of Temperance's lashes. "We should probably repair there directly after supper."

"Yes, Lieutenant."

There was no missing the slight edge in her tone.

Before he could address it, the waitress entered bearing a tray. She distributed bowls and spoons, inquired about their comfort, and then departed with Ansel's reassurance.

"Miss Scott..." Ansel swallowed. Temperance's stiff posture as she poked her spoon into her serving of cabbage and beef forbade the familiarity of first names. "Before we left Savannah, I expressed how honored I was to escort you for a holiday in the country. To introduce you to my family. This may have been your father's idea, but I asked if you were content with the arrangements." Indeed, he had taken her aside privately to ensure it. "Has that changed? Because if it has, we will turn around in the morning and ride back to Savannah."

Her watery eyes shot up to meet his. "And return me to my father's tender care? No, thank you."

"Do you suggest another alternative?" Ansel opened his hands.

"I fail to see why I couldn't spend a month at the plantation instead."

"Your father thought you would enjoy some time in company."

"In *your* company, and the company of your loyalist family, you mean." If anger could translate into heat, those tears in her eyes would have evaporated into steam. "Do you listen to everything my father says? And act accordingly?"

Where was this ire coming from? He chucked formalities in favor of directness. "Temperance, you have always known my family, like yours, supports the king and the royal government."

"Tolerating it in theory and expecting it to rub off on me by forced proximity are two very different things."

He sat back, rubbing his chin. Egads! "What a relief that your sense of justice has helped you find your tongue."

"How can you expect me to be civil when I am merely exchanging one jailor for another?"

"Miss Temperance." The low warning came not from Ansel but from Cecily, who stared at her mistress with wide, dark eyes. "Lieutenant Anderson has been nothing but kind to us."

Temperance glanced at her. She bit her lip, then turned on Ansel, speaking in a rush. "I heard what Father said to you."

His skin went cold. "And what was that?" Had Judge Scott told her of his suggestion of a betrothal? He'd indicated to Ansel that would be something Ansel could pursue, as the lady made herself willing...or not. He was not in the business of coercion. Even still, his agreement with her father left a hollow spot in his middle.

She set her soup aside. "The night he told you about the Townsman letters."

Ansel stilled. It had been Temperance's shadow he'd spied under the door.

"He said you needed to help him find out who sent them."

If she knew that, she'd heard Judge Scott say the name of

the stamp master. He drew a deep breath. "It should not surprise you that your father asks my observations on the mood of the town and the military. He is, after all, responsible for my promotion."

"Perhaps so, but is that all there is to it? For soon after, he told Frankie the Governor's Council was onto him. And then he sent him away. Who made the Governor's Council suspicious, I ask you?" Temperance rose, bracing herself on the table.

Cecily watched her from the corners of her eyes, her brow puckered, her posture tense, as if prepared to spring up at any moment.

Ansel extended his hand. "Miss Scott, I understand if you are upset about your cousin—"

"This is not about Frankie! It is about you." The twist of her voice at the end, the inherent threat of another descent into tears, stopped Ansel's heart. There was more, much more, they needed to discuss than political maneuverings.

He stood and dared to touch her arm. "Temperance..."

She flinched away but did not flee. She watched him with a furrow between her brows, so he met her eyes dead on.

"I know you don't trust me right now. And frankly, I don't trust you either. By our very stations in life, we've been at cross purposes. But I don't think we are really opposites in what we believe. Our conversations have shown that. So I'm asking you to at least believe me when I say that I wouldn't have invited you to come home with me if I did not truly think it best. Best for you."

He stressed the last word, but she repeated another one. "Home. What's it like?"

"In November? Peaceful." Ansel gestured to chairs, and they took their seats again, Cecily relaxing in hers. "Mother will be setting food stores and candles by for winter. My brother, Martin, will oversee the slaughtering." When Temperance's eyes widened, he chuckled. "We raise hogs and cattle, in addition to wheat, corn, flax, and indigo."

Her brows lifted. "No rice?"

He shook his head. "We leave that to the big planters on the marshy land south of Savannah. Father may be away for court in Augusta, so Mother will be delighted for your company. I sent notice ahead. Everything will be prepared. I promise, everything will be done for your comfort." Ansel leaned forward, holding out his hands.

She drew hers into her lap, her mouth tightening. As he slowly straightened, she said, "I want more than comfort. I want honesty." Tears pooled in her eyes. "I'm weary of games."

His heart squeezed, even if he couldn't squeeze her hands. "That is why we are leaving Savannah. Give the country a chance. Give my family a chance. All will be just as it appears. And we will talk. There, not here."

A high-pitched squeal from the alley punctuated his statement and drew a laugh from all three of them.

Temperance met his gaze and tucked up one corner of her mouth. "Promise?"

"I promise."

That honesty might cost him any chance of a future with her, but they could not build a future on secrets and half truths.

CHAPTER 14

The scent of coffee the morning after her arrival at Resthaven—as she'd learned Ansel's family farm was appropriately called—woke Temperance from her deep slumber. She turned over on her feather mattress to find the trundle bed below her unoccupied. Cecily already stirred about the room, quietly unpacking the contents of their trunk.

"Good morning, Miss Temperance. I laid out your blue light-woolen gown and quilted petticoat." She pointed to the garments draped over a nearby chair, then she gave a shiver. "There be a chill in the air."

So the tip of Temperance's nose told her. "Yes, it's colder here, this far inland." She nestled under the covers for another moment. The ecru bedspread featured intricate patterns of tiny knots she'd not seen before. When she'd turned it back yesterday, she'd found dainty bundles of minty-smelling herbs on the pillows.

"Good thing we did not pack many fancy dresses." Cecily shook out a silk taffeta sack of French style before she hung it up. "I don't care to fold them in a clothes press, and there aren't that many pegs."

Temperance had been so beleaguered from the journey when they arrived late last night that her surroundings had scarcely registered. She retrieved her spectacles from the bedside table so she could survey the room. Substantial but functional walnut furniture complemented ochre-yellow-painted wainscoting and white muslin curtains. "Things do seem a bit more Spartan, perhaps, but there's a country charm." Something about the simplicity was restful—like the name of the place.

Temperance struggled out of the dent her body had made in the mattress and went to the washbasin behind a tapestry screen. As she completed her toilette, her mind went to Ansel. How would he seem in this different environment, among his family? A nervous eagerness spurred her to hurry. Or maybe that was the hunger-hollow spot beneath her breastbone.

Over the course of their four-day journey, Ansel's thoughtfulness had eroded her reserve. She'd left Savannah brimming with resentment at her father's treatment. Convinced Ansel was not only a party to it but the reason for it. For if he'd pointed a finger at Frankie, he'd surely set her domestic captivity into motion. And yet, a person of his direct demeanor could not fake the regard he showed her—or the eagerness he couldn't conceal at the prospect of bringing her home to his family. Any of her father's cronies could have decried Frankie. She would give Ansel the forbearance he asked for, the opportunity for them to start afresh in a new environment.

Most likely, he was waiting for her downstairs. But once Cecily helped her into her stays and gown and secured her hair into a bun and cap and she descended the steps, she met a quiet house. On one side of the hall, she peered into a parlor and a study, finding no one. The painted dado trim of both reflected the cohesive earth tones she'd noticed upstairs—raw and burnt sienna, somehow grounding after the Prussian blue and busy, printed chintzes favored by Temperance's mother. A dining room across the way featured verdigris-green trim, a long table, and candles stubs burning under silver warmers on a sideboard. She was just peeking into one when someone spoke behind her.

"Good morning, miss."

Temperance dropped the lid over the thick-sliced bacon with a clatter. She whirled to face a middle-aged woman in gray linen and a white apron. "Ah, good morning. Mrs. O'Grady, was it?" The housekeeper.

"It was, indeed. I hope you slept well, Miss Scott."

"I did, thank you." She tilted her head. "What was the herb in the nosegay on the bed? I recognized the lavender, of course, but the other..."

A smile lit the woman's lightly lined face. "Costmary. My mother says they used to nibble it to stay awake during long church services. Mrs. Anderson also makes a pleasant and healthful Sweet Mary Tea from it. She made the nosegays, too, of course. She has quite a hand with wee growing things."

"As I have heard." Temperance smiled at the creative late-fall arrangement of witch hazel branches with their delicate yellow flowers on the table. "Where *is* Mrs. Anderson? And everyone else?" As Ansel had predicted, his father was in Augusta for the year's last court session, but she struggled to suppress a sense of disappointment not to find Ansel waiting to greet her.

The woman folded her hands before her rounded abdomen. "Mr. Ansel went out to join his brother in plowing the flax field. He said to tell you—"

"They are doing the plowing themselves?" Temperance cocked her head.

"Yes, miss. Remember, the Andersons keep no slaves at Resthaven." A patient smile tugged up Mrs. O'Grady's lips.

"Of course." White servants made for a heartening change from the black slaves she'd been forced to accustom herself to.

151

Temperance stowed her curiosity for a better time—along with the desire to run to the window in an attempt to spy Ansel laboring in the fields that led down to the Little Ogeechee River. She'd never seen him out of his uniform. "I'm sorry for interrupting you. You were saying he left a message for me?"

"He wanted you to know he'll be in for dinner. He asked me to see that you had everything you need." She indicated the buffet with a sweep of her hand. "I've made coffee, but if you prefer tea..."

"Coffee is perfect. Where might I find Mrs. Anderson?" Though she'd met the woman only briefly last night, her hostess's gracious demeanor made her comfortable to seek her out this morning.

"She is in the kitchen, miss. She said if you like, you can fix your plate and we'll put it on a tray for you to take to join her."

"I would like that very much, thank you. Would it be possible to have a tray sent up for my maid too? She is unpacking in our room."

"Most certainly, Miss Scott. Cecily should make herself at home here. The servants will see that she has everything both of you need."

The woman's easy acceptance of her maid set Temperance at ease. She proceeded to fill two plates with bacon, biscuits, jam, and boiled eggs. Then she carried her own tray to the kitchen so Mrs. O'Grady could take the other one upstairs for Cecily.

A trail of smoke rose from the chimney of the kitchen behind the house. Unlike the residence, which had been constructed of wood and painted a soft gold, the kitchen was made of brick. The soft red hue complemented the russet trim around the windows of the main dwelling. Between the two, raised beds divided an extensive herb garden into sections. The soft golden sunshine wrapped in wisps of cloud had melted the early hint of frost into soft dew on the grass beyond, but from here, Temperance couldn't glimpse the fields or the river.

She found the lady of the house with a young kitchen maid behind a long table covered with ingredients. She wore an apron over her linsey-woolsey bed gown and petticoat, and strands of silvering brown hair the color of Ansel's escaped from her mob cap. Patricia Anderson came around to greet her with a bright smile.

"Oh, Miss Scott, 'tis good to see you looking so refreshed." She cleared a corner of the table near the massive open fireplace and helped Temperance slide her tray onto it.

"Yes, I'm afraid I was quite dead on my feet last night. I hope you don't mind that I join you." Temperance adjusted her spectacles, conscious of their weight on her nose. And their detraction from her appearance.

Mrs. Anderson seemed not to notice. She was pulling up a ladder-back chair. "Tis exactly what I had hoped. I felt awful not to wait for you, but I also wanted to make sure we had something to eat for dinner."

"Of course."

"I hope it did not seem rude to you. You're probably not accustomed to the lady of the house disappearing into the kitchen for the balance of the morning." Her assessing gaze held no judgment, merely apology. "Ansel tells me your household is quite extensive with many hands to share the labor."

Slave hands. Temperance flushed as she took her seat. "That is true, but you can hold your head up before God about your way of doing things." She uncovered her plate and set the silver dome aside.

Mrs. Anderson's hand rested briefly on Temperance's shoulder, drawing her gaze up to catch an understanding smile. "My son mentioned that you share our view of slavery. I'm glad to hear it."

Temperance weighed what she should say to that. "Er... thank you." What else had Ansel told his family about her?

His mother laughed softly, as if reading her mind. "Don't worry. He is a man. I don't get near the details I crave, and his letters come far too sporadically to satisfy me. 'Tis why I am so glad he has brought you to visit us. I'm sure you don't remember me, but I remember you from our days in Charlestown."

That raised a bit of curiosity. "What do you remember?"

Mrs. Anderson moved back around the table, still smiling. "A serious little girl who would get very upset when her sister's antics got her in trouble. Even then, you had quite the sense of justice."

Temperance grimaced. Not the most charming picture of herself, but accurate. "Still do, I'm afraid. Although I'm fairly adept at getting myself into trouble now." She nibbled her bacon.

Ansel's mother measured a half a teacup of cornmeal into a large earthenware bowl, then paused with the cup in the air. "I daresay you have a good reason for your trouble."

How perceptive this woman was. Temperance smiled and sipped her coffee. "It's true that my family and I don't always see eye to eye. As Ansel told you, slavery is one of the main points of division between my father and myself. He was very upset recently to discover that I'd been helping the rector with the religious education of local slaves."

"How progressive of him—the rector." Mrs. Anderson hefted a small sack of flour and poured a goodly amount into her bowl. Lowering it, she shot Temperance a smile. "And you, of course."

She paused in spreading peach preserves on her biscuit. As much as she wanted Mrs. Anderson's approval, she couldn't deceive the woman into thinking they shared all the same ideals. "We disagree about more than slavery. The Stamp Act is creating divisions in many families who have traditionally been loyal to the king." She took a bite of the fluffy bread and chewed with appreciation.

Her hostess stepped back to allow the maid to pour boiling water from a kettle into her mixture. Her lips firmed, then she spoke. "Ansel has been sharing some concerns along those lines. 'Tis increasingly hard for him to do his duty without betraying his conscience."

"Is that so?" Temperance's biscuit froze halfway to her mouth, her heart expanding with hope.

"I think you are partly responsible for his burgeoning awareness." Mrs. Anderson's lips twitched with another smirk, then she began stirring.

"He has increased my awareness as well. I am intrigued how you manage a farm of this size without slave labor." Temperance nibbled the end of a bacon slice.

"Just as you see it—at least, here in the house." She grinned as the maid held another teacup over their bowl and a measure of molasses slowly drooled downward. "We share the labor with paid servants. In the fields, 'tis a bit different. We do hire some help, but the men also have a system of swapping work. Thankfully, there are several in the area who also claim our convictions. They take turns in each other's fields at planting and harvest time."

Temperance sat up straight. "What a beautiful concept."

"Less lucrative by far than owning slaves, admittedly, but God has blessed. And as you say, we can hold our heads up before Him." Mrs. Anderson added applesauce and salt to her dough, then something from a smaller bowl before stirring again.

"What you describe is the way I long to live." Unexpected tears filled her eyes. She raised her coffee cup to hide her emotion. "In truth, such an honest existence lines up with my

155

sense that we need to be able to take care of ourselves here in the colonies."

"Then you and I are on the same page." Ansel's mother winked at her. "And if you want to live honestly, you're welcome to start right now, if you have finished with that breakfast of yours."

Temperance lowered her cup and straightened her spine. "What do I do?" What noble task would Ansel's mother set her to?

Mrs. Anderson turned her sticky white mixture from her bowl onto the wooden table. "Fetch some butter from the churn yon. You can help me make our dinner bread."

∼

*A*nsel returned that first day at dinner as promised, smelling of freshly turned earth and with a ruddy color to his cheeks and a light in his eyes which he attributed to physical labor. He took Temperance on a full tour of the farm that afternoon, but the next morning, he rode out for Mount Pleasant to deliver a letter to the militia commander there.

Martin said Ansel couldn't ignore his military obligations for more than a couple days at a time. Ansel said the quicker he went, the quicker he'd be back. But he apologized until Temperance assured him of her eagerness to absorb all his mother could teach her.

Martin snickered and elbowed Ansel at that.

Temperance flushed. But an attempt to explain that her nature demanded self-sufficiency in all things, regardless of her marital status, would require more transparency than had been called for.

Despite his teasing, Martin made her stay easy with his brotherly nature. He worked hard and played just as hard, occupying Temperance of an evening with cards and nine pins and gallops on horses from their stables.

Most of all, she loved the way Ansel behaved around him. Martin brought out a mirthful side she'd not been privy to in Savannah. Mrs. Anderson said that if their personalities were any indication, the boys should have been born in opposite order.

"Indeed, no," Martin exclaimed. "For I never would have amounted to anything as a second son."

Mrs. Anderson explained the uses of every herb in her garden to Temperance, though she'd already begun to winterize the plot. She tutored her in the kitchen without showing any judgment that Temperance had never made so much as a beaten biscuit.

As she readied herself for bed their second night at Resthaven, she told Cecily, "Ansel's mother is going to show me how to do the type of knotting on this bedspread. Can you believe she made it herself?"

Folding a petticoat, Cecily glanced over her shoulder. "'Tis beautiful. What does she call it?"

"Candle-wicking. I love how it is not only decorative but functional, unlike the fine embroidery I've done my whole life." Temperance grabbed her silver-backed brush and scrambled over to the bed, bypassing the steps and hopping up in one jump. The mattress poofed around her.

"Your fine embroidered pictures sure do look pretty framed on the wall."

"Thank you. But my point is that Mrs. Anderson runs this household with the help of Mrs. O'Grady, but she is perfectly able to complete any of the tasks herself. That is how I want to be." Temperance settled in and ran the brush through her hair.

Cecily cast her a smirking look. "You thinking the lieutenant had more in mind when he brought you here than just getting you out of Savannah for your daddy?"

She could only hope. "I might could figure that out if he'd ever come back from Mount Pleasant." A delicious shiver passed through her at the memory of the way Ansel's rough-spun clothing had clung to his strong frame. Farmer Ansel was even more appealing than soldier Ansel. "But even if I'm to be an old maid, I don't want to be a helpless one. We have no idea what the future holds. I can't rely on my father's provision forever, as his recent displeasure has shown. If I don't kowtow to his wishes, he might put me out on my own."

"I doubt that very much, Miss Temperance."

Temperance would no longer bet on it. "In any case, I don't want to end up like Mother, completely governed by his whims, with the most important thing in my life my next dress fitting."

"Now, Miss Temperance..." Cecily's sharp reprimand drew her attention. Despite the familiarity of friendship Temperance encouraged between them, her maid almost never took a tone with her. When she did, it was because she felt strongly about something. "Don't you belittle yo' own mama like that. There be more to her than you can guess."

"What do you mean?" She lowered her brush to her lap. "Cecily, you know I love Mama. We're just different."

Blowing out a little breath, Cecily turned to put Temperance's shoes in the drawer. "Not so different as you might think."

No matter how Temperance pestered Cecily, she'd give up no more information.

CHAPTER 15

The journey to and from Mount Pleasant on the bluffs of the Savannah River had given Ansel ample time to think. He had expected his family to welcome Temperance, but her reaction to them and to everything about Resthaven had made his heart surge with hope. Removing her from the intrigues of Savannah had been the right thing to do. Despite the trappings of wealth and influence with which she'd been raised, her strength of spirit and innate industry meant she would thrive in an honest, hard-working environment.

The fact that he'd rushed through his duties to return to her told him his feelings were more developed than even he'd understood. Truly, she embodied everything he sought in a wife. But before he could broach that subject, they must lay a foundation of trust. No more deceptions or evasions. And he would take the first step.

When Temperance flew out of the front door to meet him as he returned on a brisk, late-November afternoon, he could barely get off Oliver fast enough. He handed the horse's reins to a stable boy and bounded over to swoop her from the steps.

She let out a little cry as he swung her around and then, when he'd allowed her feet to plant again, went still and silent in his arms as he embraced her, his cheek against her hair. Ah, the fresh, sweet scent of her.

He whispered the question foremost in his mind. "Did you miss me?"

"Very much."

Her answer set his heart to pounding. He drew back and cupped her face. "How are you? Truly."

"I love it here, Ansel." She admitted it on a soft breath, her attention straying to their hands as he wrapped her fingers in his. How good his name sounded on her lips. "Your mother has been teaching me so much, and your brother has made me forget all the troubles of Savannah."

"Exactly as I had hoped." He beamed at her. "I'm only thankful he has a sweetheart, lest he steal you away."

Her eyes went wide, then she flapped her hand in a dismissive gesture.

Ansel instantly sobered. "I'm sorry. I should not assume so much. But seeing you here—"

"And yet you barely have."

The hint of teasing in her voice lifted his heart. That she cared enough to attempt to flirt boded well indeed.

"I will not go again until we spend some time together."

A curtain stirred at the parlor window. Ansel's mother peeked out, smiled, and when he gave her a slight wave, she returned the gesture and moved out of sight. She would give him the time he craved with Temperance.

After a glance toward the house, Temperance stepped back, assuming a casual manner. "How did you find the Mount Pleasant militia?"

"Less than open to receiving a summons to support the governor. 'Tis not just in Savannah that people grow discontent." He gestured toward the drive, where young oak trees tipped in autumn's russet hues lined the dirt lane. "Walk with me a minute?"

"But surely, you wish to rest. You just got off your horse."

"All the more reason to walk. I need to stretch my legs."

"Very well, but you shall have to wait for me to fetch my cloak. 'Tis a bit nippy out here."

Ansel shrugged out of his fitted blue officer's coat, heavy with red facing and brass buttons, and held it out. "Will this do?"

She gave a timid nod and turned for him to drape it about her shoulders.

He did so gently, lifting a strand of hair that had escaped from her bun, fingering it a moment longer than necessary. When she faced him with brows raised and lips parted, he offered a rueful smile.

"Let's walk toward the river. We should have a good view of the sunset. Where are your spectacles?"

She patted her pocket, the corners of her lips lifting.

"Don't you need them?"

"I trust you will warn me if I'm about to step into any holes." He quirked his mouth at that, and she shook his arm. "I'm jesting. See, your brother rubs off on me. Truly, I can manage well enough without them."

He cocked his head. "You settle for 'well enough'?"

Temperance pressed her lips together and fished out the glasses in question. She slid them on but did not look at him. "Happy now?"

When Ansel's finger contacted her chin, she startled. He turned her face gently but firmly toward him. "You do know you're just as lovely with them as without?"

She lowered her lashes. "If you say so."

"I do."

Her sudden reserve nudged him to drop the subject for now. He offered his arm, and she took it, allowing him to lead her down the driveway. "Forgive me for keeping you in the cold, but at least we may speak privately out here."

Temperance shot him a glance. "What must we speak privately about?" How well she must know, yet her question and its tone portrayed her nervousness. Did she fear shattering the peace she'd found here? He would make it as easy as possible, lest she erect her defenses again. And he could start with a confession of his own.

"Something has been on my conscience since the stop at the tavern in Abercorn."

"Oh? What is that?" When an eddy of a breeze sent dried leaves dancing about her petticoats, she tugged the lapels of his coat closer.

Ansel drew a breath. "You asked me who aroused the suspicion of the Governor's Council regarding your cousin's activities. I can only assume your uncle alerted them. But it was me who alerted *him*."

Temperance's head snapped toward him. When he met her gaze without faltering, she kept her hand on his arm and asked softly, "Why?"

"I saw him giving envelopes to a couple of men outside Machenry's just before the Townsman scandal erupted. I told your father I knew not for sure, but his manner was suspicious."

"Do you think he wrote them as well as sent them?"

Ansel gave a single nod. "I think it's likely." He stopped at the turn to the narrow dirt track that led between the fields, toward the river. "Was I wrong to suspect him?"

Temperance opened then closed her mouth. Finally, she said, "No."

He searched her eyes. "The night you snuck out to meet him, you were going to Machenry's, were you not?"

"Yes." Her chest rose and fell on a deep breath. "I wanted to see what the Sons of Liberty would plan for the arrival of the stamp master. They are not a violent group, Ansel. You know that now."

As much as Ansel believed that about most of the members, evidence from Sons of Liberty groups in other states showed that it only took one or two firebrands to upset the balance of peace. "Would you bet everything on that?"

Temperance hung her head. "My father certainly wouldn't."

"I know you don't trust him, but will you trust me? We both want nothing more than to keep you safe, Temperance." He raised his knuckles to brush her cheek. He had to communicate that his questioning came from a place of concern, not control. He angled for a better view of her expression. "We have to be honest if we're going to build trust, Temperance. No more games, remember?"

"I—I don't want games."

Ansel dropped his hand but did not step back. "Then is there anything else you want to tell me about you and Frankie?" *Please, God, let her trust me.*

A breath in and out. "Only that I am guilty of allowing his familiarity for what I could learn from him, not for any romantic reasons."

Ansel's heartrate picked up. Though it would be easy to let things go at that, half truths would not serve them in the long run. "As much as I had hoped that was the reason you kept him close, Temperance, I know there is more to it. I know you gave him information as well."

The sun chose that moment to paint the sky in shades of brilliant red and orange. A V-formation of geese mounted above the trees, honking as they followed the Little Ogeechee south. But Temperance's wide eyes sought his.

"How do you know that?"

"That list of dances...when I went back and examined it, I

saw the invisible writing." Probably some sort of citrus juice, not a chemical formula such as skilled spies used. It mattered not. The intention was the same. "You were warning Frankie about me, weren't you? Or is Mrs. Swinton involved also?"

"Mrs. Swinton is...sympathetic. But she has no connection to the Liberty Boys." Temperance spoke high and fast. Her fingers plucked at the collar of his coat. "What is so wrong about sharing what we know with those of a common cause? You give my father information."

Ansel dipped his head. "True. But Frankie's was the only name I offered, and only when 'twas clear his actions were misguided and threatened to incite conflict."

"And yet, you came to Savannah under false pretenses. Why should I trust anything you say?"

He stiffened but stopped himself before stepping back. "There were no false pretenses. I came to serve the governor and my officers. I have done so and will continue to. This is my livelihood, my path to a future where I might hope for a home and family of my own. But Temperance, I look for a time when that service is no longer necessary." He reached for her hands and squeezed them. "Because you and some of the very Liberty Boys I'm keeping tabs on have opened my eyes to many things I was blinded to before. We are not so different as you think. In fact, I would daresay there is little we actually disagree on."

"Truly?" Temperance's lashes fluttered against sudden moisture in her eyes. The sunlight made them look amber.

He nodded. "I see now that change is coming. Must come. But can we not achieve it peacefully? Do we want to see our city divided? Our families divided?"

"Of course not. I hate what all this plotting is doing to us."

"Then let us agree, you and I...we will work for an accord. We will allow only honesty between us henceforward."

Temperance nodded. "Only the truth."

Ansel's heart surged as he drew her close for a tender

embrace. "Good, for if we can trust each other, there is much we should discuss."

~

*A*nsel had promised his mother's harp playing afforded a soothing delight. While a delight it was, the gentle plucking of the strings failed to soothe Temperance the night Ansel returned from Mount Pleasant. Through no fault of Mrs. Anderson, to be sure. Indeed, Temperance laid the blame on her own emotions.

Or maybe Ansel was at fault. He'd greeted her with such enthusiasm. Then he'd sprung that unexpected conversation on her, and she'd found herself gushing truth like millpond water released into a raceway. And then, he'd said those words before he'd led her back inside...about there being much they should discuss. Exactly what did he mean? If his fervent glances served as an indicator, her pulse had good reason to gallop.

"Ansel, you should practice your minuet with Temperance."

Mrs. Anderson's sudden statement as her fingers stilled over her harp strings drew Temperance's head up.

From his place next to the fire, Ansel glanced her way with raised brows.

Heat crept over Temperance that had nothing to do with the flames, since she perched on the settee across the room. "I hope you don't mind that I invited your mother, your parents, to our Twelfth Night Ball." Would he think her presumptuous?

He straightened slowly, sitting up in his wingchair as he lowered to the table beside him his pewter tankard of the cinnamon-laced winter warmer she'd proudly prepared. The tender smile that enlivened his dimples poked some holes in her midsection too. "I most certainly do not mind."

Mrs. Anderson also smiled. "You should finally meet my husband tomorrow, Temperance."

She tipped her head. "I look forward to that." Although the notion made her stomach flutter. What if Captain Anderson did not approve of her? He was, after all, a loyalist like her father.

As though reading her uncertainty, Ansel winked at Temperance while speaking to his mother. "He will adore her."

"And hopefully, bring me a letter from Charity." Martin snapped down the newspaper he'd been reading in the other armchair and sprang to his feet. "Well, up, you two." He rolled his arm. "Let us behold this triumph of social artistry. I'm here to help, as I have no doubt help will be needed." He snickered at Ansel and said to Temperance, "My brother will admit, I've a good deal more experience on the dance floor."

Temperance's midsection knotted, and she shrank back on the settee. "Oh, no…this really is not necessary." Dancing a minuet with Ansel was daunting enough, but with an audience? Subject to his brother's commentary?

"It's not a bad idea." Ansel eyed her speculatively. "'Tis true that I can use the practice. I've been taking lessons with Mrs. Smith, but I'm still nowhere near the level of the other guests."

Temperance swept her hand out. "There is not near enough room in here, not with all the furniture."

"We can take care of that." Martin lifted his wingchair and carried it toward the nearest wall.

"That will not be necessary, Martin. We will use the hall." Ansel directed an arch look at his brother. "And you will stay in here."

Martin let out a puff as he lowered the chair. "Must you take all the fun out of everything, Ansel?"

"Temperance and I will have plenty of fun." He turned to her. "If you will join me?"

She stared a moment at the hand he held out to her. The

ball was fast approaching, and she and Ansel had never once danced together. Wouldn't it be wise to acquaint herself with that nerve-wracking experience in private before attempting to perform such an elegant dance in front of all Savannah society? Finally, she relaxed her shoulders and came to her feet. "Very well." She almost regretted it the moment Ansel's fingers closed around hers. How could she feign composure while performing so many intricate moves with this man whose mere presence made her heart race? He would read her every emotion on her face.

Mrs. Anderson spoke again while stroking out the introductory refrains of the "Minuet in G Major" Bach had published. "Will this do?"

"That will do nicely, Mother. Thank you." Ansel led Temperance to the door, casting his brother a smirk as Martin put his armchair back into place and collapsed in it with a gusty sigh.

They took their places at the back of the hall near the stairs, facing each other.

"We will still have to make our steps smaller," Temperance pointed out.

Ansel nodded. "Common minuet? Start simple?" He waited until she nodded, then called to his mother that they were ready.

Temperance would surely make a fool of herself.

But when they moved toward each other, rising onto the balls of their feet on certain beats and dropping their heels almost to the floor on others, circling inward in three-fourths time, she forgot herself. Ansel's grace mesmerized her. She would never have expected it from one so serious and calculated. But there he was, taking her hand, wheeling her in a three-quarter turn, casting off from her with the fluidity of a courtier.

Country ruffian, indeed.

As they proceeded through the dance, separating, meeting in a right-hand turn, separating again, the irony of the Z-figures struck her. Did the steps not reflect their relationship? Constantly at odds, but repeatedly drawn together. Closer than ever now that—

"Ow!" Temperance had turned into the small table at the back of the hall. She paused to rub her shin while Mrs. Anderson kept on playing, oblivious to Temperance's blunder.

Ansel was at her side, his hand on her back. "Are you all right?"

"I'm fine." She raised a rueful smile to him, but he stood closer than she'd anticipated. "Before you say I should have worn my glasses, my clumsiness this time was owing to the small space rather than my weak eyes."

"I would never call you clumsy."

She shook her finger at him. "Well, don't say 'I told you so' either."

He caught her finger and folded it into his palm, drawing her a step nearer. "I wasn't going to say that. In fact, I wasn't going to say anything at all."

She sucked in a breath. Did she imagine it, or was he leaning toward her? The mere imagining of his lips on hers struck her with such a thrill and terror that she planted a firm hand on his chest. "Lieutenant!"

"Yes, miss?" That one dimple winked at her, underscoring his teasing address.

"Surely, you are not about to take a liberty that is permitted only if two people are betrothed." Much of the indignation of her warning was lost in its breathlessness. He could surely feel her heart pounding against his arm bent between them.

He released her hand and swooped the same arm around her waist instead. "That, Miss Scott, should be one of the things we discuss."

Her lips parted, and his gaze went to her mouth. Undoubtedly, it was going to happen now. But before either of them could move, the door opened, and a frosty blast of wind blew them apart.

A man who could only be Ansel's father stood in the opening. He swept off his hat and chuckled heartily. "Well, it would seem my early arrival is indeed a surprise."

CHAPTER 16

*T*emperance sprinkled powdered sugar over her dried apple scones and stood back from the table to admire her handiwork. She chose to spend as much time in the Resthaven kitchen as she could, for no doubt she'd not be allowed to practice her newly discovered skill back home.

"I call that a job well done." Mrs. Anderson glanced up from chopping herbs and smiled.

"They do smell delicious. Perhaps it would be wise for us to taste them, though, before I take some to the men?"

Was she more nervous about failing at a culinary endeavor or encountering Ansel's father again? While Martin was out working late on the morning after Captain Anderson's return, the older man and Ansel were catching up in the study. Martin got his fair coloring and blond hair from his father, but the captain and his son the lieutenant shared the same formidable military bearing. She'd scarcely untied her tongue in Captain Anderson's presence at breakfast, managing only to politely answer his questions. It would seem that despite her attraction to Ansel, her fear of intimidating men held firm.

"No need. I watched you every step of the process, and I

stand behind my mother's apple scone recipe. Believe me, you will be met with great appreciation." Mrs. Anderson shooed a damp, basil-flecked hand toward the door. "Now go. When you come back, I will be finished helping Constance stuff this goose." She nodded toward the kitchen maid, who was industriously plucking said fowl. "We can pause for a cup of tea and enjoy a treat of our own."

"That sounds lovely." Temperance's mouth watered at the prospect. Even more appealing was the idea of spending a leisurely moment with Ansel's mother. Temperance had come to treasure their teatime chats. Mrs. Anderson did not keep only to the standard, formal, late-afternoon tea. Tea was produced any time one needed a rest or a talk or a book or a sigh. And one never knew what interesting herbal concoction might steam out of her teapot.

Quickly, Temperance transferred the four most perfect triangles to the tray she'd laid out, then she made her way to the main house, letting herself in the back way. The door to the study was cracked, and the rumble of the men's voices reached her in the hall. The mirror reflected a disheveled head and a forgotten apron. Setting the tray on the small table she'd danced into the night before, she paused to put things to rights.

"What does Governor Wright plan to do when the stamped paper arrives? And when will that be?" Captain Anderson's questions brought Temperance's hands to a halt as she untied the apron at her waist.

"Could be as early as next week. The plan I heard before leaving Savannah was to take the paper to the guardhouse."

Temperance removed her apron and began to fold it.

"That seems the safest place. When I was in Augusta, I heard the citizens of North Carolina confronted Governor Tryon at his home. They demanded he turn over the stamp distributor. Only when they threatened to burn him out did he produce the man. The crowd was armed." The captain's grave tone so resembled Ansel's in a similar mood that it was hard to distinguish. Quietly, she laid the apron on the table.

"'Tis why the governor wants to bring the number of officers in Savannah to eight and the privates to fifty-six."

She ought to go in. Her days of listening at doors ought to be behind her. She'd already overheard sensitive information. Temperance reached for the tray.

"I hope you do not have to hurry back. It is best you are here with the girl for a while." Captain Anderson's comment brought her up short again. "As much as I want you to do your duty, I do not wish to see either of you in the midst of a rebellion."

Ansel chuckled. "'The girl' has a name, Father. Temperance."

Now she listened without compunction, edging a bit closer.

"Yes. Temperance. If she is the one you have chosen. Although I could hardly judge her fairly, as she barely spoke last night or this morning."

"She is a bit shy at first. And you did arrive at an awkward moment."

Captain Anderson laughed, and something clunked as though he set a glass back onto his desk. "I take it you were about to press your suit. Well, another good reason to stay here longer. Take advantage of the opportunity. Your mother and I have said all along that a betrothal to one of Judge Scott's daughters would benefit you even more than loyal service."

Cold shock washed over Temperance. Ansel had come to Savannah with the purpose of courting her—or Tabitha? Of using her to leverage her father's favor? For what?

Her hands dropped to her sides, numb. Land, of course. More than once, hadn't Ansel mentioned his desire, his need, for acreage of his own? Land grants had to be approved by the Governor's Council. Did he even care for her, or was he merely playing a part as he'd played to his other patriot friends? Pretending to be open to their beliefs to engender trust.

After the long silence that had given birth to all her fears, Ansel's response finally rumbled forth. "Oh, I intend to take advantage of the opportunity. I even have her father's blessing."

Temperance's chest heaved. She whirled and ran before her desperate need for air—for escape—could betray her. No, he would not take advantage of the opportunity. For he would find her gone.

"*B*ut hear me in this, Father." Ansel met his parent's gaze over the desk. He'd striven so many years for this stern man's approval that facing him now as a man set on his own course was not a small feat. "This is no marriage of convenience. For I love Temperance."

"Love her? You have known her all of three months."

"I knew in a space of weeks. But I couldn't let myself acknowledge it until I could trust her." He'd been ready to declare his feelings the evening prior when his father had showed up.

Father's green eyes narrowed. "What do you mean, 'trust her'?"

"I told you in the letter I sent ahead that Judge Scott was concerned for his daughter's safety due to some rumors. What I did not tell you was that at least some of those rumors had substance." Ansel still had questions for Temperance, but their agreement had bridged the gap between them. There was time enough for details. And he wouldn't hash over them with his father before he'd reached his own understanding. He headed off the question his father drew breath to voice with a wave of his hand. "Doesn't matter. Suffice it to say that Temperance shares our views on slavery. 'Tis part of it. But it goes further than that. She feels that same conviction regarding freedom for the colonies from unjust laws."

Father's brows shot up. "She is a dissenter?"

"She's a patriot. But she shares my dedication to working for change within the law."

"What's this?" Father rose with his hands on his desk. "You have been taken in by the same rhetoric you went to Savannah to quash?"

"I went to keep the peace. I've helped Judge Scott do that very thing. And I will continue to, God willing, with Temperance by my side. With both of our contacts..." Why hadn't he seen it sooner? They would be far more effective working together than apart.

His father lifted his hand. "I wish to hear no more. Not now, Ansel."

"You think I've defied you." Ansel's shoulders sagged on a deep breath, but the burning in his middle remained.

"I—no. You took me off guard. If you want a fair response, you should give me time. Time alone." When Ansel hesitated, he snapped, "Now." His hand went to the Bible lying on the corner of his desk. "With the Good Book."

Ansel's chair scraped as he shot up. "Yes, sir." He recognized—and thanked the Lord for—wisdom when he saw it. Meanwhile, he could pray. This wasn't the first time his father had shown discretion by withdrawing from a potential upset to seek God's guidance. It never turned out badly.

As he closed the door to the study, the faint scent of apples drew his notice to a tray of scones sitting on the table just outside the door. Had his mother left them there, not wanting to disturb them? But why would she leave her apron too?

As he fingered the folded chintz material, another possibility hollowed out his gut. And then made his heart race as someone dragged something heavy across the floor of the bedroom just above.

Temperance's bedroom.
Something heavy like a trunk.

~

At the knocking on her bedroom door, Temperance's gaze flew to Cecily. She'd told her moving that trunk would be too loud.

The maid straightened from placing undergarments into the bottom compartment. "You want me to get it?" she whispered.

"Don't you dare."

"Temperance? It's me. Open up." Ansel's familiar voice bore pleading and a hint of panic. How did he know already?

"I'm sorry, Ansel. I can't do that right now." Somehow, she'd managed to sound halfway normal.

Cecily fixed her with a slit-eyed stare. "Miss Temperance, you gonna have to talk to him. How you expect we get back to Savannah without a carriage?"

Temperance shushed her with a gesture fit to decimate any insects in arm's reach. "I shall speak to Mrs. O'Grady." She just couldn't face Ansel. Not with the shame of knowing how he really viewed her. No doubt, if Lord Riley hadn't been in the picture, Tabitha would've been the recipient of his attentions.

"Temperance, open this door." Firmer now. "You can't leave."

"I can't leave?" The statement fired her nerves, sending her stalking to the threshold and jerking the door open. She glared into Ansel's startled face. "Am I your prisoner now, just as I was my father's?"

"Of course not. I only meant that we should talk—"

"Oh, I think you have talked enough."

The color drained from his face. "How much did you hear?"

She whirled away from him, shoving her shaking hands

beneath her folded arms. "Enough to know that I was but a pawn in your plan for advancement."

"You were anything but. I did not come to Savannah looking for a bride. Of course, my parents want that for me. But it was your intelligence, your passion for your causes—"

"Don't." When he attempted to touch her arm, she pushed his hand away and marched to the bed. "Keep packing, Cecily." Then she turned back to the man in the doorway. "If I am not your prisoner, Lieutenant, you will kindly inform your groom to prepare a carriage." She started pulling her books and journals off the shelf and carrying them over to the trunk. Cecily should have started with those.

Despite her dismissal, Ansel stepped farther into the room, holding his hands palms out. "If you had but eavesdropped a moment longer outside the study door, you would have heard me tell my father that while yes, I planned to propose to you, the last thing I would consider the marriage was one of convenience."

Temperance's steps slowed. But of course he would say that. He would say anything to retain his dream of becoming a landed gentleman like both of their fathers.

He continued entreatingly. "I told him who you were, what you believed. What *we* believed. And I told him...I told him I loved you."

Her grasp on the books she held loosened, and the top one thudded to the floor. She paid it no mind. Instead, she turned to Ansel. "You told him what?"

He did not meet her question with the ardent declaration she breathlessly awaited. His attention was fixed at her feet. He pointed. "What is *that*?"

Temperance swallowed a cry of frustration. With a brisk shake of her head, she looked down. And gasped. For a blank page had spilled out of the book she dropped—a blank page with the shape of an eye mask cut out.

CHAPTER 17

*A*nsel strode toward the strange paper and picked it up. "Is this what I think it is? A page meant for encoding messages?" Temperance's blank look as he shook it at her gave him answer enough. "And you brought it here, intending to send secrets you might overhear to your cousin? Intending to betray the family that sheltered you?"

"No, I-I would never..."

To be fair, she'd left Savannah angry at him. Comparing him to her father. Was it any wonder she'd brought along tools of her spy craft, however rudimentary they might be? 'Twas only a guess that a message might be written in the mask opening, then a letter carefully composed around. He must've been correct.

Ansel forced himself to take a calming breath.

Cecily stared at him wide-eyed.

If he looked anything like his father in a temper, 'twas no wonder the maid seemed afraid. He lowered his arm and met Temperance's eyes. "Well, did you?"

"Did I what?" The three words escaped on a puff of breath.

"Did you hear anything of note?"

"Yes, I did. Just now. But I was not going to write it down."

"You were simply going to leave."

She nodded.

"Why write it down when you could report it in person?" Ansel scoffed.

"No...I just need to go home." Temperance's head drooped.

"Because you're angry? Or because you're guilty?" He tossed the mask page at her. It fluttered back to the floor at her feet.

"Guilty for what?" She raised her chin. "For not wanting to be used as leverage for your advancement?"

Ansel likewise hardened his heart. "Oh, what a crock, Temperance. You heard what I just said to you. If you still want to leave, what harm is there in putting all our cards on the table? Tell me the rest. Tell me everything."

Tears flooded her eyes, and she laid the other two books in the trunk, then clenched her hands into two small fists. 'Twas hard to remain angry with her, with her looking like that. "What do you want to know?"

"Your sewing circle..."

"Is a Daughters of Liberty group." His eyes went wide, but she sucked in a breath and continued more steadily. "We are making a Stamp Act Congress flag and our own material to support non-importation."

"And the Townsman letters?"

She wrung her hands, a look of pleading in her eyes. "I wrote some of them, but only as examples for the Sons of Liberty, to see if they wanted to send something similar. They were never meant to be mailed. Someone took them from my desk."

"Who?" The demand came out harsher than he'd intended.

"I don't know." She threw her hands open. "It could only have been Tabitha. She denies it, but she came in while I was writing one. I have no idea how she knew about the secret compartment."

A CONFLICTED BETROTHAL

"You expect me to believe you wrote letters you never intended to send and that someone stole them from a secret compartment in your desk and gave them to your contact to disperse." Even saying it aloud as flatly as he did, it sounded ridiculous.

"I know it seems crazy, but that is what happened. And I did not write the one to Habersham at all. After Frankie brought me the newspaper article about the letters, I was going to destroy them, but Frankie—"

"Stop." Ansel held up his hand, just as his father had done, but unlike his father, he had no desire to pray. He couldn't think past the many avenues of betrayal twisting in his mind.

She took a step his direction. "You have to believe me, Ansel."

"I don't believe you. But what's more important, I don't trust you. You had more than one occasion to tell me the truth about the letters, but instead, you let me go on with my suspicions about your cousin. Did you even feel a moment's guilt?"

"Yes." She spoke emphatically and reached for his arm, but he shook her off. She tried again. "Ansel, I'm glad for *this* moment. To explain."

"And yet you were not going to give me the same opportunity." He straightened and turned away. "Go ahead and pack. I will order your carriage."

"Ansel!"

Temperance's cry tore his heart, but he still headed for the door.

She burst into sobs behind him.

Another voice broke over them. "I did it! I took the letters!"

They both whirled to stare at Cecily, who stood there like a pop-eyed statue, clutching the sides of her petticoat.

"Cecily, you didn't." Temperance gaped at her. "Why would you do such a thing?"

"Why else but to protect you?" The maid's thick lashes fluttered. "Oh, miss, you were getting in so deep. I heard how Miss Tabitha threatened you. I saw how rash Mr. Frankie be. And I remembered seeing you open that secret part of the desk not long after you got it. So I took the letters to Miss Marjorie."

"To Mama?" Temperance gasped. "Why?"

"I figured she'd know what to do. I thought she'd burn them. But she made me tell her everything, even about the sewing circle and how you passed messages to Mr. Frankie at Mrs. Swinton's. I think she suspected it all along."

Temperance's gaze swung to meet Ansel's. "Mama never said a thing to me." She looked back at Cecily. "But then, how did the letters get to Frankie? He said he found them in the dead drop. If you did not put them there..."

Cecily shook her head. "Your mama must've."

"There's no way." Temperance's stunned expression said she'd thought her mother as shallow as Ansel had. "She is no patriot."

"I told you that you were more alike than you knew." Cecily lifted her shoulders. "Once upon a time, Miss Marjorie had a lot more opinions than she does now. At least, what she lets your daddy see."

"To live like that, divided, must bring such pain." Temperance drew in a shuddering breath, and the raw vulnerability in her gaze pierced Ansel's armor. She held out her hands. "Please, please, let us not be like that."

He couldn't help himself. His heart drew him back to her. He ignored the outstretched hands but walked across the room and wrapped her in his arms. The relief to the crushing pain in his chest was almost instantaneous. Tears filmed his own eyes.

Temperance spoke from a muffled place against his chest. "Cecily, will you please go?"

"You have every right to be angry with me, Miss Temperance—"

"I'm not angry with you." Temperance turned her head

toward her maid, but Ansel couldn't bring himself to loosen his grip. Having her in his arms put everything to rights. "You are more a Daughter of Liberty than I am. And Mother, apparently, than both of us. But right now, I need a moment alone with Ansel."

"Now, Miss Temperance, I'm not leaving you in your bedroom with a man." Given the indignation in her tone, Ansel could practically picture the slight woman drawing herself up to her full height.

"You can stand in the hallway and leave the door open. Just give us a minute."

"Miss Temp—"

"Now, Cecily."

Ansel did not look to see if the maid obeyed. He cared not. He couldn't wait another moment to raise Temperance's dainty chin and put his lips on hers. He hooked one hand behind her neck to brace her for the impact of his emotions.

Apparently, she needed no bracing, for her arms came around his neck, and she kissed him back with an ardor that left him breathless. They broke apart for only a moment, then came back together again.

She gasped his name. "Ansel...I do believe..." He pulled back to look into her eyes. "A kiss of that consequence merits a proposal."

"If you would ever give me the chance, I'd like nothing better. I love you, Temperance Scott. You. Not your sister. Not your family's money. Not your father's power."

She cocked her head. "Even if I came without a land grant?"

"If you can live as a soldier's wife." Did she have any idea what that meant? He released her but clasped her hands between them. "Although that would require me to extend my enlistment."

"Thankfully, I do come with a land grant, one my father will be more than pleased to provide." A twinkle of mischief ignited in her eyes.

"Only if I fulfill my terms of service to him and the governor. Can you countenance that? And abstain from the activities that made him offer your hand to me in the first place? Because that is what he would require." When the enthusiasm drained from her expression, he tipped her chin with his index finger. "You see now how our options are limited?"

She lowered her gaze, then suddenly looked back up. "Couldn't you resign your commission? I don't mind if we don't have our own place for a while. I love your family...well, except for maybe your father..."

"He will come around." Ansel could speak with confidence on that, if not on the rest. "And perhaps we could live for a while across the hall from my brother and his bride, but Martin inherits this place, then his children. What would we have to give a family of our own? And no, I cannot just resign. I could be fined. Even brought up on charges. The latter is more likely in a time of conflict. I can't leave the rangers until next autumn."

Temperance pursed her lips, then nodded. "Very well. I will do as you ask. I will step back from the action if I return to Savannah as your betrothed."

"'If?'" Ansel tenderly cupped her face, aching to taste the sweetness of her lips once more. When they spoke thus, words seemed so unnecessary. "So do I have your permission to get down on one knee now?"

"How about if I just say 'yes'?" And so saying, she drew his head toward hers again.

He'd just clutched her close when a voice spoke from the doorway.

"Miss Temperance, Mr. Ansel, my congratulations. But your moment is over."

The whole household turned out to welcome Temperance and Ansel back to Savannah. The brilliant smiles on everyone's faces proclaimed that Temperance's letter announcing her engagement had already reached them. 'Twas as she had hoped, since she'd passed another two weeks with the Andersons after mailing it while Ansel made his trip to Fort Augusta.

In his absence, she'd strengthened her relationships with his family, including his father who, as it turned out, had decided the positives outweighed the negatives in favor of their betrothal. They'd set the wedding date for the beginning of next autumn, when Ansel would be released from military service. Temperance and Mrs. Anderson had lingered over many a tea, discussing plans. And of course, the Andersons would attend the Twelfth Night Ball, where the betrothal of Temperance and their son would be announced.

Temperance's own mother was first down the front steps, sweeping Temperance into her floral-scented embrace. She drew back to cradle her cheeks and spoke softly for only Temperance's ears. "My dear, forgive me for pushing you toward your cousin. I knew you shared ideals, and I mistakenly thought he offered your only chance to wed. I am so much happier that you have found love."

"Thank you, Mother." Temperance captured her mother's hands and patted them.

"Even with a love match, Temperance, you must always be true to yourself. Do not change who you are to please your beloved."

Her mother spoke with an intensity that confirmed Temperance had misjudged many things about her. They would need to have more conversations, but her father approached. He boomed his hearty felicitations, shaking Ansel's hand and kissing Temperance as though they had accomplished some herculean feat. She flushed under his approval, strange as it was.

One person clearly did not share that approval. Tabitha remained on the front porch and disappeared inside the house before Temperance and Ansel reached her.

Mother had prepared a light buffet in the dining room to welcome them home, but Temperance found Tabitha in the parlor, looking out the window. Probably at Ansel, who was still outside speaking with the servants.

Tabitha spoke without turning around. "You'd better go eat. Our Advent fast resumes tomorrow."

Temperance wouldn't tell Tabitha that at Resthaven, they hadn't observed the Congregationalist custom that always made Tabitha so cranky. If anything, Temperance found herself in need of a fast after so much time in the kitchen with Mrs. Anderson. "First, I want to greet my sister." Removing her gloves, she cocked her head.

"So you can rub in your joyous news? My hearty congratulations."

Tabitha's sarcastic tone stung. She'd sought Tabitha out with the purpose of making amends, but she'd hardly set foot in the room before her sister had launched a fresh attack. "Can you never just be happy for me, Tabitha? Must I always be overlooked? Second place?"

The full-length Watteau pleat at the back of Tabitha's burgundy embroidered silk dress flared as she spun to face her. "Forgive me if my charity falls short of yours. For not only did you take the man I wanted, but yours is not the only engagement that will be announced at the Twelfth Night Ball."

Temperance blinked at her. "Lord Riley?"

"Yes, Lord Riley. Father's dear friend who is old enough to be my father."

Compassion replaced Temperance's hurt. She approached her sister, reaching out. "I am so sorry, Tabitha."

Tabitha flicked her hand in Temperance's direction, circumventing her gesture of comfort. "No need to act surprised. We all knew it was coming. Was it so awful that I hoped for a love match as well?"

"No, of course not." Just not with Ansel. Temperance folded her hands.

Tabitha squared her shoulders. "Well, someone has to fortify the family finances, since your fiancé is poor as a church mouse. At least Lord Riley knows what he is getting and accepts me as I am. I can't say the same for you."

"What do you mean?"

"Even if Ansel agrees with you in principle, he is still a king's man. Can you live with that? Can you kowtow to what he and Father expect of you?"

Temperance took a slight step back. "There will be compromises, yes, for both of us. That is what marriage is."

"Oh, and you are such an expert on that." The brusque swipe she took at the corner of her eye removed some of the bite from her words.

Temperance raised a little prayer for grace. She could afford to take the high road. "I'm truly sorry about Lord Riley, Tabitha. But I did not come in here to fight with you. I wanted to apologize for accusing you of taking the letters out of my desk. I know now it wasn't you. Will you forgive me?"

Tabitha's gaze locked on hers. "Who was it?"

Temperance nibbled the inside of her lip. Telling the truth might temporarily buy her sister's approval, but she couldn't bring herself to trust Tabitha with information that sensitive. "I'm not at liberty to say. But I *will* say I've misjudged more than just you. So will you forgive me?" She pressed her point with a direct stare.

"Fine." Tabitha's chest caved on a sigh. "I would have

suspected me too. And I wouldn't be so hard on you about Ansel if I did not see how he looks at you. I know you're finally getting what you deserve, my prim little sister. But naturally, I'm jealous." She threw her hands up. "What would you expect? I always want the best. It's just how I am. And right now, I'm famished."

Before Temperance could close her gaping mouth, her sister flounced past her toward the dining room.

A smile spread over Temperance's lips. That was the best she could expect from Tabitha. She'd take it.

CHAPTER 18

On Christmas Eve morning, scents of evergreen and fragrant herbs filled Christ Church. Temperance had accompanied her mother to the sticking of the greens. Her heart softened as she watched her mother across the sanctuary with another society matron, securing little bundles of lavender and rosemary to the ends of each box pew. She'd not found the courage or the private moment yet to ask about the Townsman letters, but a new respect marked their relationship. Everything in her family had been better since her return. Since her engagement.

"Temperance, are you bringing the ivy? I can't judge how much holly to place without it." Elizabeth Patterson motioned her over to one of the recessed windows where they were adding greenery around bayberry candles in glass hurricane globes.

"Sorry. Here you are." Temperance propped her basket on the nearest pew and selected a couple strands of ivy, which she arranged to droop elegantly past the edge of the windowsill. "How's that?"

"Perfect. I can't believe you will soon be overseeing decorations for your wedding." Elizabeth stood back and peered at her as though she'd sprouted wings.

"Next autumn is hardly soon." In fact, it seemed forever.

"But still! And to a ranger. I never would've figured."

Was that a bit of judgement in her tone? Temperance pressed her lips together as they moved to the next window. "The Andersons are old friends of my family. Very fine people." Must she defend Ansel to everyone?

"I'm sure. I just...you know..." Elizabeth shrugged, focused on her holly arranging. "I always thought if not Frankie, one of his friends, perhaps."

A Son of Liberty, she meant. "Ansel and I agree on most things, and where we don't, we give each other leeway."

"Enough leeway to continue our sewing circle?" Elizabeth faced her with a straight brow raised. "We have not met since Ann had to disassemble the storeroom."

Temperance winced. "I hate to hear that. Either you or Ann would make a wonderful leader." She bent to add her ivy, tucking some behind the candleholder.

"Then you won't be coming back?"

She straightened with a sigh. "Not right now. I need to give my father time. I can't do anything to break his trust or he'll send me away." Not that that would be so bad, but it would be nice to get through her betrothal announcement before being packed off to the country again.

Elizabeth tucked a stray curl back under her mob cap, surveying Temperance with a touch more understanding. "I can see why he thinks this engagement will be good for you. I'm just not so sure. I want to be happy for you, but I don't want you to lose who you are."

Her trusted friend's concern—expressed uncannily like her mother's—twisted her stomach, but she lifted her chin a notch. "Once Ansel finishes his term of service and he and I are wed, I

A CONFLICTED BETROTHAL

won't have to worry what my father thinks. Until then, you and Ann should keep the group going."

Elizabeth shook her head. "Ann and Button are moving to St. Catherine's Island. They couldn't make a go of the store, so he is going to try farming."

"Farming?" Temperance put a hand to her mouth. "Oh, no. It wasn't because of the rumors, was it?"

Elizabeth lifted one shoulder. "Probably more to do with non-importation. And I don't think he has found his niche quite yet. But with a woman like Ann supporting him, he will."

"Why don't you hostess? Everyone looks up to you."

"We'd be awfully cramped in my little parlor. Perhaps one of the other ladies could. Not the Mabrys. Their father is suspicious too."

Temperance moved to the window nearest the door into the vestry. This was supposed to be fun, but the heaviness of her abandoned responsibility weighed her down. "Where is Lydia? She would have us singing 'The Holly and the Ivy.'"

"You're right. I'm sorry. I did not mean to be the voice of doom and gloom." Elizabeth drew Temperance into an impromptu hug. "You have found true love. And it's Christmas Eve. We *should* be singing." She positioned a holly branch in the windowsill and led forth in a ringing alto, "'The holly and the ivy, when they are both full grown...'"

Temperance smiled and joined in. "'Of all the trees that are in the wood, the holly bears the crown.'"

The other women in the sanctuary took up the refrain, so that she almost missed the "psst!" that hissed from the cracked vestry door. It farther parted to reveal a peering eye and a motioning hand. Frankie? Temperance hesitated until her cousin pointedly cleared his throat. He wouldn't leave until she attended to him.

"Um, would you pardon me a moment?"

189

Elizabeth's eyes widened, but she nodded and took Temperance's basket.

Temperance hurried into the vestry, where the rector stored his robes in a large walnut wardrobe. Frankie looked thinner than before in a dark-green velvet coat, beige knee pants, and ribbed stockings with brown buckled shoes. He shut the door and faced her with his back to it.

"Is it true? Tell me 'tis not true."

What kind of greeting was this? She frowned. "Is what true?"

Frankie's expression waffled between anguish and anger. "You're to marry a king's man. That country lieutenant, of all people."

"Yes. It is true." Drawing a longsuffering breath, Temperance clasped her hands before her. "Our betrothal will be announced at the ball."

"To which I am not invited." Definite bitterness. He did not allow her the opportunity to explain as Elizabeth had but snapped out his next query. "Why have you not checked the dead drop?"

Her hands fell open. "Why do you think I have not checked the dead drop? You know what Father's surveillance is like."

"Is that why you agreed to this engagement?"

The sudden switch back to the previous topic had Temperance giving her head a quick shake. "What?"

"For appearance's sake. Did my uncle tell you to do this so the loyalists would be mollified? So they would lose interest in you?"

"No, the engagement is indeed fortuitous in that manner, but..." She touched her temple. "Frankie, I love the man. And he loves me."

His brown eyes hardened and glittered in the winter light from the narrow stained-glass window. "How can you love someone who would bear arms against those of the cause you claimed loyalty to?"

"Ansel would never point his weapon at anyone, much less fire it." Even as she said it, she struggled to strike such a circumstance from her mind. What *would* Ansel do if Captain Powell commanded him to fire into a crowd of protestors?

"Are you so sure? Or has your newfound passion for him changed your allegiance?" Frankie's thin face twisted. "All this time, working together for a common cause, and you never showed such devotion to me."

Her heart galloped like a hare stumbling over a tripwire. She started around him for the door. When he grabbed her arm, she attempted to shake him off but only managed to upset a brass cross atop a table. She righted it, then faced him. "Ansel was right. You are controlling. And right now, you are inappropriate. Release me at once."

He retained his hold on her but loosened his grip. His angry expression melted like heated wax. "I'm sorry, Temperance, but I fear I only grow more inappropriate. This is the face of unrequited love. Yes, I admit it, although I daresay you have known it for months, maybe years."

"Stop, Frankie." She pulled away, but angled his body to continue to block her escape back into the sanctuary.

"I understand—you found a more appealing prize. I'm but a shadow of him, with my plain features and pock marks, and I lack the sabre or pistol that would make me more a man."

What he had said about being a shadow—had she not felt similarly about Tabitha? "That is not it."

He held up his hand. "I also understand that your father has you in his vise grip. Perhaps in pity, in the interest of our past endeavors, you will answer me just one small question."

She firmed her jaw, eyeing the door. If she gave him the information he wanted, he would let her go. He wasn't her enemy, after all. "What is it?"

A slight tip of his head indicated satisfaction. "This month has been quiet only because the stamp master has yet to arrive, and we knew not where they took the stamped paper when it arrived on the fifth. We thought it was in the guardhouse, but we recently learned it's in the King's Store at Halifax."

"And?"

"How many men does Wright have there? We need to know if we can storm the fort."

Temperance's eyes went wide. "Do not attempt it. The governor has called rangers in from the other forts. It would be foolhardy to attack them at Fort Halifax."

"How many?" His fingers dug into her arm again.

Temperance turned her face aside, for it would surely betray that she possessed the knowledge he sought.

"Don't attempt to look innocent. I know you, remember?" His hot breath fanned her face. "You might as well tell me because this attack is going to happen regardless. Giving me a number will help us be better prepared."

She snapped her focus back to him. "Better prepared to attack my fiancé?"

Frankie's neck bulged, and a vein pulsed in his forehead.

And then the door behind him swung open into his back, and he hunched over with a cry of pain. Temperance took a quick step back.

Mother stood behind him, lifting her hand to her ethereal lace fichu. "Oh, excuse me. *Frankie*?" Her tone instantly turned leery, and when she beheld Temperance's frozen expression and heaving chest, her eyes widened. She held out her hand, and Temperance flew to her. Mother threaded Temperance's arm through her own. "Come, dear. Elizabeth says you have abandoned her."

Drawing Temperance through the door, Mother let it swing shut as though Frankie weren't still standing there, red-faced and spluttering.

A CONFLICTED BETROTHAL

Temperance clung to her mother's hand. Perhaps she should have stayed in the country. She hadn't been in Savannah two weeks, and already she found herself enmeshed in its intrigue. And she'd never expected her own cousin, a man she'd relied upon as an ally, to become a threat.

~

*A*nsel rode at the head of his small contingent of rangers from Fort Halifax toward Wright Square, where the governor had ordered them to muster. The day Temperance had warned him about—intelligence he'd passed to Captain Powell—had come to pass.

He never would've thought when he'd found Temperance ruffled at the Christmas Eve service that it would take this long —until January second—for the Liberty Boys to act. But finally, they had succeeded in rallying approximately two hundred people to assault Fort Halifax and destroy the stamped paper.

No doubt, the Sons of Liberty had delayed their action until today's scheduled muster, since that offered an excuse for armed patriots to assemble. There had already been news of a tavern brawl. Hopefully, all the rangers could gather in Wright Square before those at the muster betook themselves to Halifax. His old captain from Argyle, John Milledge of the First Troop, would join Savannah's Second Troop, believing their increased numbers would ensure the peace.

Drums beating from the west caused Ansel to draw up on Oliver's reins as they reached Broughton Street.

Jack spoke from behind him. "That's coming from Governor Wright's residence."

"Why would militia assemble here?" Ansel swiveled in his saddle to share a concerned frown with his friend.

"For no good purpose."

193

And within feet of Temperance's stoop. Ansel gestured west on Broughton. "Let's go."

The troop followed him without question to the turn on Barnard.

"Halt." Ansel held his hand out to stop the men before they turned the corner and drew the attention of the protestors—a small group of civilians and off-duty militia with waving flags congregated before the governor's front door.

A man at the front of the crowd took up a chant. "Send us Wright! Send us Wright!"

Jack drew even with Ansel. "The governor is probably already at the guardhouse. Should we fetch him?"

Behind Ansel, a Scottish private named McCleary scoffed. "By all means, let us tell him he has callers and see how that goes. Nay, we should disburse the rabble."

"Silence, both of you." Ansel needed to think. The differing opinions warred in his head. The goods in Fort Argyle's storeroom had never talked back in such a manner. Commanding men did not yet rest easy on his shoulders, especially when their lives might be at stake. "We will skirt around on Broughton and inform the governor so he can make his own decision."

He was about to turn Oliver when a cry and a flurry of struggling arms and flashing petticoats caught his eye from the far side of a massive live oak thirty or so yards away. A brown-haired man in civilian clothing wrestled with a young woman in a gray maid's ensemble.

The girl gasped. "Unhand me, sir!"

"I know who you are—one of Governor Wright's servants, no doubt bearing a message calling for help." The maid's attacker ran his hands over her bodice. "Now just where might you be hiding it?"

Ansel swung off Oliver and tossed the reins to Jack. "On second thought, stay with the men and monitor the protest. I'll handle this miscreant." Nothing was worse than the type of lowlife who used civil unrest as an excuse to indulge his own vices.

"Stop, sir." Ansel barked the command as he strode toward the two. But when the man glanced back at him, Ansel's steps faltered.

Frankie.

Heat swept through Ansel as he beheld the face of Temperance's cousin, twisted with unhealthy glee—which quickly hardened to undeniable hatred upon sight of Ansel.

Fine with him. His feelings for Frankie Scott hovered just the forgivable side of the same mark, especially since Temperance had related how her cousin had roughed her up in the church vestry, of all places. And now here he was, accosting a defenseless maid.

"You," Frankie said. "I don't take orders from loyalist lackeys, especially those who turn my own family against me." He released the servant girl, only to drag her back flat against his chest.

"You will unhand her this moment." Ansel drew his pistol. The sight of it should be enough to show Frankie he meant business, even if he never intended to fire it. Doing so would only incite a riot in this crowd...although something—or someone—had drawn their attention. A murmur rippled through the protestors.

"Not until I have discovered the treasures the wench conceals." Frankie grinned and reached around her waist to drag up a handful of her petticoats, eliciting a strangled scream and a backward kick that must have made little impact through his boot, for he slid his hand beneath her petticoat. His gaze challenged Ansel. "Just as I will my dear cousin, soon as you are out of the way."

How dare he? With a growl, Ansel lunged and grabbed

Frankie's arm with his left hand, breaking him away from his prisoner.

She shot free and ran toward her employer's house.

Frankie attempted an uppercut.

Ansel brought the barrel of his pistol down on his temple.

Frankie cried out and stumbled. He righted himself and touched the wound on his head. Blood sprouting from a cut near his hairline covered his fingers.

Ansel leveled the pistol at him while he was still bent. "You ingrate. I'm taking you in. You'll be brought up on charges of assault."

Frankie sneered at Ansel. "Go ahead. The Liberty Boys would love the excuse that one of their own has been arrested to incite a riot. Especially now, with the governor standing in their midst."

Ansel's stomach dropped. The governor had arrived?

One of the protesters yelled, "Will you appoint a temporary distributor of stamps?"

In response, an authoritative voice rang out over the crowd. "My people...this is not a manner to wait upon the governor of the province."

Ansel's head swiveled. He'd just caught a glimpse of the governor at his gate, his musket in his hand, his silvering blond hair unpowdered, when Frankie plowed into him, knocking Ansel into the street. His pistol went flying.

Ansel scrambled to his feet, but Frankie dove in front of a passing wagon loaded with barrels and disappeared into the crowd.

~

Temperance stood inside her gate facing the square, straining to catch the governor's words. He was telling the crowd outside his house that he was more a friend to liberty than they were and that his actions would uphold liberty while theirs would destroy it.

Such claims would only anger them into action. Even more protestors were said to be assembling to march to Fort Halifax.

A view out an east-facing window of their upper story had disclosed the ever-growing presence of rangers around the guardhouse on Wright Square. Father had joined them, along with a motley crew of sailors, merchants, clerks, and loyalist landowners.

Was Ansel there yet? Here she stood, right in the midst of the two factions—symbolically and literally. The city was in uproar around her, and all she could do was flit from one side of her yard to the other like a caged canary.

Tabitha appeared on the porch. "Temperance, come inside."

She glanced back across the square as a man bleeding from the temple stumbled by. "Frankie!"

He turned to her, pressing a handkerchief to his wound. "Temperance. Forgive me. You were right." He leaned in, his fingers curled around the gate. "They are too many for us. It is hopeless."

She rushed forward, offering her own handkerchief. "Who did this to you?"

His hand closed over hers as she blotted his forehead. "Who but your own fiancé?"

CHAPTER 19

After Temperance stitched up Frankie's wound, he guzzled their whiskey and made liberal use of his snuffbox in their front parlor while spilling his remorse for his behavior at Christ Church. He'd been desperate to gather intelligence that could ensure the success of the assault the Sons of Liberty had planned on Fort Halifax. Not to mention, out of his head with jealousy of the man who had edged him aside in Temperance's affection. He'd taken temporary leave of his better judgment. Could she forgive him?

In light of his profuse apologies and his painful injury—which he said Ansel had inflicted when Frankie attempted to question one of the governor's servants—Temperance had offered grace. Her cousin's explanation about the encounter with Ansel made little sense, but why would Frankie lie about it? He knew she would ask Ansel.

Thankfully, the violence Frankie had forecasted did not come to pass. After being chided by the governor, the crowd in front of his residence dispersed with promises to gather again when a stamp master was appointed.

The rangers mustered on Wright Square departed, presumably to Fort Halifax, only to return not long after with a heavily guarded cart. That night, Temperance's father told the family that the governor had forty rangers and armed civilians patrolling the streets and surrounding the guardhouse where they had moved the stamps.

The next day, Ansel did not come or send word. Where was he? Why did he not come to her? His absence gave credence to the story Frankie told her and her family.

The day following, Father departed suddenly for a mysterious meeting. Why would no one tell Temperance anything? Was this how it would be? She would be kept in ignorance, closeted at home, of no more use than a piece of furniture to be of service as needed and shoved aside when not in use.

Her betrothal to Ansel would be announced the next day at the Twelfth Night Ball. But unease and unanswered questions swirled in her stomach as she helped Cecily refresh the greenery around the house.

She was retying the bows on the stairway garland when a knock sounded at the door. A flash of blue in the side window shot energy through her, and she flew to answer ahead of Jonas. Upon opening the door, she spied the visage of the man she loved and, for a moment, forgot everything but longing and flung her arms around Ansel's neck.

"My darling." He gathered her hands and kissed them. "I have but a few minutes. Your father told me I could come over. And my captain, of course."

"What?" She peeked past him but saw nobody else. "Where are they?"

"Across the square at the governor's."

"Why?"

He eased her backward and closed the door behind them. Studying her face a moment, he drew a quick breath. "The stamp master is being sworn in."

Temperance's middle hollowed out. "And you were involved in this?"

Ansel released her and stared askance at her. "We were ordered to fetch him on the *Prince George* from Tybee Island and escort him here. What did you expect me to do?"

"I don't know." She tossed her hands up. "Collaborate with First Lieutenant Jones to approach Captain Powell. Perhaps the two of you could talk sense into the governor. You could try to convince my father that this will only bring more unrest. You should do something, anything to prevent that man from becoming the only stamp master in the colonies to take office."

"Temperance, your father and Captain Powell are in full agreement with the governor. They have no choice but to enact this law. What do you think will happen to them if they refuse? They could lose everything."

"That is just the problem." She whirled and took a step away from him. "No one is willing to lose anything."

He touched her back and spoke more softly. "I'm not willing to lose *you*."

She closed her eyes, drew in a breath, and crossed her arms. "I suppose the governor will also give clearance to all the ships waiting in port."

"If he doesn't, the city will starve. Even the Liberty Boys know this, Temperance." With a gentle hand on her arm, Ansel turned her to face him. "But 'tis my understanding that is all he will do. Wright is no fool, and no ogre. He understands the people's demand to wait upon the king's answer to their request to repeal. He will not issue any further papers."

Temperance worried her lower lip between her teeth, searching Ansel's eyes. "And where will they keep him while they wait, this stamp master?"

He hesitated. "I cannot tell you that."

"You think I will tell my friends." She squared her shoulders, letting her arms hang at her sides.

Ansel's brows drooped. "I am only doing my duty, Temperance. I have been ordered to share the information with no one."

"And what of the pledge of honesty and truth between us? How quickly that goes out the window when your duty calls." The sense of constantly being watched, of tongues being guarded around her, eroded her poise and made her own tongue sharp. But she couldn't seem to stop herself.

"That pledge was not a requirement to reveal military secrets."

"Like the ones you tell my father?" She balled her fists. "Perhaps I *should* call Frankie. Let him know the stamp master has been sworn in and is right across the street."

His face paled. "You wouldn't do that."

"Are you afraid he might tell me something else? Such as how you pistol-whipped him at the protest?"

Ansel took a step toward her, letting out a hiss of breath. "That snake. I'm sure he didn't tell you why."

She lifted a brow. "Because he attempted to detain a servant of the governor's when she went for help?"

"Because he accosted her most indecently and also spoke indecently of you!"

Ansel's forceful declaration drew Temperance up short— and her mother down the stairs.

She paused on the landing, one hand on the banister and a furrow between her brows. "Is everything all right, my dear?"

"Yes, Mother." Temperance caught her head between her hands. All this mistrust and maneuvering was driving her mad. A swift prayer and a beat of silence allowed her finer sensibilities to triumph. Gratitude for her mother's concern and yearning for peace with the man she loved softened her. She looked up and reached for Ansel's hand.

"Then would the lieutenant care to stay for tea?" Mother wanted to know.

Ansel turned to address her, still holding Temperance's hand. "Thank you, ma'am, but I must rejoin your husband in the governor's mansion. I only came to tell Temperance how eagerly I am awaiting tomorrow night."

Her mother's guarded smile made Temperance's heart skip a beat. "As are we all, Lieutenant." With a nod, she disappeared back up the stairs.

Temperance looked after her. Had Mother heard them arguing? Did her doubts about their relationship now override the joy she'd expressed that Temperance had found love?

"Temperance." Ansel spoke her name low, drawing her attention back to him. "Do you believe me? About Frankie?"

She squeezed his hand. "I know you would never set upon him without cause. It's just hard for me to believe he would behave in such a manner."

"Is it really? After his actions at the church? I assure you, he would be locked up at the fort now if he hadn't managed to escape." His face hardened. "And with good cause."

"I suppose...it's me I don't trust. My judgment. How can I not have seen the kind of person Frankie was all these years?" Temperance dropped her head.

"Because you cared about him—as family and as a fellow patriot. That's nothing to be ashamed of. You see the best in people. That's one of the many reasons I love you." He chucked her chin with his index finger.

She looked up, a smile taking over her face. She would never tire of hearing those words from him. "I love you too."

"I cannot stand to be at odds with you, Temperance." He touched her cheek, searching her eyes. "Don't you know, I'm playing the long game? Everything I do now is for you. For us."

Her heart twisted. Temperance groaned and fell into Ansel's arms, which came around her with firm desperation, and before she knew it, he was kissing her with the same emotion.

The slight growth of bristles on his jaw raked her cheeks as he showered kisses along her hairline. His fingers pushed into her curls. Their desire for each other could burn all other concerns away—at least for a time. But those concerns had a way of constantly resurrecting.

Temperance cupped Ansel's face. "Why does it seem the whole world conspires against us?"

"Then we'll just have to conquer the whole world. Because our love will be worth it. Don't forget that, Temperance." He pressed his mouth to hers in another brief kiss. "Please."

He left her standing there with her lips swollen and her heart pounding. Had she ever imagined herself with such a man? Never in a million years. And yet the very things that appealed to her also divided them. Was she letting infatuation take over her reasoning?

She sought out her mother in the ballroom, where she was arranging white poinsettias in preparation for the ball. She turned to Temperance with a muted smile—the same kind that had sparked Temperance's wariness earlier. "Is everything well with your lieutenant?"

"No, Mother." She rushed to her mother, who opened her arms. "I love him so, yet we are so often at cross purposes. But I think you know that." She drew back to assess her mother's expression.

Mother pressed her lips together, then allowed a tiny, genuine smile and a brief nod. "It is no easy thing to spend your life with a man you do not see eye to eye with. I have sacrificed much for love. Turned my head to injustice and swallowed many words."

"And yet you found the courage to speak out when you felt strongly about something. About the Townsman letters?" Temperance whispered the last.

Mother released her and turned back to her arranging. "A mistake. I shouldn't have done that, and it could have gone very badly. Even now, I am not certain we are safe."

"Yet you acted with bravery on your deepest convictions. I admire that. I never suspected."

Mother's gaze flicked to hers. "It is best your father and those in our circle think me brainless. Opinionless. I greatly regret putting you in danger, Temperance. I hope you can forgive me."

"There is nothing to forgive." Temperance squeezed her arm. "And look what good came out of it. Soon I will be married to a man I love more than anything." Well, except for God.

At her declaration, her mother looked at her with more openness and affection than Temperance could ever recall—but then her lips firmed. Her lashes fluttered down. Something lay heavy on her heart.

Temperance took a small step back. "What is it? You can speak your opinions to me. I want you to." Hadn't she sought out her mother for this very purpose? To give her a perspective that would put her emotions in place?

Mother drew a deep breath. "If you are certain Ansel agrees with you on the deepest issues and will allow you to be yourself, you should not allow any act of Parliament or governor or stamp master to come between you. But if marrying him will make you sacrifice the core of who you are, Temperance, it will not be worth it."

~

"The governor has shown great discretion in dealing with these revolutionaries." The voice of a large, bewigged man in royal-blue velvet rang out from the other side of the holly-encircled silver wassail bowl in the Scotts' dining room. "Now, if we can just keep those South Carolina firebreathers from coming down here and destroying our hard-won peace."

Ansel didn't know to whom the man spoke, for the one next to him angled away as though he suspected his neighbor had already partaken too much spirituous liquor—or else was spraying him with spittle as he made his noisome pronouncements. But 'twas already the second volatile conversation Ansel had steered Temperance away from as guests flowed into the residence for the Twelfth Night Ball's seven o'clock refreshment hour.

"'Tis too crowded in here." Ansel spoke into Temperance's ear—or as near he could get to it without the feather drooping from the top of her mounded and powdered hair tickling his nose. "Would you like me to bring your sweetmeats and wassail into the hall?"

"Please." Temperance grimaced. "But instead, I shall be in Father's study." The one room on this floor off-limits to guests. "You might not find me in the hallway, flattened to a wall as I would surely be."

Overlooking her in the vivid green painted silk gown she wore would be an impossibility. Wide panniers added width at the hips while her hair added height. She would fit right in at Buckingham Palace. Was her lavish ensemble an attempt not to be outdone by her sister?

Tabitha flitted among the guests like a butterfly in the bright yellow she favored, laughing and showing off the pearl bracelet that had been a Christmas gift from Lord Riley. It matched the seed pearls she had clipped into her dark tresses.

Like Ansel's engagement to Temperance, the betrothal between Tabitha and Riley would not be officially announced until the seated supper at ten. But it was widely put about that the two couples were the special guests of the evening, and the fact that they were leading off the minuet rather than taking a place far down the line of prominent citizens silently proclaimed what would occur after that initial elegant round of dancing. By midnight, when everyone would kick up their

205

heels to jigs, reels, and hornpipes, Ansel would be officially engaged.

At last, he had a clear path to his future—one he could be excited about. With land of their own, he and Temperance could build a house and grow a reputation in their new community as fair and liberty-minded people. Perhaps he'd eventually serve as a militia officer, like his father.

After Temperance eased out of the room, Ansel waited in line at the wassail bowl until someone recognized him and ushered him to the front. Drinks in hand, he managed to cross the foyer without spilling anything.

The door to the study stood partially open, and a red-haired girl in a lavender-striped silk dress blocked Ansel's view of Temperance. She spoke in a clear voice. "Does this engagement to the ranger lieutenant mean you're done with the sewing circle?"

"For a time. Father only allowed me back home because my betrothal to a king's man would allay suspicions."

The pile of red curls shook back and forth. "I never pegged you for one to lay down for any man, Temperance. Your father *or* a husband."

Ansel cleared his throat as he slid the door open with his foot. The girl spun around, and Temperance's eyes went wide. He crossed the room and handed her a drink, then bowed to her companion.

Temperance presented Lydia Harrison, who quickly congratulated him on capturing her friend and excused herself with a meaningful glance over her shoulder at Temperance.

He looked after Lydia. "Was I wrong, or were her felicitations rather forced?"

"Lydia is nothing if not forthright, but she is a good friend. She's here to support me."

Ansel tilted his head. "Against laying down for your father and me?"

Temperance flapped her hand. "Don't take it personally. She is just jealous because she has yet to find someone herself. But she knows how these formal events cow me. And if I hear one more person praise the governor's heavy-handedness..." She drained the wassail with uncharacteristic speed and set the glass on her father's desk.

"He is doing what he must to keep the peace." Forty men remained on duty every night since they had transferred the stamps to the guardhouse and the stamp master to the governor's residence. For obvious reasons, neither man was in attendance tonight...even among such a sympathetic crowd. The governor had sent express riders with letters to important people in the area, calling on them to help check any unrest.

"He failed to do that when he swore in Mr. Angus and stored rather than burned the paper."

Ansel drew a deep breath. What had gotten Temperance's dander up tonight? Surely, she'd overheard more than a few opinionated guests at a ball. "Can we not talk about politics?" He placed his glass beside hers and twined one of the ringlets hanging over her shoulder around his finger. Stiff with pomade and powder, it barely uncoiled. "Tonight, of all nights?"

Her mouth firmed, then relaxed, and she nodded. "We should go find your parents. They must feel as lost as I do."

Ansel chuckled. "No doubt Father has found some militia commanders to talk to. Mother, however, would love to see you. But first..." He lowered his head and brushed her lips with his. Her body went soft, and his grew hot. If only they could wed sooner, they could face the conflict around them with a unified front. It seemed every time he left, doubt whispered in Temperance's ear. So much could go wrong in nine months.

Their camaraderie restored for now, they mounted the two flights of stairs to the ballroom. He and Temperance had practiced here before Christmas, but tonight, the space had been transformed into a winter wonderland. Small silvery-white trees in silver pots lined the periphery, candles in glass holders dangling from their branches. Light from the candelabras glowed on the polished wood floor, and sheer white organza banners draped from the ceiling. On a small dais, a quartet of two violins, a French horn, and a harp played a concerto for the colorfully clad guests beginning to congregate for the minuets.

Ansel's mother hurried to Temperance's side with hugs and compliments. Her own ivory silk *robe à la francaise* was more the style Ansel had expected his fiancée to wear. Temperance looked beautiful, but why was she trying to be something she was not?

His suspicions were confirmed after Judge Scott announced that Tabitha and Lord Riley would open the evening's festivities. Tabitha danced like a golden flame. One would never know she held anything but passion for her intended, so intensely did she look at him. As they performed the intricate variations they had prepared with polish, Temperance's fingers on Ansel's arm kept tightening. Her eyes never left her sister.

He leaned around the feather to whisper, "You do not have to be like her. I love you because you are not."

She flashed him a grateful smile, but it quickly faltered. "What woman would not want to be like her? She makes even Lord Riley dance with vigor."

"We dance to our own tune."

But would she wear her glasses? Ansel had mentioned it too many times. Now would be the wrong moment to do so again. Instead, he patted her hand, and when the applause faded and Judge Scott announced them, he led her forward as gracefully as possible. No spectacles.

Temperance held her chin up so high that Ansel could only pray she'd memorized all her steps. He'd taken it as a military maneuver, rehearsing the whole thing in his head every night before sleep. As long as he did not think about the rather ridiculous mincing involved, he could pretend it was a drill.

With the measured cadence of pliés and rising steps, they curved sideways to meet at the back of the ballroom. He took her inside hand. It shook in his. He wheeled her in the three-quarter turn, and they separated again. Whispers followed their progress through the Z-figure of the movement. As Temperance danced diagonally toward him, her gaze flitted along the line of spectators.

He clasped her right hand tightly. "Look at me." Moving his mouth as little as possible, Ansel breathed out the directive.

She did not respond. Her focus was all in the wrong place. Another Z-figure and her face had flushed pink. Her chest rose and fell in double time to the music. She extended her left hand, and—her foot flew to one side!

Her other arm flailed. A cry left her lips.

Ansel shot out both of his arms just in time for her to collapse into them.

Gasps echoed around the ballroom. The musicians stopped playing. Temperance panted softly against his shoulder while the tiny seed pearl she must have slipped on rolled across the floor.

"Are you all right?" he whispered in her ear. He wanted to rip that dratted feather from her hair.

She nodded.

Ansel set her upright on her high-heeled silk shoes. Across the room, the musicians looked from him to Judge Scott, who stared at his daughter with a thunderstruck expression on his face. "Shall we continue?" Ansel asked softly.

But Temperance turned her head toward the murmurs rippling through the guests. Her eyelashes fluttered as though she attempted to bat away a nightmare.

Then someone giggled. A high-pitched, mean-sounding giggle.

Temperance swallowed hard and attempted to speak, but

nothing came out. Shooting Ansel a stricken look, she fled for the exit, feathers bobbing.

Ansel did not hesitate. He followed and chased her all the way to the second floor, where she collapsed against a wall, covered her face, and drew in a shuddering breath.

"I knew it. I knew it!" she cried as he wrapped his arms around her.

"You knew what? That you would step on a pearl in the middle of the minuet?"

She dropped her hands. "Is that what it was?"

"Yes. Had you seen—"

"Had I worn my spectacles, you mean." Her face went pale. "I might have been prepared for my sister to once again sabotage me? Spare me the rebuke. Every person in the ballroom is laughing at me right now." She pushed his arms down and stepped back.

"First of all, no one is laughing. If you had stayed, we could have completed the dance, and they all would have congratulated you on not letting a stray pearl ruin the evening."

"But it's not just a stray pearl! Don't you see? It's everything!" Temperance gestured with each exclamation. Tears ran down her cheeks. "She outshines me in everything. For once, just this once, I wanted to be her equal."

Ansel's chest constricted, and he stroked her arm. "Temperance, when you are true to yourself, you are far her superior. Why do you think she works so hard?"

Temperance's eyes flashed. "When I am true to myself? Who are you to lecture me on that? You who believe one thing and do another."

Ansel's mouth dropped open. "I do what I must, to make a home for us." She attempted to pull away, but he maintained his grip on her arm. "Did you even hear what I said? No, you are only hearing yourself tonight, your own insecurities and doubts."

She went still. "I do have doubts. If you love me for who I am, why do you go along with my father? You're making me...*this*." She flung her hands down along her dress.

"I would have you in linen and wool."

"Oh, you would, would you? You know that is what people are wearing to balls who want to protest the establishment. But you are part of the establishment. What would you truly have done if I had showed up tonight dressed like that?"

"Temperance, stop this. You're upset. You need to cool off." How did he reason with this complete desertion of logic? She left him reeling. Desperate to anchor her.

The lines of her face hardened. "I think that may be the problem. I *have* cooled off. I've let other people tell me who to be and what to do. Well, maybe you can believe one way and live another, but I cannot." She ripped the offending feather from her hair.

He had a bad feeling this wouldn't stop with the feather. "Temperance, what are you doing?"

"I'm calling off our engagement, Ansel." Tears flooded her eyes, and she shook her head. "I'm so sorry."

She left him standing there as she ran down the hall to her room.

CHAPTER 20

Two weeks had passed since the disastrous Twelfth Night Ball. Ansel had called countless times at the Scott residence, but on each occasion, he'd been received by the judge or Cecily, both of whom explained that while Temperance regretted fleeing the scene and leaving him to face humiliation alone that evening, her feelings had not changed. She could not consent to marry him so long as he was in the king's service.

Would she rather him be brought up on charges? Put before a firing squad?

Of course not, Cecily had said. He must tread his own path just as she must tread hers. But for now, they must do so separately. Temperance was no more willing to compromise than she had been willing to admit anyone to her room the night of the ball, though a procession of pleas had passed through her door. Ansel had finally departed in a state of shock and despair, and only one betrothal announcement had been made at supper.

Now, standing before Judge Scott's desk, he swallowed the

same frustration he'd marinated in half the month as Cecily reported that Miss Temperance was "not at home."

"Of all the poppycock." Judge Scott shot upright in his leather chair. "She has not *left* home since the ball."

"Begging your pardon, sir, but she has." Cecily clasped her hands tightly together. "She has been out calling with Mrs. Scott."

But she had not been to church, or Ansel would have seen her there.

"Her mother is the only one she will speak to. Well, and this one here." The judge shot Cecily a sideways glare. "I have not locked the girl in her room. But neither have I permitted her to wander about the city on her own. She says that if she cannot actively aid her causes, she will remain true to herself alone in her chambers. She continues to bring me shame. But you must know, I have done my utmost on your behalf, Ansel."

"I know, sir. Thank you." Ansel faced Cecily. "Did you tell her I was leaving town and would not be back for a while?"

Cecily bobbed her head. "That I did, sir. I'm very sorry."

His shoulders slumped. He'd expected this, but the rejection and Temperance's unwillingness to even converse wore him down. He reached into his jacket and pulled out a wax-sealed paper. "Will you give this to her, then?"

Cecily took it and curtsied. "Of course, Lieutenant." She glanced at Judge Scott, who waved her off with a dismissal.

Ansel released a heavy sigh. "Will you let Temperance know I'm gone on official business?" Of course, he could not disclose the nature of it to her—a perfect example, she would point out, of how his duty erected walls between them.

Judge Scott nodded. "Of course. 'Tis a wise decision for the governor to send Mr. Angus into the countryside until things quieten. Perhaps you will find your time there reflective."

"I don't know about that, sir." More likely, he would stew, while his absence would only allow Temperance to forget him.

"Do not despair. I yet hope that once this situation is resolved, my foolish daughter will come around."

Ansel dipped his head. But was Temperance the foolish one? Or was he?

~

*W*hile her mother examined the velvet winter hood she'd commissioned at the counter in the milliner's shop on a mild Tuesday the last week of January, Temperance listlessly surveyed a collection of black woolen bonnets displayed in the front window.

Black. That was what she felt like wearing. What a fool she'd been, to think she could compete with Tabitha. And the love match she'd been so proud of? A dream. How could she move forward with it if it required her to sacrifice her very identity?

But, oh, the gaping ache in her midsection. Day and night, night and day, it did not abate. Even when she shoved a pillow into it. Even when she paced and prayed. Even when she finally agreed to accompany Mother on her errands.

Fresh air wasn't doing the trick.

On the other side of the wavy glass, a head slid sideways into her line of vision, right between two bonnets. Her eyes went wide. "Frankie!"

Had Mother seen him? Temperance glanced over her shoulder, but her mother was talking with the shopkeeper.

When Temperance turned back around, her cousin beckoned her emphatically.

Ansel's description of Frankie's assault of the governor's maid flashed through her mind. But the desire to learn what was happening in town—and to buck her father's control—was stronger. On the public street, Frankie would be the model of propriety. Especially since he thought he'd weaseled back into her favor after the protest.

Temperance pushed open the door. The bell rang, and this time, her mother noticed. But she said nothing, just turned around again. Temperance was still gawping at her back when Frankie snagged her elbow and drew her onto the boardwalk.

"Frankie. I-I don't know—"

"She doesn't mind." Frankie's hasty reassurance stunned Temperance into silence. Surely, her mother hadn't arranged this meeting. Had she? "I've been dying to speak with you. I heard what happened at the ball. It's been killing me, to think of you locked up in your room again like Rapunzel. Who does your father think he is?"

"My father. And he has yet to give up hope on my betrothal to Ansel."

Had *she* given up? If the governor put the stamp agent on the next ship back to England and dumped all the paper into the harbor, would she take Ansel back?

No. Not even then, for as long as he enforced the king's authority here in Savannah against the patriots, he opposed everything she believed in. It had taken her too long to see that. But if he was free...

Yes. The enthusiasm of that response resounded through Temperance's heart. She would never wish Ansel to bring trouble on himself by attempting to resign before his enlistment expired, and thus, their impasse. But if they could be together away from this cauldron of political turmoil which threatened to boil over daily, she would run to him so fast it would make his head spin. If he would still have her...

The letter he'd left for her said he'd call one more time when he returned. He prayed she'd reconsider and at least talk with him because he was certain they could find common ground. Find a compromise.

Temperance was done with compromises. But those words,

one more time, rang in her head with the hollow dread of a death knell.

"Betrothal? What betrothal?" Frankie spat the word, jerking her attention back to the conversation at hand—one she wasn't sure she should be having. "Will your father take all your decisions from you? Force you to wed a man whose beliefs are polar opposites to yours?"

"Not polar opposites." Temperance's protest sounded weak. "But neither can I marry a man who isn't true to himself."

"Of course not. You say he is a secret patriot. I have yet to see it. Patriots act on their convictions."

"There are plenty of patriots in the rangers and militia." Why was she still defending Ansel? Probably because her cousin spoke with such vitriol.

"It doesn't matter. I'm just thankful you came to your senses." Frankie grasped her gloved hands in his, too tightly for her to easily pull away. "Speaking of acting on one's convictions, you will also want to know that this city is about to stage a protest the likes of which we've never seen."

She'd heard that before. "What do you mean?"

A boy running past in raggedy clothing bumped Temperance against Frankie.

He responded by slipping an arm about her, taking the opportunity to lean close and lower his voice. "Friends from Charlestown have rallied our sagging aspirations. Invited us to lay a new plan."

"Or maybe 'twas the threat to punish anyone selling provisions from Georgia with death that did that." Temperance used a wry tone. Even she had heard through her mother that South Carolina had been furious when Georgia had failed to oust their stamp agent. And, no doubt, jealous of the trade Savannah received whilst their own port was closed.

Frankie's brows nested. "Their anger was justified. We are the shame of the colonies, and we have to do something about that. So we're going to try again. This time, we truly will storm the guardhouse and destroy the stamps."

She swallowed hard. "Frankie, the guards will fire on whomever tries such a thing."

"Yes." He drew himself upright, giving a sober nod. Despite his shortcomings, Frankie's courage was admirable. "They might wound or kill some. But we will have three times the number we did before. Our Charlestown friends will stand with us. And after we destroy the stamps, we will take into custody any friends of the government."

A shiver coursed through her. "Are you saying my father would be at risk?"

Frankie shrugged. "If he were arrested, that would work to our advantage, would it not? It would free you, and I... Well, I could renew my suit...were you willing." Sudden splotches of red stained his neck and face.

Temperance blinked at him. "Frankie, I told you, I don't feel that way about you."

"Could not love be borne out of common goals and admiration?"

"Yes, at times, but..."

"But what?" He lowered his arm from around her but remained in her personal space.

"Ansel told me you were indecent when you accosted the servant girl, and that you spoke disrespectfully of me." Temperance glanced through the window. How long did it take her mother to purchase a hood?

"Lies," Frankie hissed. "What do you expect? Another attempt to sour you against all you hold dear. And you cannot deny, there is a bond between us, cousin. One I have worked a long time to deepen."

The hungry way he scoured her face wrought a shiver through Temperance, and not the delightful kind that Ansel often caused. But something told her not to argue. The

217

memory of Frankie's forcefulness in the vestry, no doubt. Plotting with her cousin had always ignited a sense of excitement, but his intensity burned too hot. Right now, she needed to get away from him.

He resumed before she could formulate an excuse. "At the moment, that matters not. If I can give you sufficient notice, can you rally your women to join us?"

Temperance gasped. "To march on the guardhouse?"

His eyes were bright, almost wild. "When the time comes, we want you beside us. The Liberty Boys would show everyone that we value the support of the women of Savannah. We need numbers. We need you beneath that flag you made."

Ann had given the flag to Elizabeth before she left town. Elizabeth had told her so at the Christmas Eve sticking of the church. "I don't know." Temperance's heart pounded so loudly in her ears that it drowned out the noise of the street. "How would I get word to them?"

"I can help with that. Think, Temperance. This is your time to make your stand."

To expose herself to potential musket fire? Were a bunch of stamps worth such a risk?

Was *freedom* worth such a risk?

The shop door opened. Her mother was coming.

Temperance met Frankie's blazing eyes. "I will be ready."

At least with Ansel gone, she wouldn't have to add facing him across protest lines to her fears.

~

Was it just another rumor, or would the Liberty Boys succeed in stirring an actual riot this time?

Ansel rubbed his chin, gazing over a rear-facing caisson at Fort George. One would expect the threat to materialize from a frontal direction, from the sea, in this case—where the flag pole

A CONFLICTED BETROTHAL

and front gate faced. Fort George wasn't much to look at, just a raised wooden blockhouse in the center of four mud-and-upright-palmetto walls, but situated as she was on Cockspur Island between the north and south channels of the river, her guns would hold off any enemy ships approaching Savannah.

Ansel did not miss the irony that 'twas toward Savannah he gazed as he pondered rebellion. And the implications made him sick. This in-fighting had to end. His troop of escort for the stamp master had been called back, along with extra rangers from the outlying forts, when word reached the governor that Charlestown incendiaries bestirred local patriots. He had ordered the stamped paper moved from the guardhouse to Fort George. The present guard of two captains, two subalterns, and fifty rangers awaited further instructions.

"Does it not strike you that our mad scramble here has left the city veritably defenseless?"

The voice next to Ansel made him turn.

Jack drew alongside him, smoking his clay pipe. "If the Liberty Boys were smart, they could take over the government."

"Let us pray that does not occur to them." A coup would mean a battle. Was he willing to kill his fellow Georgians to maintain royal control? No. If it came to that, he would sacrifice his future, even his own life...

Ansel drew himself upright. Was he really thinking that, in the face of actual revolt, he would defect? *Oh, God, what am I doing here?* He groaned and scrubbed his face. "Why can't we come to an agreement? Why has diplomacy failed us?" His internal struggle made him speak as a friend, not an officer.

Jack braced Ansel's shoulder with a firm hand. "Because the man for whom this fort is named does not wish to grant colonists equal rights, and our own legislative houses are split, upper against lower."

"What will it take to unite us?" Ansel eyed him with anguish writhing in his chest. "To truly be one people?"

"Maybe these stamps." Dropping his hand, Jack shrugged. The salty wind ruffled strands of blond hair loose from his queue. "Maybe something bigger. If not this, mark my words, something else will bring us to the point of decision."

"Surely, there is some way the governor can smooth this over."

"Maybe temporarily. But too much discontent surges beneath the surface. And Parliament has made clear that they will levy taxes as they see fit. One more thing, and...*poof.*" Jack made a blowing sound and spread his fingers to mimic an explosion.

He was right. That was why Ansel needed to get out of the royal rangers. But how? His hopes hinged on that fragile peace Jack had intimated might be established for a season, buying him time to complete his commission. But would Temperance wait for him? If she wouldn't even see him, how much of their relationship could he hope to salvage once he was free of all this?

Jack nudged him, and Ansel looked at him again. He'd fallen to staring over the wide expanse of the river, rubbing the back of his neck. "What?"

"Methinks 'tis not just the city that gives you such a long face. Pining for your girl?"

"I don't know that she is mine...much as that pains me to say." Ansel leaned a booted foot on the caisson.

"What would it take to make things right with her?"

He huffed and dragged his hand over his collar again. "Leaving the rangers, which I would consider if..."

"If you might not forfeit your very life, thereby negating the whole purpose?"

"Exactly."

Jack took a few short draws on his pipe, then puffed out a smoke ring. "What if there were a way to step back from active duty here in Savannah?"

"To return to Fort Argyle?" Ansel shook his head. "I would still be within the governor's reach."

"Fort Augusta, then. Not so far from your family, is it?"

Jack's suggestion lit a spark of hope in Ansel's chest, like an ember in the fireplace that refused the imposition of a curfew. "I hadn't thought of that." Augusta was far enough away that rangers from there were rarely called to Savannah. And he had not heard of protests in the smaller city, the colony's second-largest.

"There's usually a way around." Jack nudged his arm and winked. "If I had a girl like Temperance waiting in the wings, I'd find a way to start the next act."

The cry of a seagull drew their notice. No, not a seagull. A man. A scout boat approached. Most of the men on duty, Ansel and Jack included, hurried out the gate and on to the landing. The lettering on the side of the craft became visible as the sailors inside pulled up to dock. *Speedwell*.

Captain Powell's boots thudded as he stepped onto the wooden planks. "What news, men?"

The oldest sailor among the group stood and saluted. "*Speedwell* has returned to Tybee Island. We're to load the stamped paper aboard, out of reach of the rebels."

The captain gripped the hilt of his sabre. "Protestors have gathered as predicted?"

"Aye. Several hundred backwoodsmen have arrived, promising to shoot the governor and raze the city. Wright wants as many soldiers and sailors as can be spared to return to defend Savannah."

CHAPTER 21

*A*nsel and several of his privates were mounting up to patrol the streets early the morning two days after their return from Fort George—Tuesday, February fourth—when one of the local boys paid to run messages jogged through the gate of Fort Halifax.

Spying Ansel, he altered his course to more quickly spill his breathless report. "Sir, some women are at St. James Square, putting up a liberty flag outside the governor's house."

Ansel exchanged a glance with Jack. Such a banner would serve as a rallying point for the malcontents who had been swelling the city for the past few days. It had to come down. However Ansel felt about the Stamp Act, the recent threats on Wright's life necessitated rapid action.

Ansel tossed the boy a coin before he swung up into the saddle. He led the privates down mist-shrouded Bryan Street. Their horses' hooves rang out on the cobblestones surrounding the market, where fishmongers and bakers and weavers set up their stalls for the day.

After they turned away from the river on Barnard, Private

McCleary rode up close behind him. "Captain Powell will want the miscreants brought in for questioning, sir."

"Thank you, Private. I believe I know my duty." Ansel clipped out his response. The action-hungry Scot always seemed to look for an opportunity to put himself forward.

"Just sayin', Lieutenant, it would look good on us..." He allowed his suggestion to fade and his mount to fall behind while Jack's drew alongside Ansel's.

As they entered the open space of St. James Square, Ansel gave thanks for a friend at his side, for he could not have hidden from McCleary his reaction to the scene unfolding before him. Two women and a man stood beneath a ladder. On that ladder, a slightly built woman wearing a cloak with the hood raised reached up to secure a red-and-white-striped flag to the top of the imposing wrought-iron gate directly before the governor's door.

Ansel would recognize that form anywhere. He exhaled her name on a whisper to Jack. "Temperance." It was more a plea for help than a revelation.

Jack nodded, understanding writ in his tense features.

Frankie's cocked hat did nothing to hide his alarmed countenance as he glanced their way. "Rangers!" He released the ladder, and—though it wobbled and one of the women had to help Temperance step down—he took off west on State Street, coat tails flying.

"Go!" Ansel waved McCleary and his friend after him. "Arrest that man. We will take care of the women."

Temperance needed only a moment to dart a look his way before grabbing the hands of her friends and running into the square. He lost sight of her among the live oaks and draping moss.

"She'll go this way, toward her house." Ansel tipped his head east at the Scott residence. He and Jack rode across the

223

grass to cut them off. They must at least be seen to pursue the women.

But the ladies did not emerge on the expected side.

"Wait here. I will see if I can find them." Ansel dismounted to blend in better with the handful of individuals beginning to mill around the square. He led Oliver south to York Street, and there, emerging from behind a boxwood hedgerow, was the cloaked figure he sought.

"Ansel!" Temperance stepped back between her friends, pulling the edges of her hood forward as though she could disappear into it. "Please. We're not doing anything wrong. Is it not a citizen's right to assemble?"

"Assemble?" He almost choked on the scoffing word. Did she really think she could play naïve with him? "You're raising a flag that defies the king. The captain will expect me to bring you in."

Tears shimmered in her eyes, and she extended both hands, palms reversed, as if to shield the women accompanying her. "I know you don't want to do that. I beg you, at least let my friends go."

"Walk this way, all of you." He gestured ahead of him, brusquely, as though giving a command, should anyone be observing. Then he spoke again in a low timbre. "At the side alley that leads to your house, I will let you go."

"Oh, Ansel. Thank you." When Temperance shot a grateful glance over her shoulder, he prodded her to keep moving.

"Do you think I could do otherwise?" His words caught on the sudden lump in his throat. The severing of their betrothal had in no way freed him of the need to protect her. Unlike Frankie, who hadn't hesitated to abandon Temperance when she needed him the most. "I can't say the same for your cousin. 'Tis my fondest hope that my men have captured that rapscallion."

Her jaw firmed. "I hope they do. I could have broken my neck falling from that ladder."

Where two-story frame buildings rose on either edge of the narrow side street heading north, the brown-haired woman whose name might be Elizabeth turned back and spoke with tense emphasis. "Come, Temperance, we must go." She met Ansel's eyes. "Thank you, Lieutenant. I know you truly care for my friend, and you will do the right thing."

What was the right thing? What did she mean?

Temperance cast him a wavering smile, but he caught her arm before she could follow the others. "I won't ask you to remain inside today, but will you at least be careful?"

She bobbed her head. Would she request he come to her after this was over? Hope struggled against the hurt in his heart. No, for neither of them knew how this day might play out. But she did raise her hand to touch his face, her fingers lingering in a soft caress before she turned and hurried away. The longing in her eyes had told him she'd far from forgotten him this miserable month apart.

God, watch over her. Watch over us.

Ansel led Oliver back to the square.

Jack no longer waited at the northeast corner.

The crowd in the square grew, people mumbling and gesturing toward the governor's residence, where Temperance's flag still blew in the breeze. Ansel's men were nowhere in sight.

Horse hooves approached from the north, and Lieutenant Jones rode into view at the head of most of the Second Troop. "Somebody get that banner down!"

Two privates hastened to dismount and do their officer's bidding.

When Jones's gaze swept in Ansel's direction, Ansel snapped off a salute.

Jones did not bother to return the acknowledgement. "Why was this not already taken care of, Lieutenant?"

"We were pursuing those who raised it, sir."

"'We'? Where are the rest of your men? And the guilty party?"

"Here, sir," Jack called out from State Street. Still mounted, he led McCleary's horse. Another of the men rode behind him.

Walking after them, McCleary dragged a struggling Frankie before his first lieutenant. "Here's your man. Took him down meself, and a fair scrapper he be." With a nudge of his boot to the back of Frankie's knee, McCleary forced him to kneel.

The man's pock-marked face now bore a reddening patch around his eye, which Ansel could only wish he'd put there himself.

"And the others?" Jones sought an answer from Ansel. "I was told there were several women." The stiffness in the first lieutenant's frame betrayed the tension of conflicted loyalties Ansel experienced. Would he understand what Ansel had done?

He had to chance it. "They escaped up a side street, sir."

"Escaped! Hah." Frankie tilted his head up to Ansel, an ugly grin splitting his mouth. "He's sweet on her. He let them go."

"Be silent." Lieutenant Jones made a slicing gesture toward Frankie. Relief caved Ansel's chest at the close call. Even if Jones might have his back, most of the rangers did not entertain patriotic sympathies. Jones barely looked at Frankie. "We will hear nothing further from you until our captain asks you to speak. He will decide if the Governor's Council should interview you."

"Jones, you know me..." Frankie began his ill-timed plea in a whining voice.

Lieutenant Jones turned a look of wrath upon him, but it wasn't that which silenced him.

It was the marching of many feet, the murmuring of the crowd.

People nearby turned and pointed, and Ansel followed their gazes.

Entering the square with muskets at their sides and flags waving, several columns of men in civilian clothing made their way to the governor's house. They marched silently until one at the front shouted, "Give us the governor! Give us the stamps!"

Those behind took up the chant.

Lieutenant Jones raised his voice to be heard above the mob. "Rangers, cover the front."

The privates wheeled their horses to obey, creating a long line before the governor's house.

Ansel's heart pounded. This was it, the confrontation they had all feared.

"Lieutenant Anderson," Jones shouted. "You will take Mr. Scott to Fort Halifax and let Captain Powell know what is happening here."

What? How could Ansel protect Temperance if he wasn't here? For he had no doubt that within minutes, she would join the crowd filling in the square behind the newly arrived men. Which was probably why Jones ordered him away, so his loyalties wouldn't be tested.

Frankie broke into high-pitched laughter, further grating on his frayed nerves. "By all means, take me to your captain. He will find what I have to say most interesting."

McCleary stepped forward. "With all respect, sir, I captured the rebel. Should I not present him to the captain?"

Jones had time only to spare the Scotsman a glance, but Ansel read his concern just the same. If they allowed Frankie to be taken in for questioning, especially by one such as McCleary, what might he reveal about the patriots among the ranks? Ansel could handle Temperance's cousin more to their advantage, but the decision wasn't his.

Jones flicked his fingers toward McCleary. "Very well. Anderson, with me."

As McCleary prodded Frankie from the square, Ansel mounted up and edged Oliver to the end of the line. His one consolation was that if it was in his power, Jones would prevent violence. Though many unfamiliar and angry faces confronted them, demanding that the governor pledge to issue no more stamped papers and turn over the stamps, there were also people Ansel recognized in the crowd. No doubt, these were men Jones would consider close friends.

But surely, nothing was worse than looking across an angry mob and seeing the face of the one you loved.

Temperance and the women he'd just released edged up behind the men, joining the cry. "Give us the governor! Give us the stamps!" As their fists punctuated every syllable, her eyes met his, and his chest clamped in a vise.

Tangled emotions rose from deep within. The fear, he understood...even the frustration over his impotence at such a volatile moment. But shame? For doing his duty? Never had he thought it would come to this.

Most astonishing of all, perhaps, was the lack of feelings of anger or betrayal. He did not blame Temperance for joining the protest. In fact, the admiration he'd first felt when she'd spoken of her convictions in her garden swelled within Ansel's heart. There might be danger in what she was doing, but there was no deceit. And that was good.

But what would happen if the armed citizens stormed the rangers' line?

Ansel could only pray.

~

Three hours. That was how long they had made their unacknowledged demands and traded insults with the sailors and sundry loyalists the governor had rallied to stand with the rangers. Even though the patriots had more than double the number of their foe, disagreement among their ranks had allowed the confrontation to fizzle, just as before.

Temperance gritted her teeth when she thought of it, returning home that night. She carried the folded flag the rangers had trampled, a painful reminder of her ineffectiveness. She'd gone back to gather it after the mob dispersed, uncloaked, unhooded.

That was something, wasn't it?

Now everyone in town would know Judge Scott's daughter had defied him. She was a Daughter of Liberty.

When Temperance paused in the doorway of the parlor where her mother and sister sat sewing, Tabitha rose, tossing her embroidery onto the settee next to her. "How dare you come in here with that? You have placed your family in an awful predicament, and for what?" She flung her hand toward the window and the empty square beyond. "Everything is as it was before."

"Not everything." Temperance murmured the response as the realization dawned fully. "I followed through on my convictions. I was true to myself."

Mother lifted her gaze along with her needle and gave her a slight nod.

The back door banged open, and Father shattered Temperance's brief moment of satisfaction as he stalked in. "I have been apprised of all that transpired today." His narrowed gaze shifted from Temperance's flushed face to the flag she held. "Get that thing out of my sight." His additional use of a rare explicative froze her in place. "Now!"

She clutched the folded banner to her chest, shielding the ache within. If her father had a choice, he would want her out of his sight as well...permanently. She couldn't seem to take a step.

"Very well." He practically growled the words as he started toward her. "If you won't remove it, I will." He seized the edges of the heavy silk, but she held firm. An awkward wrestling match ensued.

Mother leapt to her feet. "Bazel, please!"

Temperance lost her grip, and the flag unfolded. Father grabbed hold. He balled the material up, strode into the parlor, and flung the flag into the fireplace.

Temperance let out a cry as the spluttering flames roared to life, hungrily devouring the fabric.

"No!" The visual of all she held dear being destroyed at her father's hand wrenched her heart. She made to dart around his substantial form, but he caught her, keeping her from shoving a hand into the fire to rescue the flag.

A hammering on the front door froze them in place. Whoever it was did not wait for the butler. The door flew open, and a figure in blue and red dashed into the hall.

Ansel froze at the threshold when he saw her. "Temperance!"

Her heart sputtered as he hurried to her side. "Ansel."

Father released her to face his unwanted guest. "Why do you barge in here?" Clearly, his embarrassment at being caught in a compromising position overshadowed his usual regard for his lackey, for ire sharpened his demand.

Ansel barely took his eyes off her as he answered her father. "Frankie has betrayed you."

"What?" Her stomach plummeted to her toes.

"Yes. And he has done so publicly. James Habersham got word Captain Powell was holding him and insisted on being present when he was questioned."

Father made a sound deep in this throat. "Habersham was never satisfied after the Townsman affair."

Ansel shot him a glance. "Frankie has admitted he delivered the letters, but he named Temperance as the author. He says he has encoded messages she sent him that he can offer as proof."

"Oh, no!" The cry came from Mother, whose hand flew to her heart.

Temperance met her eyes and gave a quick shake of her head. No matter how guilty Mother might feel, Father must never know her part in this. What Frankie said was true, anyway. No doubt, he'd saved her messages, and the handwriting would match Temperance's. She alone must take the blame for this. The time for hiding in her house or running to the countryside had passed.

Father stepped toward Ansel, all business. "What will happen next?" Even as the flag turned to black shreds in the fireplace, he was figuring how to maneuver them out of this.

Temperance's heart softened toward him. He did love her, in his way.

Regret filled Ansel's face as his gaze swept her. "Habersham has insisted that Temperance be brought before the Governor's Council first thing in the morning."

In his pause, her mother gasped softly.

"I only know this because...a friend warned me. He wanted to give me time to take whatever steps I could to protect you." His eyes latched onto hers, pleading.

She forced herself to speak calmly. "Thank you, but I am not in need of protection."

Father inched forward. "Temperance, my influence has its limits, and we have reached them. I cannot stop this." He looked to Ansel before she could protest. "What do you have in mind?"

When Ansel dropped to one knee, it was Temperance who gasped. What was he doing?

He clasped her hand in his. "Marry me. Tonight. I can send you to my family." He must have seen the rebuttal forming in her mind, for he hurried on. "Or if you stay here, my name may provide you some leniency."

"Your name?" She whispered the question almost compassionately. "The name of a loyalist?"

Father rounded on her as though he might slap her. "You ungrateful chit!"

Ansel rose and held out a hand toward him. "It's all right, sir."

"It is not all right. This brazen child would spurn the efforts of any good man on her behalf. She deserves what she gets." He turned his back on her.

"Father is right." Temperance offered Ansel a faltering smile. "'Tis time I own up to my doings. I will welcome the chance to speak the truth."

He reached out as though to touch her, then thought better of it and curled his fingers tight. "You will not do yourself any favors. If the Council accuses you of treason, you could be sent away for a trial." They all knew that meant Admiralty Court, where the nearest crown-appointed judge presided...in Nova Scotia. Beyond that, she could not bear to imagine.

A groan rippled from her mother's throat, but Tabitha comforted her, allowing Temperance to remain focused on Ansel. "I understand," she said softly. But her voice wavered.

The hint of weakness was all her father needed to try again. "Don't be a fool, girl. Take this man up on his offer. He may be a loyalist, but he obviously loves you."

"And I love him." She needed Ansel to know that, especially if they were about to be parted for good. She reached for his hand as wonder flared in his green eyes. "But I can never again stand across a divide from him as I did today."

"Nor can I." Ansel squeezed her hand. Then he looked at her father. "And I'm not a loyalist."

"What?" Father barked the question that had frozen in her throat.

"I agree with your daughter," Ansel said. "Only sworn duty kept me away from her today. But never again."

A CONFLICTED BETROTHAL

Temperance's heart swelled as Ansel shifted his attention to her.

"I will tell Captain Powell my sentiments have changed. He can discipline me or send me from the city. But I will stand by you tomorrow, if not as your husband, then as your friend."

Temperance flung her arms around his neck. How could she experience such joy and terror in the same moment? "God willing, you shall be both forever."

A roar came from her father. "God may be willing, but your father is not." His hands tore her arms from Ansel's neck. "Get out. You! Get out." He jerked his head between Ansel and the door as he propelled Temperance to the hallway.

"Father, please!" Even Tabitha sounded horrified by his rough treatment.

Ansel started after them, but Temperance shook her head. "No." She couldn't allow him to get into an altercation with her father, who could have Ansel thrown in the guardhouse. "Tomorrow."

He would understand and come to her wherever they took her. She caught one last glimpse of his anguished expression before she shook free of her father's grip and ran for the stairway.

Minutes after she shut herself in her room, a key turned in the lock.

CHAPTER 22

The evening should have been a glorious one for Temperance. Ansel had realized where his true sympathies lay, and he loved her enough to own them at risk of great harm to himself. But she was the cause of that potential harm. She had used her quill and her needle to further the cause of liberty, and now she might pay for it with her own freedom. And Ansel's too.

All night long, she cried out to God and wracked her brain for a way of escape that would honor their dreams for the colonies and for a life together. Every path she mentally traced ended in despair for one or both of them.

At the very least, she could save Ansel. If she got but one glimpse of him tomorrow, one smile, it would make her strong enough to do what she must. She would say goodbye and bid him to fulfill his term in silence, as so many of the patriots who were also in the military did. By autumn, he could be free. Even if she was sent to some faraway penal colony, she could think of him, working his family's land.

But surely, it would not come to that. Her father might in his anger and unbending judgment take her to appear before the Council tomorrow, but he would use his influence to bargain for mercy. She knew it.

She also had her mother on her side. Marjorie Scott had proved surprisingly courageous before when her conscience demanded. And she would attempt to right this, for Temperance would never be in this position if Mother hadn't sent the letters—though Temperance couldn't bring herself to blame her mother for her one brave act of rebellion.

Temperance did not think she slept, but she must have, for when she sat up with a start, faint gray light edged the curtains. Not moonlight. 'Twas almost dawn. And something had awakened her.

She slid her feet onto the cold floor, eschewing her slippers, and darted to the window. The creak and jingle of a single enclosed coach moved down the street. Temperance turned back toward the bed, but a white rectangle on the hardwood caught her eye. Someone had slipped a message beneath her door.

She hastened over and picked up the unsealed note. She took the letter to her small table near the window and lit a candle. Temperance gasped. Feminine, looping script filled half the page. Not her mother's, but Tabitha's.

Dear sister,

We both know it will not go well for you today. Therefore, it falls on me to rescue you. I suppose I owe you that much. I made your life miserable and tried to steal your beau. Since I failed and I must wed Riley, anyway, I might as well do so in a style worthy of my reputation.

Ansel's pleas for you last night made me realize what a man will do for the woman he is besotted with. Riley is besotted. He came at my summons after Father locked you away and immediately agreed to my plan. Just a little deception, and he will get what he wants sooner rather than later—and he knew I had intended on much, much later.

Do not try to stop us. I will already have appeared before James Habersham by the time you read this. However, after this, you may consider yourself in my debt. Until such a time as I call in that debt, have a lovely life with Ansel.

Tabitha

The letter gripped tight in her hand, Temperance ran to the door. She beat on it and yelled with all her might. "Father! Father!"

~

The morning following the St. James Square demonstration, Ansel stood before Captain Powell in full uniform. He clasped his hat under his arm. "Sir, I request to lead the escort of the prisoner to the Council House." Even now, saddled horses were being led into the fog-laden yard of the fort. Soon, Frankie would be brought out of the King's Store.

Captain Powell did not even look up from the letter he was writing, but his lips raised at the corners. "So you can lose him too?"

Ansel frowned. "No sir. I bear the man no fondness."

A brief chuckle. "I have heard."

"I wish to see him answer for his part in the Townsman scandal."

"And your sweetheart?" The captain did meet his eyes then. As Ansel stiffened, he made a slight scoffing sound. "Please. All Savannah knows how she left you on the ballroom floor before your betrothal could be announced on Twelfth Night. Perhaps you are still angry about that. Do you wish to see her answer for

A CONFLICTED BETROTHAL

her patriotic plottings as well?" He slid his quill back into its pottery holder.

Ansel's heart hammered. "I am not angry. Temperance will do whatever she must to remain true to her convictions. As should I. That is why I am requesting to stand beside her today...and throughout whatever else may unfold. I also would like..." He swallowed.

Captain Powell's brows elevated.

Ansel drew a quick breath. *Help me, God.* "I would like to request a transfer to Fort Augusta, far from this noxious political cauldron. I have done my best to serve my benefactors whilst I was here, but I can do so no longer, not in good conscience. It is my plan to leave the rangers when my term expires, and hopefully, to start a life with Temperance Scott. If you cannot see clear to transfer me, sir, well, I am...at your disposal." The rush of words ceased, and Ansel bowed his head.

Did Captain Powell understand what he'd just confessed? The man merely sat silently, softly drumming his fingers on his desk.

The fire snapped behind him.

"You do know Frankie Scott named you as well as his cousin last night."

Ansel tightened his jaw. He'd suspected as much. "Am I to be questioned also?"

The patient smile returned to the captain's mouth. "If I questioned every man he accused, half the Second Troop would stand before the Council this morn. I am no fool. I'm well aware that sentiment against the governor and the king pervades these ranks. But neither can I afford to take the word of a Liberty Boy desperate to save his own skin. I must maintain a ranger force...and a strong morale. Most of those with conflicted loyalties are honorable men like yourself. So you

237

won't be questioned, and you won't be brought up on charges. But neither will you be going to Augusta."

"I won't, sir?" Panic spiraled through Ansel. He hadn't made himself clear enough. He could not remain in service in Savannah.

"No, but if you are willing to accept a demotion, the man who filled your position at Argyle was caught embezzling goods from the storeroom this past month. Captain Milledge might be persuaded to take you back."

"Oh, yes, sir. I will accept a demotion." And be grateful for it, if it got him out of Savannah. "But—"

Powell lifted his hand. "'Tis unlikely a quartermaster would be called to the governor's aid."

"Yes, sir. Thank you, sir." Ansel's shoulders relaxed a bit as he let out his breath. His commander understood him, after all. His prayers had been answered. But the pressing danger remained. "About the escort? I would serve you with honor on my last assignment in the city."

"If I did not believe that, I wouldn't have allowed you to remain in those colors. But there is no need."

"No need?" Ansel's heart thudded again. Had they taken Temperance during the night? Had they already reached a decision?

"You may go with the prison detail if you wish, but your Temperance will not be there."

"Where is she?" The question rasped out of Ansel with physical pain.

"At home, I expect." Captain Scott took up his quill again. "Someone has already confessed to writing the Townsman letters."

Ansel gawped at him. "Who?"

"Her sister. Tabitha. She presented herself to James Habersham at dawn, copied his letter in the exact same hand, and identified the location of the dead drop she used to communicate with her cousin. Lord Riley was so disgusted by her betrayal that he took her to the Council House to await the legislators himself."

~

*A*nsel couldn't get to the Scott residence fast enough. But what would he find there? Would Judge Scott even admit him? He was prepared to throw pebbles at Temperance's window if necessary. Or, if he could get a message to Cecily, he and Temperance could elope this very night.

Amazingly, the door flew open before he even knocked, and Temperance herself stood there, her hair flowing down her back and high color in her cheeks. She'd never looked so beautiful.

He stepped in and, after shutting the door behind him, flung his arms around her and lowered his mouth to hers. Her kiss offered a surrender sweeter than he'd ever imagined.

"You came." She breathed it out against his lips. "How did you know?"

"Captain Powell told me. Your sister would really do such a thing for you?"

"Oh, Ansel." Temperance laid her head against his chest and wept. "We tried to stop her."

From inside the parlor, another bout of tears began.

He peeked through the door. Mrs. Scott slumped on the settee in a flowered morning bed gown. "My poor, darling girl! So brave. So unselfish. She has sacrificed herself for us."

Temperance's tears dried up, and she raised her face with a wry look at Ansel.

He lifted one side of his mouth and swiped the moisture from her cheek. "Let us see if we may comfort your mother."

"Yes, come in, and you can read the letter Tabitha left me." She led him by the hand into the adjoining room.

239

Mrs. Scott mopped her face with her handkerchief. "Oh, Lieutenant Anderson. Do forgive me. I am overcome."

"'Tis perfectly understandable, ma'am. We all are." He bowed to her, then accepted the folded paper Temperance offered him. She indicated a chair across from her mother, which he took. Temperance sat next to Mrs. Scott.

The woman sniffled and squared her shoulders. "Allow me to say, sir, you demonstrated great bravery in the face of my husband's displeasure yesterday eve."

Displeasure, was it? Ansel had thought the man might kill him. He'd been willing to risk it before Temperance ran upstairs. Now he understood her healthy fear of her father. "I thank you, ma'am."

"I was wrong about you. And wrong about my nephew." Mrs. Scott shuddered, her handkerchief clutched in her lap. "For him to turn on his own kin in such a manner..."

Temperance reached for her hand. "Tabitha has shown him how it should be, Mother. She is the heroine of this chapter." The look Temperance cast Ansel revealed not only her sincerity, but her concern. "Father has gone to see what can be done. But read the letter. What Tabitha says about Lord Riley makes me believe she has a plan."

He perused the contents of the message, then folded it with a frown. "I see what you mean. But Captain Powell said that Lord Riley was disgraced by Tabitha's behavior. In a vindictive rage."

"It is as I imagine he would be." Mrs. Scott twisted her handkerchief. "He is a fool for Tabitha, but he would not suffer her making him one."

Ansel cocked his head. "What if she did not? What if she made him a proposal? Much like the one I came to make you." He turned to Temperance, assuming he could now speak freely in front of her mother. "I've told Captain Powell where I stand.

A CONFLICTED BETROTHAL

He asks me not to leave the rangers but to accept my old position at Fort Argyle...with the understanding that I will not be called back to defend Savannah in cases of unrest. I know you wanted me out of the service entirely, but this would allow us to make some arrangements. And provide income for a while. Both necessities since we will no longer have your father's support."

She drew in a soft breath. "Are you asking me to elope?"

"If you will accept a humble home outside a fort on the Ogeechee River for now, yes. It is the only way I can think of for us to wed."

Mrs. Scott groaned, but when Temperance's face lit, Ansel's heart leapt.

She jumped up to come slip her arm around his shoulder. "Then I accept."

"That will not be necessary." The rumbling decree came from the door to the parlor, and they all froze in place.

How had Judge Scott entered with them unaware? He must have come in the back door.

Ansel rose as Temperance's father walked toward him. The man's face was inscrutable. Ansel slid Temperance behind him. This time, he would fight the man before letting him take charge of the woman he loved.

Judge Scott stopped a few feet away and gazed beyond him at Temperance. "When I called upon Mr. Habersham, he informed me that Lord Riley had driven your sister to the Council House. But when I went there, I found it locked."

"Where were they?" Mrs. Scott asked breathlessly. "Did Riley take her by his home for some reason?"

Her husband looked at her. "I rode there next, thinking the very thing. And lo and behold, the man's housekeeper informed me her master had packed in a hurry during the night and sent for the captain of his sloop."

"Eloped." Ansel spoke the same word he'd earlier thought.

241

A wild desire to cheer the black-haired vixen rose within him. She had cheek—he'd give her that.

"Oh, my Tabitha. Married. And a lady now!" Mrs. Scott clutched her lacy square of fabric to her mouth.

"One can only assume. The harbormaster did not have a record of Riley's sloop departing, but they must have sailed for his plantation on the Altamaha. Under any other circumstances, Tabitha's reputation would be ruined." Judge Scott shook his head. "But her little scheme just may have saved us all."

"Exactly as she intended," Temperance whispered. "I *am* in her debt. But is she safe? The Altamaha is not that far."

Her father palmed off her query. "No one will risk the snakes and gators and Riley's wrath to seek her out, not once she is his wife. She has removed herself from the field of play. I admit, she has shown more cleverness than I would have anticipated." A small flame of admiration lit in his eyes.

Had Tabitha banked on that too? She must have craved it, with Temperance being their father's longstanding favorite.

"And more sacrifice." Temperance gazed at Ansel with wonder. "I would say it is just like her to steal the scene, but this time, I don't envy her. For she did not love Riley."

"She will come to." Judge Scott collapsed into a chair as though his legs had given out. "He will treat her like a queen. You shall see."

Ansel stepped forward. "And what of us, sir? You heard my plan to take Temperance away in a similar manner. Will you attempt to stop us?" Hopefully, his tone and posture promised he wouldn't stand for that without his having to voice the words. If he could salvage a modicum of respect between them...

The judge dragged the back of his hand across his face. "I do not agree with your politics. I do not give my blessing. But you will persist despite that, with my wife on your side, nagging, nagging..." He fluttered pinched fingers together with a scalding glance Mrs. Scott's direction. "As she has been doing all night. So, honestly, I'd just as soon have you out of sight, and maybe we can return to a semblance of peace."

Temperance peeked around Ansel. "Does that mean you will let us go?"

Judge Scott let his arm fall by his side. "Well, I would rather not both my daughters wed in scandal. If you will stay while Ansel prepares a place at Argyle, I will see what I can dig up at the land office."

Ansel's eyes flashed open wide. "You would do that still?"

The man flung out his hand as he abruptly sat upright. "You prefer to support my daughter forever on a ranger's salary?"

"No, sir." Ansel swallowed hard, his mind racing.

"Then get out of my sight before I change my mind. And don't come back until you have a house to take her to."

"Yes, sir." Ansel grabbed Temperance's hand and pulled her toward the foyer.

Mrs. Scott rushed to her husband, kissing his forehead. "Oh, we'll plan a beautiful wedding, my dear."

He brushed her off, but Ansel saw no more, for he stepped onto the front porch with Temperance. They stared at each other in stunned silence.

Finally, she asked, "What just happened?"

His heart raced. "Our future just happened." And he couldn't help but notice that only after he'd stood up for what he believed had God made a way. *Stand fast therefore in the liberty wherewith Christ hath made us free.* Thankfulness overflowed, bringing moisture to his eyes.

"I am to be your wife." Temperance cupped his face with her small hands, her expression aglow.

"It won't be easy." The need to manage her expectations spilled over into warning. "It won't be what you are accustomed to—being wed to a ranger or a farmer, either one."

"No. But it will be exactly what I prepared for. And your mother will help me."

"'Tis true." His mother had been praying ardently ever since the disaster at the Twelfth Night Ball. "She never wavered in her belief that we were meant to be together. And Cecily? What of her?"

Temperance missed not a beat. "I will ask my father for her manumission as a wedding gift. She will come with us. And later, once everything is settled, we will go visit my sister and thank her in person for what she did for us."

Ansel smiled and slid his arms around her waist. "Perhaps it will be the start of a new era for you two."

"I would like that." She sobered. "I have a feeling we're going to need strong family ties for what the future holds."

"Indeed." Jack's words came back to him. Even if a compromise were reached over the Stamp Act, the discord it produced sowed the seeds of rebellion. "I pray not only our families but our colonies can come to an accord. But whenever the fight for freedom may come, we will face it together."

Did you enjoy this book? We hope so!
Would you take a quick minute to leave a review where you purchased the book?
It doesn't have to be long. Just a sentence or two telling what you liked about the story!

Receive a FREE ebook and get updates when new Wild Heart books release: https://wildheartbooks.org/newsletter

AUTHOR'S NOTE

I hope you have enjoyed this love story and journey toward freedom. For this novel of my Scouts of the Georgia Frontier Series, we moved from the wilderness to Georgia's leading Colonial city, Savannah. Exchanging battlefield action for parlor intrigue was quite the challenge, but the little-known history behind the Stamp Act riots in Georgia was too interesting to pass up. Since Georgia is often deemed to have lagged behind the other colonies in patriotic fervor, I found it surprising just how extensive the unrest actually was.

In February of 1766, Benjamin Franklin convinced the Committee of the Whole of the House of Commons that enforcing the Stamp Act would be impossible. His efforts restored him to the good graces of colonial patriots, who felt he had initially been far too accommodating. On March 4, 1766, Parliament repealed the Stamp Act. Non-importation had put such a hurting on British merchants that it took King George several hours to reach the House of Lords on the eighteenth due to the number of people cheering in the streets.

Only a week after the repeal, however, Parliament passed the Declaratory Act, which stated that they had the right to

AUTHOR'S NOTE

legislate for the colonies in all cases. Despite this, a spirit of goodwill and reconciliation prevailed—for a time. Governor Wright and the Commons House congratulated each other that no violence had occurred in Georgia, and the joint legislatures thanked the king for considering the happiness of his American subjects. However, heated and extensive exchanges in the *Gazette* that summer showed a colony still divided.

A *Conflicted Betrothal* includes mentions of and cameo appearances by a number of real-life individuals. Some of these were: Governor James Wright, Captain John Milledge, Captain James Edward Powell, First Lieutenant Noble Wimberly Jones, Second Lieutenant Moses Nunez Rivers, Button and Ann Gwinnett, Peter Tondee, James Machenry, James Habersham Jr. and Sr., Alexander Wylly, Rev. Bartholomew Zouberbuhler, Joseph Ottolenghe, the recipients of the Townsman letters, George Angus, Joseph Habersham, and Joseph Clay. In *A Conflicted Betrothal*, I had Ansel basically take the place of the historical third lieutenant, Mungo Graham.

The Townsman Letter debacle occurred mostly as described, with the exception of the involvement of my Scott family fictional characters. The sending and publication of the cryptic missives created quite the furor, which appears to have petered out when the true identity of the stamp agent came to light. To my knowledge, the author and/or sender of the letters remains anonymous to this day.

Button Gwinnett became one of Georgia's three signers of the Declaration of Independence. When I learned he opened his store in Savannah in 1765, he had to become a small part of this story. For a time, I worked for Gwinnett County, interpreting history at their museums and telling visitors about Button's life. I don't know for sure that non-importation played a part in the failure of his merchant establishment, but it did fail, and he did purchase land on St. Catherine's Island. He soon fell into difficult financial straits again. The Revolutionary

AUTHOR'S NOTE

crisis brought him into politics, where he ran afoul of Lachlan McIntosh, who ended up commanding the Georgia battalion instead of Gwinnett. Gwinnett became speaker and then president of Georgia's Provincial Congress. When he proposed a military foray into British East Florida, McIntosh opposed him, and the expedition did fail. This led to a duel in which each man shot the other. Gwinnett's wound proved fatal. He was buried in Savannah's famous Colonial Park Cemetery, but the exact location of his grave is unknown. I would tell young people who visited the museum that Button is case in point that even if life gives you some hard knocks, you can still become famous.

Ann Gwinnett was something of a shadowy historical figure, so my portrayal of her is mainly fictional.

While Tondee's Tavern became the 1770s hotspot for meetings of the Sons of Liberty, during the Stamp Act crisis, that honor went to Machenry's Tavern. Unfortunately, little could be found about the building or its proprietor, so I based my depictions on generalized research.

Bartholomew Zouberbuhler did serve as rector of Christ Church from 1745 to 1766, and he was known for baptizing the first Africans into the denomination and entreating England to send a catechist for slaves, Joseph Ottolenghe. I included some historical details of their lives and service in the story.

The First and Second Troop of Rangers were described as accurately as possible, though it proved challenging to determine which commanders and portions of troops were actually stationed in Savannah/Fort Halifax in 1765. Making this decision for the novel sometimes came down to the process of deduction after studying sources that gave greater detail for other forts in 1760s Georgia—Fort Augusta, Fort Frederica, Fort Argyle, Fort Barrington, and Fort George. Two sources that were especially helpful were *Militiamen, Rangers, and Redcoats: The Military in Georgia, 1754-1776*, by James M. Johnson, and *Ft.*

AUTHOR'S NOTE

Argyle: Colonial Fort on the Ogeechee, by Daniel T. Elliott, printed through the Legacy Resource Management Program of the United States Department of Defense and available online.

While we do not know the inner beliefs of Governor Wright's ranger captains, Milledge and Powell both warned him when insurrection threatened and fully supported him with their men. Therefore, I allowed Powell to lean toward loyalism in the story. However, Noble Wimberly Jones was later known to become a patriot, so I depicted him with corresponding beliefs in the decade prior to the Revolution. Governor Wright did not know who among the militia he could trust. I depicted that to be true to a lesser degree among his royal rangers.

The identities of the 1760s Liberty Boys were not publicized, but many sons of prominent Savannah loyalists went on to become patriot leaders in the next decade. While I did not find reference to an actual Daughters of Liberty chapter in Savannah at this time, such groups were documented in other colonies, making it believable that a Savannah sewing circle might identify in such a way. The Daughters of Liberty supported non-importation and developed their own flag as described in the story.

I'd like to take a moment to thank the team at Wild Heart Books—including my publisher, Misty M. Beller, and my editor, Robin Patchen—for your skill and vision in helping me bring this story to my readers. Also my launch team, especially my beta readers—Gretchen Elm, Jennie Webb, Johnnie Steinberg, Ann Ferri, Becky Dempsey, and Catherine Patton. And you, my amazing readers, who love history as much as I do and support me as an author so well.

I hope the themes of *A Conflicted Betrothal*—being true to oneself and one's own convictions, and determining the point at which it is not only appropriate but imperative that we speak out for freedom—resonated with you. Alongside that, Ansel

AUTHOR'S NOTE

and Temperance's story illustrated the necessity of honesty and finding common ground in a loving relationship. If you enjoyed *A Conflicted Betrothal*, your reviews let publishers know my stories are worth continuing to publish. I notice and treasure each one. Please visit me at https://www.deniseweimerbooks.com, and I'd also love to connect on social media.

Monthly e-mail list: http://eepurl.com/dFfSfn
https://www.facebook.com/denise.weimer1
https://twitter.com/denise_weimer
https://www.bookbub.com/profile/denise-weimer

Interesting to note, Fort Barrington on the Altamaha River changed hands several times during the Revolution, becoming Fort Howe. Perhaps you're as curious as I am to see what happens to Tabitha down there with the snakes and gators and a husband she doesn't love. Find out in A Calculated Betrothal, book five of the Scouts of the Georgia Frontier, coming this fall.

Don't miss the next book in The Scouts of the Georgia Frontier Series!

A Calculated Betrothal

EARLY FEBRUARY, 1777

The morning after her husband's funeral, Lady Tabitha Gage opened her eyes to bright winter sunlight and shuddered —with relief.
She was free.
But a lady no longer.
Terror crowded out the relief. Free, yes, but also alone on a thousand-acre South Georgia rice plantation. Across the Altamaha River, Creek and Seminole Indians, allied to the British who held East Florida, roamed the no-man's land of tangled swamps and bogs. Lord Riley's allegiance to the Crown had not kept his cattle from being raided. Should an invasion come, her late husband's loyalty would not protect this plantation, either—especially now he was gone. After Henry's name appeared on the St. Andrews Parochial Committee's list of twenty-nine suspected Tories last autumn, River's Bend was equally susceptible to Patriot retribution.

And yet it was to River's Bend Tabitha had returned—fled, more like—the day after she'd seen Henry laid to rest in the Christ Church burying ground following his extended bout with lung sickness. Keeping up appearances in Savannah had required more fortitude—and fortune—than she possessed now. Not to mention that her twin, Temperance, was too apt to see past Tabitha's façade. And their father, too apt to pull her back under his control.

Tabitha sat up but clutched the covers beneath her chin, not yet ready to relinquish their warmth for the chill of the January morning. Maybe she could stay here all day.

When she'd first set eyes on her new husband's country house, she'd cried with dismay. The white frame home with its two tiers of piazzas and saltbox-style extension in the rear set among the live oaks and palms appeared so parochial compared to his elegant brick Savannah residence.

What a little fool she'd been to think that if not love, luxury at least would reward her sacrifice for her sister.

Her upstairs room, with its twelve-foot ceilings, walnut furniture, and tapestry curtains and counterpane, had since become her refuge. Lord Riley had sought her out here less and less frequently as his hope for an heir dwindled over the eleven years of their marriage.

Now, the burden of that expectation was gone, along with the silent judgment of the man who'd imposed it. She knew not whether to stretch her shoulders with the relinquishment or continue to cringe under the accusation she'd come to expect. Her own head supplied it in the absence of Henry's voice. What kind of wife was she to not mourn her husband?

Tabitha released a shaky breath and rubbed the sleep from her eyes.

The strips of light slanting through the cracks of the shutters promised a warm midday, and flames crackling on the hearth reminded her she was not alone. Dulcie had already been in to light a fire. The daughter of the white overseer and the enslaved cook, Dulcie had every right to spend the winter as she normally did with her husband across the river. She was free, as was her husband, Cyrus. But she was here instead. For Tabitha.

A brief knock sounded on the door.

Pushing her dark braid back, Tabitha called a "come in."

As if summoned by Tabitha's thoughts, Dulcie entered bearing a breakfast tray. "Good mornin', Miss Tabitha. How are you?" Sliding the tray onto the foot of the goose-down mattress, the golden-skinned woman peered at her. Looking for signs of grief?

Dulcie had served as housekeeper and lady's maid to Tabitha long enough to know better. And that silent sensitivity of hers meant she'd long ago discerned the way of things with Lord Riley. Tabitha had glimpsed Dulcie's firmed lips and tightly clasped hands on plenty of occasions when Tabitha had stumbled into another of Henry's verbal ambushes.

She might as well be honest with the servant now. "Terrified."

Dulcie poured steaming coffee from a pewter pitcher into a cream-ware mug, picked up a tiny silver spoon, and stirred the brew. "I put chocolate in your coffee," she said, as if this were the answer to all her problems.

Tabitha stifled a laugh. The sound so surprised her that her hand flew to her mouth. She choked on a tangle of emotions that rose into her throat and promptly started crying—something she never used to do. She instantly hated herself for it. But nearly a dozen years with a man who despised her had eroded her spirit until she'd become an emotional weakling. "What am I to do, Dulcie? How am I to manage on my own?"

Dulcie touched the hem of Tabitha's linen nightgown. "You aren't alone, Miss Tabitha. Pa and I will help you."

Dulcie spoke like a white woman, thanks to the tutor her father had hired when she was a child. Henry had permitted it, he'd told Tabitha, not because he approved of educating a woman, especially a mulatto, but because Marcus Long was the best overseer in St. Andrew's Parish and he wasn't willing to risk losing the man over something some trivial.

Tabitha had shared her husband's views about slavery when they'd first wed. But now she knew what it felt like to have a master. And Dulcie's discretion and wisdom had helped Tabitha avoid many a misstep over the years, even when Tabitha had not condescended to acknowledge her.

"I know not where to begin."

"You have time." Dulcie handed her the mug. "Planting's not until March. But Pa says you should meet with him. Talk about clearing another section."

Tabitha sipped her favorite combination of coffee and chocolate. The warm liquid soothed her empty stomach. "That would be a good idea." She should learn just how bad of financial shape they were in while she was at it. "I shall meet with him this afternoon."

"There's no hurry, Miss Tabitha. If you need a few days—"

"No." Tabitha lowered her cup to the tray. "The sooner the field gets cleared, the sooner we can plant more rice and hopefully get us out of the mess Lord Riley's brother-in-law got us into." Henry had sent more and more money over the last few years to his sister, whose wastrel husband continued to indebt their ancestral estate back in England—though he'd gone to great pains to conceal their genteel poverty from Tabitha's family.

Dulcie uncovered Tabitha's porridge and sprinkled some cinnamon on top. "'Tis all over now. You have a new start. A chance to change things. At least..." She glanced up from under her dark lashes. "The lawyer in Savannah said Lord Riley left everything to you, did he not?"

Tabitha had made sure of it before leaving the city. "The house in town, River's Bend, and even his grazing lands across the river." Where Cyrus tended to Lord Riley's pinewoods cattle herd. When she'd expressed amazement at the cattle ranging free south of the Altamaha, he'd told her they were *criollo*, cows born in America but descended from European herds—Spanish, to be exact. The animals browsed the wiregrass and bluestems in warm months and the switchcane at the edges of the savannahs and streams in cooler months, often retreating to the thick stands of great cane in the winter. Herders like Cyrus moved or secured them with a series of wilderness cattle pens.

Dulcie's eyes sparkled. "That makes you one wealthy woman."

"Once we can get things turned around now that we no longer must send funds every few months to England, perhaps." Tabitha reached for her spoon and tasted her porridge. Delicious, as always. Dulcie's mother, Annabelle, was an excellent cook. "I expect it shan't be long before all the toothless widowers in the parish are tapping their bejeweled canes on my door."

But she could ignore them all once she got on her feet. A sliver of something warm and precious slid through her—independence. With it, hope stirred. Her appetite sharpening, she dipped her spoon back in for another bite.

"Speakin' of that ..."

Tabitha's gaze snapped up. She cared not for Dulcie's uneasy tone.

"You already have a caller. Two, actually."

Her chest tightened. "Who?"

"Hugh and Julian Jackson. They be waitin' in the parlor."

"At this hour?" How dare they? When she had yet to set her foot out of bed the day after returning from her husband's funeral?

"Said they missed catching you at the townhouse and wanted to pay their respects. But I suspect ..."

Tabitha's stomach bottomed out. "They have something else in mind." The Jacksons owned the vast plantation adjoining theirs just southeast, closer to Darien, the town settled by the Scottish folk on the coast. The reputations of both father and son with the ladies and the ruthless manner in which they drove their slaves made Julian Jackson the last man she'd allow to call. Or to purchase her land.

A flicker of the spirit Henry's disapproval somehow hadn't managed to snuff out had her throwing back her covers. "Help

SNEAK PEEK: A CALCULATED BETROTHAL

me get dressed, Dulcie, for I shall have no avaricious men sniffing around River's Bend."

ABOUT THE AUTHOR

North Georgia native Denise Weimer has authored over a dozen traditionally published novels and a number of novellas —historical and contemporary romance, romantic suspense, and time slip. As a freelance editor and Acquisitions & Editorial Liaison for Wild Heart Books, she's helped other authors reach their publishing dreams. A wife and mother of two daughters, Denise always pauses for coffee, chocolate, and old houses.

You can visit Denise at https://www.deniseweimerbooks.com, and connect with her on social media.

Monthly e-mail list: http://eepurl.com/dFfSfn

Want more?

If you love historical romance, check out the other Wild Heart books!

A Winter at the White Queen by Denise Weimer

In the world of the wealthy, things are never quite as they appear.

Ellie Hastings is tired of playing social gatekeeper—and poor-relation companion—to her Gibson Girl of a cousin. But her aunt insists Ellie lift her nose out of her detective novel long enough to help gauge the eligibility of bachelors during the winter social season at Florida's Hotel Belleview. She finds plenty that's mysterious about the suave, aloof Philadelphia inventor, Lewis Thornton. Why does he keep sneaking around the hotel? Does he have a secret sweetheart? And what is his connection to the evasive Mr. Gaspachi, slated to perform at Washington's Birthday Ball?

Ellie's comical sleuthing ought to put Lewis out, but the diffident way her family treats her smashes a hole in his normal reserve. When Florence Hastings's diamond necklace goes missing, Ellie's keen mind threatens to uncover not only Lewis's secrets, but give him back hope for love.

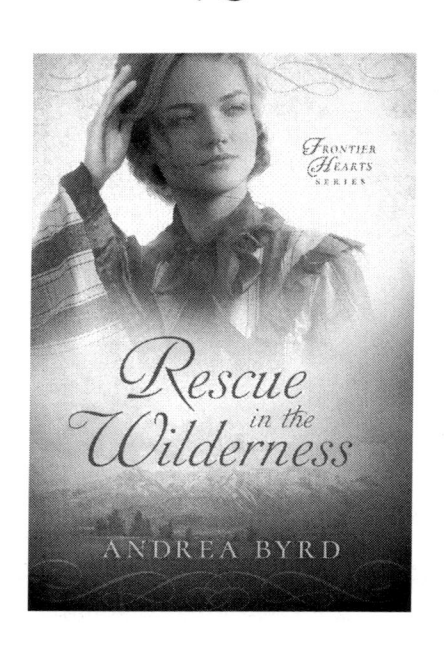

~

Rescue in the Wilderness by Andrea Byrd

William Cole cannot forget the cruel burden he carries, not with the pock marks that serve as an outward reminder. Riddled with guilt, he assumed the solitary life of a long hunter, traveling into the wilds of Kentucky each year. But his quiet existence is changed in an instant when, sitting in a tavern, he overhears a man offering his daughter—and her virtue—to the winner of the next round of cards. William's integrity and desire for redemption will not allow him to sit idly by while such an injustice occurs.

Lucinda Gillespie has suffered from an inexplicable illness her entire life. Her father, embarrassed by her condition, has subjected her to a lonely existence of abuse and confinement. But faced with the ultimate betrayal on the eve of her eighteenth birthday, Lucinda quickly realizes her trust is better placed in his hands of the mysterious man who appears at her door. Especially when he offers her the one thing she never thought would be within her grasp—freedom.

In the blink of an eye, both lives change as they begin the difficult, danger-fraught journey westward on the Wilderness Trail. But can they overcome their own perceptions of themselves to find love and the life God created them for?

Love's Winding Road by Susan F. Craft

They were forced into this marriage of convenience, but there's more at stake than their hearts on this wagon train through the mountain wilderness.

When Rose Jackson and her Irish immigrant family join a wagon train headed for a new life in South Carolina, the last thing she expects is to fall for the half-Cherokee wagon scout along the way. But their journey takes a life-changing turn when Rose is kidnapped by Indians. Daniel comes to her rescue, but the effects mean their lives will be forever intertwined.

Daniel prides himself on his self-control—inner and outer—but can't seem to get a handle on either when Rose is near. Now his life is bound to hers when the consequences of her rescue force them to marry. Now it's even more critical he maintain that self-control to keep her safe.

When tragedy strikes at the heart of their strained marriage, they leave for Daniel's home in the Blue Ridge Mountains. As they face the perils of the journey, Rose can't help but wonder why her new husband guards his heart so strongly. Why does he resist his obvious attraction for her? And what life awaits them at the end of love's winding road?

Made in the USA
Columbia, SC
09 June 2024